SONG OF SOLOMON

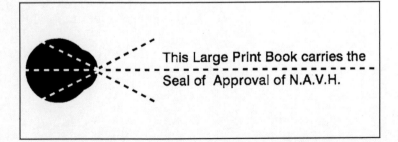

This Large Print Book carries the
Seal of Approval of N.A.V.H.

SONG OF SOLOMON

KENDRA NORMAN-BELLAMY

THORNDIKE PRESS

A part of Gale, Cengage Learning

GALE
CENGAGE Learning·

Detroit • New York • San Francisco • New Haven, Conn • Waterville, Maine • London

GALE
CENGAGE Learning™

LIBRARY OF CONGRESS CATALOGING-IN-PUBLICATION DATA

Norman-Bellamy, Kendra.
    Song of Solomon / by Kendra Norman-Bellamy.
      p. cm. — (Thorndike Press large print African-American)
    ISBN-13: 978-1-4104-3469-2
    ISBN-10: 1-4104-3469-9
    1. Soul mates—Fiction. 2. Christian fiction. 3. Large type
books. I. Title.
PS3614.O765S66 2011
813'.6—dc22   2010045472

Published in 2011 by arrangement with Urban Books LLC and Kensington Publishing Corp.

Printed in Mexico
1 2 3 4 5 6 7 15 14 13 12 11

DEDICATION

I will sing of the mercies of the LORD for
    ever:
with my mouth will I make known thy
    faithfulness to all generations.

(Psalm 89:1)

To my best loved gospel music legend. You know who you are, and you need no introduction. Long before I finally met you live and *In Living Color,* the powerful lyrics you wrote and sang somehow always took me *Back to the Cross* and blessed me beyond measure. Even if I had *Never Seen Your Face,* I'm convinced that your music would still be a melody that I would not only *Love Like Crazy,* but it would be music for which I'd still possess this same level of *Crazy Like Love* that I have today.

    After years of only knowing you as an anointed voice, a messenger of hope, and a minister of song, I feel blessed to now also define you as a faithful supporter and a cherished friend. Thanks for five decades of groundbreaking, uplifting, soul-stirring, Spirit-filled, life-changing music. Thank you for sharing *The Best Of* you with the world.

After all these years, I'm glad that you're Still Standing Tall.

ACKNOWLEDGMENTS

In everything give thanks for this is the will of God concerning you.

(I Thessalonians 5:18)

Thank you, **Jesus,** for without you, I am nothing. You are worthy to be praised!

Jonathan, Brittney and **Crystal:** You share my life, and you know better than anyone how involved I am when God is creating these stories through me. Thanks for lending me to my ministry (even when you don't want to) and for cheering me on as I endeavor to write stories that touch hearts and change lives.

To my parents, **Bishop H.H. and Mrs. Francine Norman:** Because of you, I know Him. Thanks for loving me enough to raise me according to His will and for being living examples of how it looks to grow in Him.

Crystal, Harold, Cynthia, and **Kim-**

berly: Thank you for being proud of me and supporting me in all that I do. You are siblings extraordinaire!

To **Jimmy** (1968–1995): Just because.

To **Terrance:** Thanks for wearing all those hats for all these years. I appreciate you, cuz.

To **Aunt Joyce** and **Uncle Irvin:** I'm not certain of the origin of the title "godparents," but if it means a second pair of parents sent from God, then you're it.

To **Carlton:** As my attorney/agent, you represent me well. I thank God for your legal eyes and your honest heart. I know you're looking out for my best interest.

To **Rhonda:** Thanks for promoting me every chance you get. You're awesome.

To **Heather, Gloria,** and **Deborah:** I love y'all dearly. BFF, ladies . . . BFF!!!

To **Lisa:** Psst! Look for your deserving plug in Chapter Seven of this story (smile).

To **Tia, Michelle, Vivi, Norma, Shewanda** and **Vanessa:** Thank you for sharing in the vision that is Anointed Authors on Tour. I'm flashing our AAOT "gangsta sign" right now. LOL!

To **Dwan:** I don't know when we became so close, but I thank God for your friendship and trustworthiness. You've become like a sister to me, and I cherish that.

To the esteemed ladies of the **Iota Phi Lambda Sorority, Inc.** (and especially to Atlanta's **Delta Chapter**): You've been a tremendous addition to my life. Thank you for your love, support, and sisterhood. Y'all some baaaaaad sistas! (((Turtle hugs!!)))

To my **Urban Christian** family: Thanks for continuing to be a vehicle that allows me to share my gift with the world. It has been an amazing ride.

To the members of **The Writer's Hut** and **The Writer's Cocoon Focus Group:** When I created these specialized writing fellowships, I had no idea they would bring me so much fulfillment. Thank you for pouring into me and allowing me to pour into you.

To **Revival Churches, Inc.:** Without good roots, a plant can't grow. Because of my connection to you, I have flourished.

To **Bishop Johnathan and Dr. Toni Alvarado** and the **Total Grace Christian Center family:** Daily, I thank God for you. My cup runneth over every single time I worship with and among you. There *is* no place like Total Grace!

To **book clubs** and **all other readers** who continue to embrace me: I don't take a single one of you for granted. Your support is appreciated to the highest level.

Lastly, to **Brian McKnight, Fred Hammond, India Arie, Joss Stone, Vanessa Bell Armstrong, Ruben Studdard, The Williams Brothers, Antonio Allen, Jonathan Nelson & Purpose,** and **Melvin Williams:** Music is so often my muse, and you all provided the melody that helped me get through this project. For the positive and uplifting lyrics and music that you imparted — thank you!

PROLOGUE

The worst day of Shaylynn Ford's life was the Wednesday her soul mate was murdered. Gunned down in cold blood at the age of twenty-six. No witnesses, no arrests, no suspects, no leads. And seventy-two hours after his assassination, as she buried him, Shaylynn could feel a piece of herself being laid to an eternal rest too. Eternal. Forever. Dead. Just like her husband, she was never to live again. But as lifeless as her body felt, her mind was alive and well, being bombarded with the one question that would likely never be answered.

Why?

It was a sad day. Even the heavens cried, rendering scattered showers that sprinkled the ground around the tent that had been provided for shelter. But the rainfall had done nothing to hamper the steadfast crowd. The graveside service was attended by some of the state's most elite dignitaries, all of whom seemed genuinely affected by the unexpected loss of their young colleague. Men hung their heads in sorrow, and women wept quietly into lace handkerchiefs. It was an insurmountable loss for the city. "Insurmountable loss." That was what the *Milwaukee Journal Sentinel* had called it. Everyone was saddened by the unexpected tragedy — or so it seemed.

Helicopters, displaying news channel logos and bearing cameras that captured footage of the ritual, hovered above the cemetery. Uninvited guests pressed in great numbers against the iron gates that surrounded the cemetery, trying to catch a glimpse of the burial. Camera bulbs flashed, and supporters yelled out their condolences. All of it was done in total disregard for the family's public wish to have a private ceremony. But while the unethical and sometimes callous actions of the city's residents were unwanted, none of it was unexpected. After all, the deceased had made history in the city.

Election polls showed that Emmett Ford was a crowd favorite, leading in double digits throughout the milestone race. It was astonishing that in a city that had a 44% to 39% white/black ratio, the major political race wasn't even close. Emmett had won by a landslide. It was as if the dream of a colorblind society had been birthed in Wisconsin's largest city. But a swarm of recent rumors had accused the metropolis of being relieved that they'd only had to recognize their city's first African American mayor for a few short weeks.

Could his killing have been racially motivated?

Shaylynn's eyes darted to the former long-standing mayor, whom Emmett had easily defeated. His head was covered by the blackness of the raincoat that he wore, and his eyes were cast downward in a sorrowful manner, but when she looked at him, Shaylynn's mind immediately took a quick journey to a thriving county in Atlanta, Georgia, where a former incumbent sheriff was serving a life sentence for orchestrating the murder of the man who had defeated him in his bid for reelection.

Could Emmett's killing have been politically motivated?

"God bless you," the funeral attendant said in a solemn voice that matched his facial expression with perfection as he handed Shaylynn a neatly folded American flag. It had once draped Emmett's expensive black marble coffin.

When she didn't readily reach for the

13

honorable banner that had been folded into a perfect triangle, the finely tailored gentleman laid it in the limited space that her lap provided. From behind the dark sunglasses that covered her face, Shaylynn watched the tears from her own eyes be immediately absorbed as they fell onto the red, white, and blue fabric. Twenty-three seemed far too young to be a widow, but apparently it wasn't — because she was.

The program was brief, and although well-wishers passed by and voiced remarks of how proud Emmett would have been of the noble ceremony, Shaylynn was left to take their word for it. Grief had rendered her numb and barely able to comprehend anything that had taken place since the two officers stood at her door with stoic faces and gave her the news of the shooting.

As the people filed by her, patting her shoulder, shaking her hand, and sometimes kissing her cheek, Shaylynn couldn't even rally a smile. Judas had kissed Jesus' cheek too. It meant nothing. Any one of their lips could be a mark of betrayal. Each and every one of the faces she saw, whether Democrat or Republican, was a suspect. The killer was still on the run, and as far as Shaylynn was concerned, it could be any one of them, or none of them at all. She trusted no one.

Without Emmett, she had no friends. Even the in-laws who sat in the chairs nearest her were estranged.

She wasn't exactly the bride that his parents wanted their son to take. According to them, Shaylynn was too young, too uneducated, and far too poor to qualify for the awarding of the Ford name. They'd never bothered to build a relationship with her before, and without Emmett, the one person who linked them, Shaylynn didn't expect to have much of a relationship with them at all from this point forward. And in her opinion, that was just fine.

Life as Shaylynn had known it for the past five years would never be the same. The long term plans to repeat their marriage vows on their tenth anniversary would never be a reality. The newly constructed four-bedroom home that she and Emmett had just moved into in preparation for their expanding family would now seem larger and emptier than ever. And just like his life, Emmett's mounting excitement about the pending birth of the child that had taken them three years to conceive, had been cut short by an assassin's bullet.

The family was asked to stand in preparation for being escorted to their cars, but Shaylynn wasn't ready to leave. Not yet.

And she dared anybody to try to make her. That was *her* husband's body that would be encased in a casket until his flesh rotted away from his bones. It was *her* life that was being buried under six feet of filthy dirt, never to breathe again. She dared them — any one of them — to tell her how long she could linger.

Shaylynn stood as directed, but as others began dispersing, her feet remained planted. Firm. She made no effort to leave. Her eyes burned from days of crying. Her body ached from lack of sleep. Her heart bled from the hole that wouldn't heal.

Inhale.

Exhale.

Even breathing was painful. With one hand, Shaylynn clung to a cluster of violets, Emmett's favorite flower, and with the other, she hugged the flag close to her protruding belly. The damp soil beneath her feet held her in place as steadily as stood the two fully dressed and alert armed bodyguards who positioned themselves on either side of her. They hadn't been able to protect her husband, and as helpless, lost, and hollow as she felt right now, Shaylynn hoped to God that if somewhere in the distance, a sniper had his gun pointed in her direction, they'd fail to protect her too.

ONE

Seven Years Later

"Have a good evening, Dr. Taylor."

"See you on Monday, Dr. Taylor."

"Bye, Dr. Taylor. Enjoy your weekend."

Neil Taylor, Ph.D. stood in the entrance-way that led to his office and answered the remarks with quiet waves and an occasional cordial nod of his head. As one of only a small handful of available men on staff, it wasn't uncommon for the women around him to vie for his attention; or at least, that's the way it felt. Neil wasn't complaining about it, though. In fact, though he never voiced it, he rather enjoyed the admiration. Most of the women he worked with were easy on the eyes; however, dating any one of them was totally out of the question. Business and pleasure could make for a lethal mixture, and he loved his job too much to place it in jeopardy.

Neil cherished his profession as Director

of Kingdom Builders Academy, the private school that had become an essential part of Kingdom Builders Christian Center. The responsibilities of his vocation made him feel as if he were making a genuine difference in the lives of the children of his community. Under Neil's leadership, the number of students at the academy had doubled, with a current enrollment of 576 children, ranging from pre-K to fifth grade. And they were a lively bunch.

"High five, Dr. Taylor!" a group of four boys said in chorus as they raced up to the man they saw regularly throughout each school day. Running was disallowed in the halls of Kingdom Builders Academy, but it was the end of the day, and Neil was too tired not to let it slide.

Answering the call of duty, the handsome, well-dressed faculty leader lowered his moderate five foot seven stature to their levels and slapped each of their awaiting palms with his. "Down low, down low," Neil challenged, dropping his hands so near to the floor that the giggling first and second graders had to practically kneel to reciprocate. "Have a good weekend, boys." He rubbed their heads in signature fashion. "See you on Monday. Be good now."

"Okay!" they vowed before dashing toward

the three sets of double doors that led outside.

Neil wondered how many of the rowdy boys would keep that promise, but whether they did was out of his control. Once they left Kingdom Builders Academy, they were their parents' responsibility. But Neil couldn't help but pray for them. All of the children who spent nearly eight hours with him on a daily basis were special to him.

"Is there anything else you'd like me to do before I leave, Dr. Taylor?"

The question came from Margaret Dasher, Neil's dutiful administrative assistant ever since he took the job five years ago. Her impaired hearing, coupled with the noise of the dismissed children who crowded the halls en route to their buses or guardians' cars, made her talk louder than normal. Most days Margaret refused to wear her hearing aid, citing that it made her feel old. Neil was amused by her line of thinking. Seemed to him that she'd feel even older knowing people were practically yelling at her just to be sure she understood.

"Thank you, Ms. Dasher," Neil said while accepting the folder that his assistant handed him, and quickly scanning the content. "I think that will be all." Even after years of working together and bonding on a personal level, the two of them still referenced one another by their professional titles — at and away from work.

"Good," she said, pushing her bifocals up on her nose and flashing a wide grin that displayed the good use of Kingdom Builders Academy's dental plan. Margaret ran her fingers through her short, graying hair and added, "Got anything planned for the weekend?"

The question was laced with meddlesome inquisitiveness, and Neil shook his head knowingly. "Not really. The weather is nice outside, so I plan to do a little yard work, but it should be a pretty uneventful weekend other than church on Sunday. Will you be there?"

"Of course I will." Margaret sounded like she was offended that he would even ask. Pausing, she peered at him over the same lenses that she'd just pushed up a few moments earlier. "My niece is coming into town for the weekend. She's a nice-looking girl with a college degree . . . a teacher, no less. And she's single. Why don't you come over for dinner and a chance to meet her? I think you'll like her. What do you say?"

Neil had a healthy chuckle at his assistant's expense. Margaret was forever trying to set him up with one of her many female relatives. She seemed to have more available nieces, goddaughters, and cousins than most families, and every time one of them came through Atlanta for a visit, Margaret became an instant matchmaker. Neil had only taken her up on the offer once, and that experience had been quite enough for him.

"Why are you laughing?" she asked, easily reading his thoughts. "You're still holding that two-month-old incident against me, aren't you? Listen, I'll admit that what happened with you and my late husband's half brother's second wife's oldest daughter was disgraceful, but this is different. Lawrence was a good man — God rest his soul — but his family has always been half crazy, and I should have never even suggested that you go out with that gal."

Margaret paused long enough to catch the breath that her long spiel had required. Then she shook her head and dove right back in. "But you don't have to worry about that with the McBride women." She tilted her head to the side and gave her chest five quick, proud pats like the ladies in her family were Mary's sisters and Jesus' aunts. "The McBride women are law-abiding citizens. None of them would ever be caught dead with a bench warrant against them.

They would never be so trifling as to get arrested at the dinner table in an upscale restaurant for cutting another girl over some man who was serving time in jail for stealing live shellfish out of the tank at Red Lobster."

Neil could barely contain himself. It was a situation he could laugh heartily about now, but at the time of the public arrest, it was both unnerving and utterly embarrassing. Fortunately for him, none of the patrons in the restaurant on the night that his "date" had been hauled away in handcuffs were friends or colleagues of his. Had they been, he would have had to resign from the job he loved and move to another city. Maybe even another state. Maybe another country.

Wiping moisture from the corners of his eyes that resulted from his fit of laughter, Neil calmed himself. "Thanks for the invitation, Ms. Dasher, but I think I'll just spend a quiet Saturday at home, taking care of some things around the house that I've allowed to go undone."

Margaret shrugged. "Okay. It's your life."

One . . . two . . . three . . . Neil counted the seconds in his mind, knowing full well that Margaret wasn't going to leave it at that. If history was any indication, he guessed that it would only be a matter of time before she said more. And he was right.

"I don't know what you're afraid of, Dr. Taylor. The Bible says he who finds a wife finds a good thing."

"Been there, done that, and the souvenir T-shirt that I have is all the memento that I need, Ms. Dasher. I'm not afraid; I'm smart."

"As the saying goes, marriages are made in heaven," Margaret quickly emphasized.

"And as another saying also goes, so are thunder and lightning."

Margaret wasn't the least bit amused or deterred by Neil's retort. "Okay, so your first marriage failed. Big deal. So did mine. But I didn't write off love or marriage because of it. As far as I'm concerned, it was his loss. Any man who is too stupid to appreciate all this deserves to be by himself. And he found out quickly the grass on the other side ain't always as green close up as it appears to be from afar. And he had the nerves to try and come back to me." Margaret scowled, propped both hands on her full hips, and began craning her neck back and forth like a chicken on amphetamines. "Please take you back? Are you crazy, fool? Do I have 'big dummy' written 'cross my forehead?"

Neil held his hands up in surrender and

laughed as he cowered away. "Hey, hey, hey. I'm not him, okay?"

Margaret crossed her arms in front of her body, and the amplified breath she released sounded like one that was meant to calm her. Seconds later, she'd regained her composure and was back to her previous line of reasoning. "All I'm saying is that the last thing you should do is let the person who broke your heart also break your spirit. If that woman didn't have the common sense to see that you were a catch, then maybe the relationship had to be severed in order for God to send you what you deserve. If you don't at least open yourself to that possibility, then God ain't got no choice but to give what He has reserved for you to somebody else who'll accept it and appreciate it."

If Neil lived to be a hundred, he still wouldn't understand why his personal life was so important to Margaret. "I just don't think it's God's will for everybody to marry anyway."

"Then why does He specifically say in His Word that it's not good for a man to be alone?" Margaret contested.

"Ah . . ." Neil held up one finger for emphasis. "But let's also remember that the Apostle Paul, who was a lifelong bachelor, said in the book of First Corinthians that he wished that all men would be like he was. Now, that was a smart man. Wish I'd have taken a lesson from him early on; but better late than never, right? Besides, being without a wife made Paul free to be used by God in whatever way God chose."

Margaret smacked her lips, and then sucked her teeth in protest. "Bologna! A man can be used by God without being single. To begin with, Paul probably wasn't the most attractive man in Corinth. The scripture don't say that, but I'll bet you anything that if cameras were around in his day and we had a bona fide picture to look at, we'd find out that the real reason Paul never married was because he looked a hot mess and just couldn't find a woman who wanted to marry his ugly self. He probably just used his servitude to God as an excuse."

A burst of laughter released itself from Neil's belly and resonated around the workspace. Margaret was as quick witted as any woman he'd ever known. Despite her flippant remarks about one of God's greatest apostles, she was spiritually grounded too. And even at sixty, with salt-and-pepper hair and a few excess pounds that had settled quite nicely around her hips, she was an eye-catching woman. Nice legs and all. She had that kind of overall appeal that had the potential to make Neil rethink his policy not to date a woman he worked with. As quiet as it was kept, he had always had somewhat of a boyish crush on his older assistant. Neil supposed that if he were a few years older, or if she were a few years younger . . .

Margaret intruded his rambling thoughts with, "You're too good of a man to be by yourself all this long time, Dr. Taylor; especially at this stage of your life."

"What stage of my life? You act like I'm an old man or something." Neil turned his back to her to look at the calendar on her desk, making sure he had no pressing appointments for tomorrow.

"You'll be forty-five in just a few days." Margaret said it as though he had no clue. "I'm not saying that forty-five is old, but it's not young either. And time doesn't wait for anybody. I remember when I turned forty-five. Seems like yesterday, but fifteen years have passed since then." He felt her finger touch the back of his head. "You ain't no spring chicken anymore, Dr. Taylor. Look how your hair is starting to gray."

"Premature graying is in my genes, thank you very much. And what my genes didn't jumpstart, my failed marriage did. So citing my graying temples just gives me one more reason to be by myself."

Margaret ignored Neil's comment like she hadn't even heard it. Then again, since his back was turned and she wasn't wearing her hearing aid, there was a good chance that she hadn't. Folding her arms in front of her, she quipped, "By the time I was your age, I'd been married twice and had six children. Just 'cause you fall off a horse one time don't mean you don't try again. Long as you didn't break your back in the fall, you're still good for another ride."

Neil swung around to face her again. "Horses? Rides? What does that have to do with anything?"

"You need to get hitched; that's what it's got to do with anything." Margaret looked at him like he was stupid. "You need to get hitched right now, while your future wife is still willing to give you some little ones to carry on your family's name. Nowadays, there are very few women who want to be in their forties with their feet in stirrups, birthing babies."

Neil shook his head, but he couldn't help but smile. The way Margaret carried on sometimes, one would think that she worried about him more than his mother did. Her persistence could be irritating, but to a degree, it was also endearing. It was kind of nice to have someone fuss over him the way Margaret did.

"Well, for the record, I have no plans to remarry, but *if* ever temporary insanity or Alzheimer's set in and I stupidly decide to do so, children will be optional, so there's no rush as far as I'm concerned."

"Optional?" Margaret gasped in dramatic fashion then grimaced like saying the word left a bad aftertaste on her palate. She walked closer to Neil, again looking over her glasses at him like one of those British ladies from *Nanny 911.* Margaret looked like she was all set to send him straight to the naughty chair. "How can you work around children every day and consider having your own as optional?"

"Working around children every day is probably *why* I consider having my own as optional." Neil coughed out a dry laugh. "And please don't give me the 'children are a gift from God' lecture. I've heard it more times than I care to tally up. It's not that I disagree. But be that as it may, my feelings about having kids of my own remain the same. And God knows I'm glad I didn't have any the first time around. Can you imagine what type of noose would have lingered around my neck if a child were involved?" He shuddered at the thought of it.

"Well, I'm glad you didn't have any either. That was God's doing," Margaret prophesied. "But Dr. Taylor, you're a natural with the kids in this school. For some of them, you're probably the only positive male role model they have in their little lives. Besides, children *are* a blessing from the Lord, and every good man deserves the opportunity to be a father. The Lord in heaven knows we have enough sorry jokers who are running the fields, planting seeds that they don't even stick around to see grow. So men like you —"

"Men like me will be just fine, Ms. Dasher," Neil interjected. "I'm not saying I won't have kids; I'm just saying that it's not a priority with me, just like a second walk down the aisle isn't a priority. I can take it or leave it. I like my life."

"How long has it been since you've been on a date?"

"Counting the unforgettable one you set me up on?" Neil grinned at his own facetious remark while he fished in his pocket for a peppermint. He always kept a few on hand. It was a habit he'd picked up as a teenager, after years of seeing his now

deceased father nurse on the candies religiously.

"No, I mean a *real* date," Margaret clarified, tossing him a don't-get-smart-with-me
look. "I'm talking about an evening out with
a special woman that you really cared for. A
woman that you saw as having the potential
to become the next Mrs. Neil Taylor."

"I'd have to give you two different answers
in order to accurately address both those
statements." Neil stepped back into his office space with Margaret following close
behind. Placing the folder in the middle of
an already cluttered desk, he turned to face
her, leaning back and using his desk for support. "The last time I went on a date with a
woman that I really cared for was about two,
maybe even three years ago. And I can't say
that I've ever been on a date with a woman
that I would classify as a potential wife other
than when I dated Audrey . . . and a lot of
good that did me."

Removing her reading glasses from her
bulging eyes, Margaret's jaw dropped.
"You've *never* — not even once — been on
a date with a woman you'd consider marrying material since you dated your ex-wife?"

Neil shook his head truthfully. "Never. So
maybe now you can understand why I'm
content. I mean, if the right woman hap-

pens to come along, fine. But if she doesn't, God has given me the wherewithal to be content in whatever state that I'm in. I'm not a man who is in need of the constant company of a woman. Anything a woman can do, I can do just as well. My parents made sure that their children were well-versed on how to do everything for themselves. Thanks to them, I'm just as skillful with domestic work as I am with manual labor."

"Yeah, well, there's one thing that a woman can do for you that you can't do for yourself *just as well.* You might be saved, and you might be self-sufficient, but you're still a man."

Chuckling, Neil said, "I knew you'd go there sooner or later."

"And I'm sure you've got a comeback prepared," Margaret replied. "But I don't care what you say; you know I'm right."

"Excuse me."

The words, accompanied by several knocks on the frame of the door, caused both Neil and Margaret to turn. Standing in the doorway was a child dressed in Kingdom Builders Academy's signature blue-and-grey uniform, and an unidentified woman who nearly made Neil swallow his dissolving breath mint.

His eyes locked onto the attractive, spruce lady, and against his will, they started at the bottom and scanned her petite, yet exceptional form. Her leather pumps bled the same red of her tapered skirt suit. Her legs flaunted sculpted calves. Hair that was braided so neatly that it looked as though it could have been styled just before she arrived at his doorway cascaded past her shoulders. Her skin tone was like Hershey's Kisses. . . .

It was a face that was oddly familiar, and Neil found himself thumbing through his long term memory bank for clues of where their paths had crossed. She was too young to be a former schoolmate, but probably too old to be one of the little ones that his mother used to babysit in their home. He hoped beyond hope that their former meeting — whenever and wherever it was — had been a pleasant one.

Her physical appearance stirred something inside Neil, but the sparkle from an impressive wedding set on her left hand drew an imaginary line that hindered his mind from crossing into impermissible territory.

Margaret was the first to step forward. "Yes, ma'am? May I help you?"

"I hope so. My name is Shaylynn, and this is my son —"

"Chase Ford." Neil found his voice just in time, and then walked toward Shaylynn with an extended hand. "We know Chase very well. He's a great kid. I believe he's this month's star student in Miss Berkshire's class. You should be very proud, Mrs. Ford."

"I am. Very much so." Her beaming smile served as an 'amen' to her statement.

"I'm Dr. Neil Taylor, the director here at Kingdom Builders Academy."

"Oh." Shaylynn's face brightened even more. "I've heard a lot about you from my son, Dr. Taylor. Chase speaks of you often."

"I told her you give good high fives," Chase reported, simultaneously raising his palm in the air and gaining the response from his administrator that his gesture requested.

"May we help you with something, Mrs. Ford?" Margaret repeated her earlier inquiry, ending the fleeting horseplay.

"Yes, I hope so. I was wondering if it were possible for me to use the telephone to call for assistance." Her chocolate cheeks flushed in embarrassment and her eyes darted toward the floor for a moment before she looked at Margaret again. "I carelessly locked my cell phone and other personal belongings in the car with the engine still running, and I need to get the door open as soon as possible."

"Sure." Margaret rounded her desk and pulled a large, worn telephone book from her drawer. "We have several locksmiths in the area, but they can charge an arm and a leg just to unlock a door. It's highway robbery, really. It'll probably be better for you to just call your husband and get him to come and bring the spare keys, if you have some."

"My daddy's in heaven."

Chase's announcement seemed to freeze both time and everyone who was in the room. In slow motion, Neil turned to look at the women, who were standing near his assistant's desk, and he noted a look of bewilderment on Margaret's face that indicated that she didn't quite understand the child's reply. Neil understood perfectly, but no response seemed appropriate, so he remained quiet.

"My husband is deceased," Shaylynn clarified, breaking the awkward silence.

"Oh. I'm . . . I'm sorry," Margaret stammered. Her countenance fell like she'd known the woman's husband personally. "Bless your heart, sugar. You poor thing. And left with such a young child, too. Lord have mercy, Jesus."

The pretty woman lifted her chin. "It's okay," she assured, all the while appearing as uncomfortable as Neil felt.

"When did it happen? How did he die? Did this happen recently?"

Neil cringed at Margaret's probing questions. They were far too personal to ask a woman they'd met less than five minutes ago. His mind raced for something to say that would end his assistant's interrogation, but Neil could think of nothing.

"It happened some time ago. May I?" Shaylynn reached for the phone book, seeming to want to avoid the current subject matter and get to the business of making her call.

"He must have been very young," Margaret pressed as though clueless. Neil looked at her, not believing her audacity. When Shaylynn didn't reply, Margaret's comeback was even blunter. "How old was he when he died?"

Finding his voice and making an executive decision to interrupt, Neil said, "You know what? Don't worry about making the call, Ms. Ford."

"*Mrs.* Ford." Shaylynn's correction was sharp and abrupt, though her follow-up was less abrasive. "It's Mrs."

Another awkward moment passed, and in

spite of the fact that Neil could make no sense of Shaylynn's statement, he respected her wishes. "I can get the door open for you, Mrs. Ford. I keep a special tool kit in my car, my office, and my house for emergencies like this. It'll only take a few seconds to get the car door open."

"You don't mind?" Her tone was hesitant, her expression almost childlike.

"Not at all. Why don't you and Chase go out and wait by the car? I don't want it to be left unattended too long with the engine running." Neil chuckled. "I might not be the only one around here who can open a locked car. You all just go and stand guard. I'll join you in just a second."

"Thank you, Dr. Taylor. I appreciate it."

"My pleasure."

With Shaylynn and her son out of listening range, Neil took quick steps into his office and retrieved the tool kit from a place on his shelf. He could hear the click of Margaret's shoes against the tiled floors as she followed him, and from his side vision, Neil could see her standing in his doorway.

"You may want to go ahead and leave before another crisis arises that keeps you here working overtime," he suggested.

"Did you hear what that child just said?" Margaret asked.

"Who? Chase?"

"No. His mother."

Neil gave Margaret a cross look, and then closed his office door. The volume of her hearing impairment–induced voice was way too loud for his comfort. Standing with his back leaning against the door and facing her, he said, "Actually, what you were saying out there was far more attention-grabbing than anything Chase's mother could have possibly said. I can't believe you asked that lady all those personal questions."

In defense of her actions, Margaret replied with, "No question is off limits when she's the one who opened the discussion. If she hadn't said he was dead, I . . . we never would have known it, and I wouldn't have asked any questions. I was just trying to show some concern. What was I supposed to do, just stand there like you did and say nothing? How much sense would that have made?"

"First of all, she didn't volunteer the information of her husband's death," Neil argued. "Chase did. And you can't possibly expect a kid his age to know any better. It wouldn't have been so bad if you'd stopped after offering your condolences. But asking how, when, and where the man died was just a little too much. You asked his age and everything."

Margaret smacked her lips in protest. "For your information, I did *not* ask where he died. You're putting words in my mouth. And none of that is the point, anyway, Dr. Taylor." Margaret rerouted the conversation back to her original point. "Even though her husband is dead, she insisted on being called *Mrs.* Ford."

"So what?" Neil pretended not to find it peculiar. "Lots of widows still use their married title."

"I'm a widow. I don't use it."

"That doesn't mean that a woman who decides to is an oddball."

Margaret paused like she was thinking it over. "Okay, I can agree with that, I suppose. But she corrected you. She *insisted.* That's what makes it strange. I could kind of see her reasoning if he'd just died last week or last month. Even a few months might be understandable. But she said he died *some time ago,* like it might have happened some years ago. Yet it was like she got offended when you called her Ms. Ford."

"What can I say, Ms. Dasher? Women are strange creatures sometimes," Neil said. "Another reason that I'm cool with being

38

by myself."

Margaret followed again as Neil opened his office door and walked into her workspace on his way to the hall. "You know that you and I are going to finish that whole 'I'm cool with being by myself' conversation next week, right? Don't think for a minute that I'm letting you off the hook that easily."

"The thought never crossed my mind," Neil said as the two of them stopped briefly in the school's lobby.

The halls were clear now, and through the main glass doors, he caught a glimpse of Shaylynn and Chase standing beside a silver Chrysler that shone like it had just been rolled out of a showroom. *Where do I know her from?* The nagging question almost haunted him as they exited the school building.

"I'll see you at church on Sunday," Margaret said as she waved at him just before making a beeline to her car, one of a very few that still remained in the faculty lot.

With his eyes locked on his destination, Neil was almost too absorbed to hear his secretary bid farewell. His sights were fixed and his gait was quick. There was a woman that needed to be rescued, and the case in his hand equipped him to do it.

"Thanks again," Shaylynn said as soon as

Neil reached her car. "I can't tell you how much I appreciate it. I don't think I've ever locked myself out of my car before. I don't know what I was thinking."

"It could happen to any of us," Neil said. He slipped a pair of sporty sunglasses on his face and pulled an apparatus from the case in preparation to work his magic. "It's easy to get distracted when there are a bunch of children around, I suppose." Neil purposely looked at her and smiled when he spoke. He wanted Shaylynn to get a good look at him in his Ray Bans. He'd gotten many compliments on how debonair the eyewear made him look. He hoped she approved too.

"I suppose," Shaylynn agreed.

"Whoaaaa." Chase stretched out the word. "Cool glasses, Dr. Taylor."

Not exactly the person he was trying to impress, but Neil appreciated the praise anyway. "Thanks, young man."

If he didn't think that Shaylynn was sharp enough to pick up on his game, Neil would have pretended that the job of unlocking her car door was harder than he'd thought. He would have loved to have an excuse to talk to her longer, maybe get to know her better; maybe figure out why she looked familiar to him; maybe find out why she was still *Mrs.* Ford though her husband was deceased. But with his tools, the job was a simple one, and the door was unlocked in a matter of seconds. As soon as the lock disengaged, Neil reached for the handle and opened the door for her to enter her car.

"Thank you so much, Dr. Taylor." Shaylynn slid onto the polished black leather seat and turned to watch as Neil helped her son secure his seatbelt. "Thank you," she repeated.

Neil closed Chase's back door first, and then stood by the still-open driver's door. Shaylynn's skirt stopped just above her knees, and the sight didn't escape Neil. *Man, does she have nice legs!* "You're welcome, Mrs. Ford. Have a pleasant weekend." The moment the words came out of his mouth, Neil again caught a glimpse of the diamond solitaire on her finger. Even his expensive shades couldn't minimize the sharpness of the sparkle that it created as it kissed the sun's rays.

"You do the same," she replied while allowing him to shut her door as well.

Neil took several steps backward, and then returned Chase's wave as he watched the New Yorker pull away from the campus. Although he had been mortified by Margaret's probing questions, Neil couldn't help but wonder the same things she had wondered. Just how long had Mrs. Shaylynn Ford been widowed, and what was making it so hard for her to let go?

TWO

After Emmett's death, and once she'd gotten over her desire to die too, Shaylynn began secretly hoping that the child developing in her womb was a girl. It was already unfair that she had to live the rest of her life without her husband. Bringing a son into the world who would have to live without the love and guidance of his father just seemed like cruel and unusual punishment. But for some reason, it was a cross that God had given her to bear. Despite the challenges of being a young, single mother, Shaylynn found a reason to be grateful each time she realized how much joy her son had brought to her life.

Whenever Shaylynn looked at Chase, she saw Emmett. The child had his father's handsome, dark eyes and perfectly shaped full lips. And when Chase smiled, sometimes Shaylynn was convinced that Emmett had been reincarnated. There were days that she was certain that Emmett Ford still lived with her. Even the six-year-old's mannerisms emulated a dad he'd never known.

Chase's likeness to his father was both a blessing and a curse. Shaylynn knew that she'd always be reminded of Emmett as long as her son was around, and that, she liked. But because Chase looked so much like his dad, she also felt the constant, inexplicable need to protect him from the unknown and the unseen. Milwaukee's police had never caught Emmett's killer, and the case had long ago turned cold. Murderous hands had taken her husband, but Shaylynn wasn't about to allow anything to happen to her son. She'd die first.

That was the reason Shaylynn had decided to move from Wisconsin. She wanted to move as far away from her past and as far away from harm's way as possible. Georgia had been their fourth move in six years, and for the first time, she felt like she had a new home and a new start. There were no family members or friends of Emmett's in or near Georgia, and that was the way Shaylynn wanted it. Born the only child to extremely dysfunctional parents, she was bounced around from relative to relative for most of her life, spending the bulk of the time with her paternal grandmother. By the time Shaylynn was fourteen, she had completely lost contact with her parents and had barely reached eighteen before her grandmother passed away, leaving her to sustain herself. Her dad didn't even bother to come to his own mother's funeral.

Until she married Emmett, Shaylynn never knew what it was like not to have to struggle. The two met on the campus of the University of Wisconsin–Milwaukee. He was a student in their criminal justice program, and Shaylynn, an eighteen-year-old high school dropout, worked as a custodian. Her grandmother had always told her that she was smart and pretty, but Shaylynn never dreamed that a man like Emmett would be interested in a girl like her. But he was.

Theirs could easily be described as a whirlwind romance. From the day they met to the day they married was slightly less than a year. Shaylynn had been reading romance books since she was a child. There wasn't a fairytale that the Brothers Grimm wrote that she didn't adore. Copies of books with heroines who bore ridiculous names like Cinderella, Snow White, and Rapunzel lined Shaylynn's childhood bedroom dresser. *Sleeping Beauty* had been her all-time favorite. In truth (and in secret), it still was. And when she met Emmett Ford, he made a believer out of her.

It was only after meeting Emmett that Shaylynn was inspired to get the GED that helped erase the shame of choosing to leave high school in the middle of her sophomore year, against the wishes of her ailing grandmother. Then, with renewed motivation and the support of her husband, she enrolled in Milwaukee Area Technical College, not only to gain an associate of applied science degree in interior design, but also to gain the respect of her new parents-in-law, who were mortified that their son had not only married a "child," but had "married down." When Shaylynn finished the program, she'd obtained the former, but not the latter. It soon became clear to the young wife that her in-laws' opinion of her would never change, no matter what she did to better herself. In their eyes, she'd always be insufficient and unworthy.

Shaylynn had barely spoken to either of them since their son's funeral. But Chase's birth wouldn't allow the pompous husband and wife attorneys-at-law team to deny her existence altogether. They'd only seen their grandson five times in the past six years, but Shaylynn allowed Chase to call them often.

He was just finishing his scheduled weekly

call to them as his mother placed his peanut butter and jelly sandwich and glass of cold milk on the dining room table.

"Mama, Grandma said that she's gonna buy me whatever I want for Christmas." Chase climbed in his chair and fixed his eyes on Shaylynn. "I want a Wii for my bedroom. Can I ask her for one?"

Shaylynn looked at her six-year-old and smiled. His taste was as simple as hers, and asking for something as trivial as a Nintendo Wii would probably insult his grandmother to tears. "Sure you can, baby. I think that's an excellent idea." Shaylynn had to get her kicks wherever she could find them.

"When I finish eating, can I play with my Game Boy?" Chase sank his teeth into his favorite lunchtime meal as he asked the question.

"Is your homework all done?"

"Yes, ma'am." The words were muffled by the sticky sandwich.

"Okay then, you can play games while I check over your lesson. If you need to make any corrections, you'll have to turn off the system until you get it right. Okay?"

This time, the mouthful of milk would only allow Chase to nod his answer.

Shaylynn was pleased with how well Chase was adjusting to life in Atlanta, and especially the way he was excelling at his new school. The large metropolitan area was much different than any of the other places they'd lived. They had moved away from Wisconsin nine months after Chase's birth. With her husband's absence and his unsolved murder, Shaylynn just didn't feel comfortable or safe there any longer. If she was going to have to live without Emmett, she needed to find a fresh start. She loathed the idea of putting her and Emmett's dream home on the market, but doing so was the only way she could completely sever ties with the city they'd called home. The city that murdered him.

Shaylynn had meticulously decorated the home to their liking, and she knew that if she sold it fully furnished, it wouldn't be on the market for long. And as soon as the home was sold, six weeks after the FOR SALE sign was erected on the front lawn, Shaylynn and Chase moved to Long Island, New York. There she easily found work that paid well, but hated every moment of every day of the twelve months that she lived in the city. Not only was the metropolis too congested and expensive for her personal taste, but when she moved there, too many people knew her from the still fresh news of Emmett's assassination. She quickly grew weary of answering probing questions from strange cab drivers who delivered her to her job, and getting looks of pity from her co-workers once she arrived. Not to mention the newspaper and magazine editors who relentlessly called her in search of a coveted exclusive interview. How was she ever going to heal?

Jacksonville, Florida became her next experiment, and life there got off to a promising start. The weather was ideal, and her chosen apartment, only a few miles from the beach, made for the perfect dwelling place. She had never been to Florida before, and it was just as beautiful as the photos in the magazines had promised it would be. Palm trees and sunshine for days.

Forgoing her initial plans to start her own business, Shaylynn joined an already thriving venture and became part of a team that decorated winter homes belonging to some of the music and movie industries' most demanding professionals. Life was on the upswing for Shaylynn and Chase . . . until she found herself huddled in the corner of her bathroom, holding on to her son, in fear for their lives as they experienced their first hurricane. Though her associates guaranteed her that storms the magnitude of that one were rare, for Shaylynn, "rare" was too often, and she chose to look for safer grounds.

Florida had caused her to fall in love with the South, and she decided that wherever she moved, it would be on that end of the country. Her relocation to Lake Charles, Louisiana brought Shaylynn the serenity that she needed and a renewed satisfaction with the prospect of the original idea of her home-based interior design company.

A keen business sense told her that moving close to New Orleans, where people were still rebuilding homes and businesses after the devastation of the infamous Hurricane Katrina, would bring an abundance of clientele. It was an innovative idea that worked in her favor on a business level, but a year later, as Chase turned five and began attending public school for the first time, Shaylynn was forced to lay aside the growing popularity of her business and do what she thought was best for her son. Her dissatisfaction with the school system and limited choices for private schools led to the folding of Ford's Home Interior & Designs and another family uproot that ultimately delivered them to Atlanta, Georgia and the here and now.

"We're going to the Georgia Aqueerium next week, Mama."

"Aquarium," Shaylynn enunciated.

Chase giggled. "I mean *aquarium.*" He spoke the word just as slowly as she had. "We're going there next week."

"I know, Chase. I signed the permission slip, remember?" Shaylynn shook her head at the boy's anticipation while she used a warm dishcloth to wipe away remnants of bread crumbs and peanut butter from her spacious kitchen countertop. He'd mentioned the impending trip several times over the past few weeks. The bonds her child had made in his first year at Kingdom Builders Academy were a big part of the reason that Shaylynn had given the city her stamp of approval in such a short time. Other than his satisfactory adjustment, she had no real allegiance to Atlanta. Had Chase not gotten into the swing of things the way he had, Shaylynn would have made move number seven without a second thought.

"Miss Berkshire said that she needs at least two adults to help watch us. None of the other parents have signed up yet. Can you come, Mama?"

"Uh . . . well . . . I . . ." Shaylynn's words fumbled in her attempt to think of a good excuse not to be available for the Tuesday outing. She didn't mind going places with Chase. In fact, she enjoyed casual days out with her son. But Shaylynn was the first to admit that she wasn't fond of having to supervise other people's children. "I don't know, Chase. Remember how I told you that I'm trying to build our family business? Well, I can't do that if I'm not at home. I need to be here to take phone calls."

"Please, Mama?"

When he begged, Chase especially reminded her of Emmett. The boy's pleading eyes were the same eyes that her deceased husband would sport when he implored her to take part in any activity that involved mingling with his uppity, well-to-do family. Emmett knew how intolerable the Fords could be, and he understood Shaylynn's hesitation, but he wanted nothing more than for his parents and his wife to find common ground. There were only a few goals in Emmett's brief life that he aspired to, but didn't achieve. Getting his family to accept his wife was one of them.

"Okay, Chase, I'll tell you what. When you go to school Monday, you find out from Mrs. Berkshire if she has gotten the adult participation that she needs for Tuesday's trip. If she hasn't, then I'll keep my calendar clear, and I'll come along."

The boy's delight spread across his entire face as he jumped from his chair and wrapped his arms around his mother's hips. At only six years old, he was already showing signs of being a tall boy. By twelve, Shaylynn guessed that he'd be as tall as she. It was another trait that he'd gotten from his father's side of the family. At six foot two, Emmett had towered over Shaylynn by thirteen inches.

After thanking her about nine times without catching a breath, Chase ran down the hall to the bathroom so that he could wash his face and hands before going into the entertainment room.

Shaylynn cleared away his vacated saucer and cup and wiped the glass-top table with the same warm dishcloth that had polished the counter. Pausing, she took in a deep breath, grimaced, and then released it as slowly as she could. It was an almost involuntary ritual that she practiced several times during the year. Her pastor in Wisconsin had vowed through a prophetic declaration that the pain of her loss would eventually dissipate, but the only breaths that didn't hurt were the shallow ones. The way that Shaylynn tested her healing was to breathe so deeply that she filled her entire chest cavity, reaching the very fibers of her heart. Since day one, an inhale like that had brought on an inexplicable pain. Seven years later, it still did.

THREE

Shaking the hands of several of the deacons on his way to his seat, Neil was glad to have been able to navigate through Atlanta's uncommonly heavy Sunday morning traffic and arrive at church before the start of service. The time-consuming yard work that he'd tackled yesterday contributed to a level of fatigue that resulted in an early bedtime last night. Neil couldn't remember the last time he'd slept so soundly. There was lingering soreness in his thighs that, no doubt, resulted from the heavy bags of fertilizer he'd carried from his garage to his yard while working to put the finishing touches on planting hedges that complemented the base of his porch. The finished product looked good, but his body had paid a high price.

Kingdom Builders Christian Center, identified by most as KBCC, had a membership of just over twelve hundred. In no way was it the largest church in metropolitan Atlanta, but it was one of the most esteemed. It was also one of the fastest growing. Its membership today was double what it had been five years ago. The growth spurt had forced KBCC to go through a construction reformation, widening its sanctuary to accommodate the demand. By the looks of today's crowd, it wouldn't be long before they'd be doing it all over again.

Kingdom Builders Christian Center was a part of the New Hope Fellowship of Churches where the nationally known and highly respected Reverend B. T. Tides served as overseer. For more than thirty years, KBCC was pastored by its founder, Dr. Charles Loather Sr. When the founding pastor died four years ago, attendance at the funeral service was expected to be so great that the ceremony had to be held at the Georgia World Congress Center to accommodate. When Dr. Loather died, there was never a question of who would fill the vacated pulpit chair. There was no man of God better equipped to carry on Dr. Charles Loather Sr.'s vision than his son, Charles Jr.

Charles Loather Jr. was young, but wise beyond his years. He knew that despite his education and spiritual insight, he needed to bring the growing congregation under more experienced covering. And connecting it to Reverend Tides and the New Hope Fellowship of Churches was quite possibly the smartest move the young pastor could have made. The association had been a good one, and Reverend Tides had passed along much wisdom to the son of Dr. Loather. The changing of the guard was given much of the credit for the church's expansion.

Neil took particular pleasure in seeing the younger Charles Loather walk through the side entrance to take his seat on the elevated platform of KBCC. Neil had been acquainted with Pastor Charles Loather Jr. since the days he was simply known as CJ. The cleric's closest friends still referred to him as such in spite of his eminent ministerial ranking at the church. Prior to his ecclesiastical ordination, CJ had served many years as a police detective in metropolitan Atlanta's DeKalb County, which was the district in which he still resided. But four years ago, the law enforcer made a choice to lay aside his badge to take up his mantle as full-time pastor of Kingdom Builders Christian Center, where he had served as youth pastor for ten years prior.

As undergrads at the same university, Neil and CJ became fast friends and had seen each other through some of the roughest times of their lives: for CJ, the death of both his parents, and for Neil, the death of his brother.

"We have come into this house to gather in His name and worship Him. . . ."

The eight-member praise team's perfectly blended harmony drew Neil's attention away from his pastor and friend. Morning worship had begun, and Neil found himself standing and swaying in sync to the music of the Hammond organ and slowly forgetting about the tenderness of his joints from yesterday's chores.

Tuning out the off-key singing of the elderly man who sat beside him wasn't quite as simple. At ninety, Homer Burgess was the church's oldest deacon by far. Some days he was sane, and others, he bordered senile. But even on his most feeble days, Deacon Burgess remembered all the words to any song that the praise team rendered. And on no day did he ever sing on key. Because of it, all of the other brothers who occupied the specified section tried to arrive as early as possible to avoid being the unfortunate one to have to settle for the seat directly beside the old man. Today's traffic woes had assigned the space to Neil, and his poor ears were burning with agony.

Praise dancers swarmed the front of the church, adding beauty and strength to the already significant lyrics of each song that was rendered. It helped to take Neil's attention off of the tone deaf deacon and meditate on the Spirit. For a while, he felt as if the entire sanctuary were being occupied by an overflow of anointing that would burst the cathedral at its seams. Every church that was a part of the New Hope Fellowship of Churches was known for radical worship, so Sunday morning services at KBCC were always uplifting. But there seemed to be something extraordinary about today. Ultimately, when the lengthy praise fest ended, the microphone was relinquished to CJ to bring forth the Word of God for the hour.

"When God is in the building, the sin sick are healed. . . ."

As soon as the pastor began belting out the song that was made popular by The Anointed Pace Sisters, it brought the praise team back to the microphones and the crowd back to its feet. He wasn't nearly as unskilled as Deacon Burgess, but singing had never been CJ's strong point, and it was rare that he ever even made an attempt at the talent.

"Come on up here and help me, Deacon Taylor."

Neil's eyes bulged at the sound of his name being broadcast through the church speakers, and he took a quick look around like there might possibly be someone else in the midst who shared his name. Surely CJ wasn't beckoning him.

Unlike CJ, singing was a forte for Neil, but it was a gift he'd chosen to shelve a long time ago . . . and CJ knew that. Neil's career was educating and mentoring children, nothing more and nothing less. But years ago, it was CJ's father who had always declared that Neil's calling was to sing.

"Sing your way into victory, boy!" he'd often yell from the pulpit when Neil took the mic.

Neil's gift for singing was discovered when he was still a child, around five years old, growing up on a deep-country farm. He and his older brother, Dwayne, would sing together while they and the rest of their family worked in the fields. For the boys, it helped lessen the heat of the sun and made the time pass quicker. But for others who were working alongside them, it was pure, unadulterated joy.

Soon after Neil graduated from high school, his family moved to Atlanta and quickly found a spiritual home at Kingdom Builders Christian Center. When they were young adults attending church with their mother, the elder Dr. Charles Loather would call on the brothers to carry out praise and worship, and sometimes, to lead the choir in songs that neither Neil nor Dwayne had ever rehearsed. Because the boys delivered with rarely ever a blunder, Dr. Loather said it was a sign of God's calling. Even after Dwayne's untimely death, Dr. Loather would request Neil's vocal assistance. But his compliance was always with much resentment.

After Dr. Loather was laid to rest, Neil asked CJ not to resume the tradition. CJ fought Neil on his decision, but ultimately, as an act of compassion, CJ gave his word. Neil's rich, raspy voice and his energetic delivery gave him the unspoken edge of favorite between him and his brother. And when Neil discontinued his frequent appearances, the church members sulked like spoiled children. But CJ understood more than most. He knew his friend didn't enjoy singing as much as he once had back in the days when Dwayne would stand by his side and harmonize.

Today, however, either someone had requested him, or the pastor must have felt a special leading from the Holy Spirit. If it were CJ's doing, Neil made a mental note to reprimand him for defying his wishes. And if it were the leading of the Holy Spirit . . . well, Neil didn't like that any better. Either way, he wasn't pleased with the open bid, and his narrowed eyes did their best to relay that message to his pastor and friend.

"Sing, Brother Taylor, sing!"

Without looking around, Neil knew that the loud coaxing came from his very own assistant, Margaret Dasher. She was easily his biggest fan when it came to just about anything, and he wondered if she were the perpetrator behind the request for him to sing today. When CJ ignored his silent protest and summoned him for the second time, Neil clenched and unclenched his jaws, then maneuvered his way past the other deacons and toward the front of the church, where the pastor met him at the foot of the pulpit with the microphone in hand. Neil took the mic, but not before giving CJ his best I'll-get-you-for-this-later look.

"When God Is In The Building" had at one time been one of Neil's favorite songs, but it had been so long since he had heard it that while his mouth belted out the tune, his mind juggled to recall the proper words. If any of the original lyrics were missed or sung out of sequence, the audience never made the detection. Neil had come to the front fully determined to sing one chorus just to show obedience to leadership, and then sit down. But God wouldn't allow it.

The tempo of the early 1990s anthem was slow, but the more Neil sang it, the more the ushers were forced to evacuate their stations and attend to congregants who had been overcome by the moving of the Holy Spirit. Neil had started out standing flat-footed on the floor at the base of the speaker's stand, directly in the middle of the church. By the time the song was over, he was leaning against the organ situated on the right end of the pulpit. Even Neil didn't understand how he had climbed the steps to the platform without cringing from painful soreness.

For a while, even after Neil ended the song, it was Sunday morning pandemonium.

"Sit down, sit down, sit down," CJ instructed the crowd, motioning with his hands as Neil returned the microphone to him. "Y'all sit down before y'all take up all my preaching time."

Although the charge was given, it was no surprise when few, if any, of the church members complied. The musicians had stopped the music, but people were still in active worship, walking the floor, leaping for joy, and raising their voices in praise and thanksgiving.

As Neil stood at his seat with his arms lifted in adulation, he felt hairs standing at attention beneath the sleeves of his shirt. It had been some time since God's hand had moved in the manner that it did today. But then again, it had been some time since Deacon Neil Taylor had sung.

For a long while, CJ stood in silence and allowed the voices of the people to fill the edifice. There was no music or singing, only sounds of worship that came from the lips of those who were allowing God to touch them. Moments turned into minutes, and there were no signs that the praises would end any time soon.

"Look around you, people of God," CJ finally said. "See Mother Turner over there? See Sister Marissa in the back? See this young man kneeling at the altar? See the choir members that have been slain under the anointing? That's what happens when God is in the building!"

Voices from the audience that had already been elevated got even louder. The noise level inside of KBCC was comparable to that of a basketball game wherein the home team was down by one point and had the last possession of the ball. CJ had approached the speaker's stand with an open Bible, ready to start the day's message, but with one motion of his hand, he reached forward and closed it, having not even taken his text.

Holding the cordless microphone in his hand, he walked back and forth on the platform, at first saying nothing. Then, coming to a stop and facing his audience, CJ declared, "I hope y'all are getting what you need from the Lord, 'cause God said that's the Word for today, saints. He's in the building. He's in the building. He's in the building. Do y'all hear what I'm saying? Do you feel His presence? He's in the building!"

CJ stepped down from the podium, holding the microphone in one hand and grabbing a portion of his clerical robe in the other so that he wouldn't step on the hem. Walking the floor, he arbitrarily touched the foreheads of several worshippers, all the while speaking into the microphone. "You're gonna leave here with a new purpose that's waiting to be fulfilled. You know why? Because God is in the building, and He's gonna show you what He wants you to do. You're gonna leave here with a new mind that's not easily confused. You know why?

Because God is in the building, and He's gonna change your way of thinking. You're gonna leave here with a new heart that loves. You know why? Because God is in the building, and He's gonna remake your heart from the inside out!"

With that last statement, he touched Neil's head, suddenly rendering him weak and overcome by a phenomenon that he could not ascertain. Neil sank onto the bench that he'd been standing in front of and wept in his hands. With each passing moment, the tears gained momentum. He couldn't recollect the last time he'd sobbed on this level. Maybe it was at the funeral of his brother, who had died more than fifteen years ago. When Neil cried at Dwayne's burial, he recalled feeling as though he was rejoicing and grieving all at the same time. Back then, he understood why. He was sad that his brother was gone and that his mother's heart was broken, but he was joyful to know beyond doubt that Dwayne had died happy and knowing Christ.

Today he had no idea why he was experiencing that same mixture of incalculable emotions. All he knew was that he wanted the tears to stop, but he wasn't in control.

"You know why?" CJ's voice echoed in a timely manner that sounded like he was

challenging Neil's thoughts from somewhere in the distance as he continued to
pace the floor. "Because God is in the building, and your life is *never* gonna be the same
again!"

FOUR

I must have been on crystal meth when I even thought to volunteer for this. Shaylynn stood in the back of her son's first grade classroom, watching the hyperactive children prance around as they waited impatiently to leave the room and head to the bus that would transport them to the Georgia Aquarium. She didn't know if it were due to her presence in the room, but Chase was one of the few who seemed content coloring the artwork that the teacher had given them to occupy the time.

When she told her son that she would fill in the vacancy, if needed, to make the trip happen, Shaylynn had been more than sure that another parent would want to ride along. She'd prayed that somebody — *anybody* — would do it so that she wouldn't have to. Yet somehow, here she stood in a room full of wired children that she was sure would push her nerves to the limit before the end of the day.

Look at all the other places in the world that I could be right now. She half-mindlessly looked at the colorful, large print map that was posted on the classroom wall. Shaylynn was left to wonder if her private thought had somehow been verbalized when she saw the teacher taking quick steps in her direction, her face bearing a troubled look.

Miss Berkshire was a thin white woman, even shorter than Shaylynn. She barely looked old enough to be out of school, let alone teaching it. She was cute in a childish kind of way, but the freckles on her face and neck were so obvious that they made Shaylynn want to pick up a marker and connect the dots. Miss Berkshire's underdeveloped body mirrored that of a twelve-year-old girl, but with the assistance of makeup, and with her red hair pinned into a neat up-do, her face looked closer to nineteen or twenty. As she neared Shaylynn, the teacher's expression became an apologetic billboard.

"I'm so sorry, Mrs. Ford. We're running just a little bit behind schedule. The other parent that was supposed to help chaperone hasn't arrived yet." She looked at her watch, and her face fell even more. "I have a full classroom of twenty-five today. Even the

69

daughter of the parent who is supposed to go on the trip with us is here, so I don't know where her mother is. My assistant had a death in her family and had to take some days off. It's against Kingdom Builders' policy for me to take the children away from the school with more than a ten-to-one student/adult ratio. If Ms. Garrison doesn't arrive soon —"

"Hey, Dr. Taylor!" a chorus of children's voices sang all at once.

Shaylynn turned to see several of the children, her son included, rush to the door, where Neil had barely had the chance to enter before he was bombarded. If she didn't know any better, she would have guessed that the new arrival was some sort of superstar. Barney, the beloved purple dinosaur, didn't get this kind of reception from the children on the television show that Chase watched occasionally. Shaylynn watched the scene in awe as Neil took the time to greet each one of the excited kids, either with high fives, handshakes, head rubs, or hugs before asking them to excuse him while he spoke to their teacher. Obediently, the children scattered and freed Neil to walk in the direction of the other adults.

"Hi, Dr. Taylor," Miss Berkshire said. Suddenly her actions mirrored her adolescent appearance. The woman shifted her feet, tucked a non-existent strand of stray hair behind her ear, and then timidly straightened the jacket of her tailored navy blue pants suit. Her already rosy cheeks deepened in an obvious blush.

"Umph." The sound escaped before Shaylynn could suppress it, and she hoped that no one else had heard.

Neil grinned at the teacher, concurrently ducking his head. "Miss Berkshire," he acknowledged. "How's it going today?"

"Good, Dr. Taylor." Her distinct green eyes batted in quick motions before she turned in Shaylynn's direction. "Oh." Miss Berkshire uttered the single word like she had forgotten a parent was even standing there. Like Neil's entrance had totally erased her short-term memory. It only took her a second to regroup and say, "By the way, Dr. Taylor, this is Mrs. Ford. She's Chase's mother."

Shaylynn watched a smile snake its way across Neil's lips as he extended his hand toward her. "I know," he admitted. "I had the pleasure of meeting Mrs. Ford last week."

His hand was warm, just like it had been when he shook her hand at their first meeting. "Good to see you again, Dr. Taylor,"

Shaylynn said, only meeting his dark brown eyes briefly before looking away. There was something about this guy that she really didn't like . . . or really *did* like. She hadn't yet decided.

"Likewise," Neil replied. Then, turning to Miss Berkshire, he said, "I was coming by to check on the class trip. The bus has been waiting outside for a while, and I believe you were scheduled to leave nearly fifteen minutes ago. Is everything all right?" He looked back toward Shaylynn as though he thought her presence was the reason for the delay.

The teacher caught his concern and swiftly said, "Oh, no. Mrs. Ford is here to ride along as a chaperone. Unfortunately, my other parent volunteer hasn't shown up yet, and I have too many children for just the two of us to monitor."

"I see," Neil said, glancing again at his watch.

Feeling a tug around her hips, Shaylynn looked down into the troubled eyes of her son.

"Mama, when are we leaving?"

"I don't know, Chase. Just be patient," Shaylynn replied, giving him advice that she was having trouble applying to her own life.

There was so much that she could have

been doing today. Having already started, folded, and then restarted her business on a couple of occasions, Shaylynn understood how important it was to be in place when potential new clients called. If she wanted to establish hers as a stable and reliable company, days like this one couldn't happen too frequently. Every second that ticked away on the clock represented lost revenue.

"Dr. Taylor?"

A familiar amplified voice broke into Shaylynn's thoughts, and she looked up to see the woman who had tried to pry into the details of her personal life.

"Come on in, Ms. Dasher," Neil said. "You remember Chase's mom," he added as she neared where they all stood.

"Of course. How are you, *Mrs.* Ford?"

Shaylynn detected the slight emphasis that the director's assistant placed on the title, but brushed off the urge to respond with the same level of sarcasm. And why did this woman always have to talk so loud? She'd done that same thing the first day they'd met. Did Ms. Dasher think everyone was hard of hearing or something? Shaylynn forced herself not to roll her eyes, but she immediately filed Margaret Dasher in the "unsure" pile too, right alongside her boss. She'd determine later whether she liked the wide-hipped, spectacle-wearing woman. Right now, the cards weren't stacking in Ms. Dasher's favor.

Keeping her voice on an even keel, Shaylynn answered, "I'm fine, thank you."

"What can I do for you, Ms. Dasher?" Despite his pleasant tone, Neil tossed his assistant a reprimanding gaze that Shaylynn didn't fail to notice.

"We just received a call from a Ms. Tomeka Garrison. She said that she was supposed to assist with today's trip to the aquarium, but she's having car trouble and is stuck at the mechanic's. She says she won't be able to make it."

Yes! Shaylynn struggled not to pump her fist in victory like Serena Williams would after acing a serve. Thank the Lord! He had answered her prayers after all. She wasted no time reaching for the purse that she'd set on an empty desk during the wait and began fishing for her keys.

As loud and lively as the classroom full of children had been prior to Margaret Dasher's entrance, each child overheard the amplified announcement, and it resulted in a collective disappointment-filled moan. Some moped to their desks while others remained standing, but slumped their shoulders in defeat. A few of them looked to be two seconds away from tears.

"I told my mama not to buy that old ugly, raggedy car," a pretty little girl in thick pigtails huffed. It didn't take a genius to figure out that she was Ms. Garrison's daughter.

"Does that mean we can't go?" Chase asked over the voices of others who were asking the same question.

"It doesn't mean we can't go," his teacher said in as sympathetic a voice as she could. "It just means that we can't go *today.* We'll just reschedule for another day when we can get the assistance that we need."

The verbal pacifier that she handed them was rejected with more whines, accompanied by fits of pouting, as more children moped back to their seats with fallen faces. And the tears that some had held back until now were skating down their cheeks.

"See, honey?" Shaylynn said, feeling ill about her own elation after noting the wounded look on her son's face. "You'll still get to see the fish. You'll just have to see them on another day."

"Sure you will," Miss Berkshire added, tweaking Chase's cheek in the process. "School rules won't allow just your mother and me to take you. It's not safe for there to be too many children and not enough chaperones. So, as soon as we get someone else to sign up, we'll reschedule."

"What about you, Dr. Taylor?" Chase said, abandoning both his mother and his teacher and taking a spot directly in front of his school's director. "Can't you go with us so we'll have enough grown-ups?"

"Chase." Shaylynn tried not to lace her whisper with harshness, but her level of embarrassment couldn't be hidden in her tone. She'd always taught her son not to beg anybody for anything, and to her ears, that's exactly what Chase's plea sounded like. "Dr. Taylor has to work. He can't leave to go on a trip. Now, those same fish will be there on the date that's rescheduled."

"Do I have anything on my desk that's pressing, Ms. Dasher?" Neil asked, bringing astonishment to Shaylynn's eyes and hope to Chase's.

"Well . . ." Margaret paused to think deeply. "Not *pressing,* I don't suppose, but unless you want me to call Pastor Loather and tell him you won't be available, you do have that conference call this afternoon."

Neil shook his head. "No, no, no. Pastor Loather is my boss. I can't very well tell him that I'm no longer available for an appointment that's been on the books for two weeks. Just give him a call and tell him to call me on my cell because I'll be away from my office for most of the day."

"Does that mean we can go?" Chase's face brightened.

Neil nodded and brushed his hand across the boy's head. "That's what it means, Chase. Miss Berkshire, if you and Mrs. Ford will line the kids up and escort them to the bus, I'll meet you there shortly."

Shaylynn could barely hear Neil's words over the cheers of the students. And as much as she wanted to be at home working on completing the setup of her office, Shaylynn smiled as she watched her son hold up his arms and jump up and down in sync with one of the other boys in the class. Knowing Chase was happy forced her to set aside her selfish desires. Just like the fish would still be at the aquarium had the class visited on a later date, the clients that would help to rebuild Ford's Home Interior & Designs would still be there as well.

God willing.

FIVE

"So what time should I tell the pastor to call you?" Margaret followed Neil around his office with pad and pen in hand while he gathered his belongings.

Neil paused long enough to face her. "Well, I understand that the kids have sack lunches and will be eating at the end of their tour, which will be around noon. That should be a good time for him to call. Let's say twelve-thirty just to be on the safe side." He scurried to his desk and pulled out a folder he would need to have for his scheduled conversation with Pastor Loather.

"What are *you* going to do about lunch?"

Neil chuckled at Margaret's maternal-like concern. "Don't worry about me, Ms. Dasher. I'll eat. I always do. I'm sure there is an eatery somewhere in the area where I can pick up something quick." Slipping on his Ray Bans and his suit jacket, and then scooping up his briefcase, Neil walked into the school lobby and stopped at the front door with Margaret still behind him. "Call me if you need me," he concluded, and then pushed through the door that delivered him outside. The heat index prompted him to remove his suit jacket during the short walk to the bus, and as he stepped onboard, the cheers of the children were deafening. Knowing he'd made them happy gave him a sense of pride.

Miss Berkshire offered him a front seat, but he declined. Immediately upon boarding, Neil noticed Shaylynn sitting in the rear of the bus and answered the calls for several high fives on his way to join her. It wasn't until he'd placed his jacket over the back of the seat and laid his briefcase on the space beside him that Neil realized Shaylynn's distracted demeanor. She looked straight ahead, closely watching her son, who sat four seats in front of her, sharing the row with two of his classmates.

"You're very protective of him, aren't you?" Neil watched Shaylynn's eyes redirect after her stare had been broken by his words. Seeing her bewilderment, he offered clarification. "Chase. I've noticed that you keep a pretty watchful eye on him."

"I'm his mother. Isn't that what mothers do?" Her reply wasn't quite a snap, but it was definitely guarded.

"You'd be surprised," Neil said. "He's a good kid, and I applaud you for being an involved parent. It's not as common as you may believe."

She seemed to relax a bit. "Thanks."

Although the forty-five minute ride to the Georgia Aquarium was noisy with the chatter of overzealous children, the back rows were silent during the first half of the trip. Periodically, Neil would steal a glance in Shaylynn's direction, but she never looked in his. If her eyes weren't observing her son's interactions, they were staring, almost robotically, out of the window beside her. Neil couldn't recall the last time a woman that he knew so little about had intrigued him more. Shaylynn's disposition almost perplexed him. She was quite pleasing to look at, but even on the few occasions that he'd seen her smile, her eyes carried a shadow of sorrow.

"Has Chase ever been to the aquarium?" Neil tried to make small talk to ease what felt like an unsubstantiated mounting tension.

Shaylynn hinted a smile and shook her head from side to side. "No. He's really excited about the visit. It's just about all he's talked about for the last two weeks. I

80

hope it lives up to his expectations."

"I'm certain that it will. The Georgia Aquarium is the largest aquarium in the world. It's like a sporting event in Atlanta; draws a lot of fans . . . and children are always captivated when they see the displays." Neil chuckled. "Heck, if most grown folks are honest, they'll admit that they're pretty impressed on their first visit too."

"A sporting event, huh? So should I expect to be awed by the little fishes too?"

Neil turned to look at Shaylynn and saw the blatant sarcasm on her face. He couldn't help but appreciate knowing that beneath the surface, there lay a sense of humor. It was an unexpected pleasure upon which he felt a strong desire to build.

"You think I'm overstating the facts, do you?"

Shaylynn shrugged and smoothed out the soft wrinkles in her grey silk slacks. "Since I've not been there, I probably don't have the right to make that call," she replied. "But one thing that I've learned about Atlantans and sports in the little time that I've been here is that you all really love your city and your teams. Personally, I think they're both overrated."

Shifting his body in his seat, Neil turned so that his legs were in the aisle, and he faced Shaylynn. "How so?"

"Are you going to get defensive, Dr. Taylor? I mean, I don't want to offend you."

Neil flashed a toothy grin and adjusted his sunglasses. He searched Shaylynn's youthful face and wondered how old she was. With a six-year-old, he guessed that she was probably at least twenty-six, and then calculated the years that separated her age from his. *Nineteen.* It sounded like too large a number to Neil, but it didn't erase his growing intrigue.

"Everyone is entitled to his or her own opinion, Mrs. Ford. Now, I can't promise you that I won't defend my hometown or the teams that represent it, but I don't think you can say anything that I would take as a personal offense."

Shaylynn looked toward Chase for a moment, and then for the first time since their conversation began, she gave Neil her undivided attention. "Well, Atlanta itself is overcrowded and riddled with crime. And once . . . just *once,* I'd like to go to my neighborhood post office without having an able-bodied man wearing a G-Unit shirt, FUBU jeans, and a pair of Air Force Ones standing out front begging for money, and then copping an attitude when I refuse to give him any."

"That's not just in Atlanta," Neil rebutted. "That's everywhere and always has been. Even the Bible tells us that the poor will be with us always."

"The Bible also says that if a man doesn't work, he shouldn't eat. I know there are some who have not because they cannot, but since I've been in Atlanta, I've seen countless people who have not because they *do* not."

She knew the Bible, and to Neil, that was a good sign. He nodded slowly and decided to move on. "And why do you dislike our sports teams?"

"I didn't say I disliked them. I said that they're overrated."

"In what way?"

"Let's take your baseball team for instance." She didn't miss a beat.

"The Braves."

"Uh-huh." Shaylynn nodded and removed the clip that held her neatly woven braids in a ponytail, and then replaced it after freeing some of the braids and allowing them to fall to the sides of her face. Then she threw him a brief side look. "They've only won one national championship, but if I recall correctly, just a few years ago, Atlanta wanted to make a very public stink about the fact that the Braves weren't chosen as the baseball team of the century."

"Well, they had valid grounds to feel slighted, don't you think? I mean, they'd won more consecutive pennants than any other team in baseball history."

"But they'd won only one World Series, whereas New York had won several."

Neil's right eyebrow arched. He was impressed by how well-informed this woman was. She must have had some northern ties. "A New York fan, are you?"

She grimaced. "No. Not at all. Not of the city or the team, but like 'em or not, they earned the title of team of the century."

The left corner of Neil's lips curled up into a half smile. Shaylynn's knowledge of sports statistics charmed him even more. "Perhaps," he said. "But according to who's doing the judging, the definition of a champion may not be so much defined by the team who wins, but rather the team that shows the most integrity during the battle."

"Is that so?"

Both of Neil's eyebrows rose this time. He realized immediately that he'd set himself up for a new challenge. "You don't agree?"

"Oh, no. Quite the opposite. I fully agree. I just think that it's funny that you should cite that when speaking of Atlanta."

"What do you mean?"

"The Falcons have only made it to the finals of one Super Bowl, right?"

Neil's grin returned and expanded, and he quietly accepted defeat even before Shaylynn made her point. He already knew where she was headed with this one, and the impression that she'd already made on him was getting deeper by the minute. When he didn't respond, she continued.

"The one time that they made it to the Super Bowl, not only did they lose the game by two touchdowns, but they showed very little integrity, even going so far as getting in legal troubles while they were there in Miami to play the Broncos." Then curling her upper lip, she added, "And the Hawks, well . . ."

Neil leaned back and broke into a hearty laugh that caused the children in the seats nearest them to briefly turn and look before resuming their own conversations. He was probably getting too much pleasure from the exchange between Shaylynn and him. Although her words were straightforward and her facial expressions matched them to perfection, Neil felt a twinge of toying in Shaylynn's interaction. He knew that it was most likely all wishful thinking, but he enjoyed it anyway.

"Come on, Mrs. Ford. Cut us a break.

Besides, the Hawks are playing a whole lot better now than they've played in recent history. You have to give us that much."

"And I will." She returned his smile. "Yes, they are doing better. Their games don't get blacked out on the cable networks like they used to. They've been impressive in a couple of playoff challenges in recent years. There's hope of a championship for them yet."

Neil laughed again, and then said, "Your knowledge of sports is commendable." His eyes followed her hands as they reached into her purse and pulled out a pair of sunglasses of her own. The studded Baby Phat emblem showed on the frame. "Not many women that I know are sports fans. Where did you get your love for the game?"

"The words *fan* and *love* are far too strong, Dr. Taylor. I assure you that." She paused as she blew her warm breath on the lenses of her glasses and wiped them with the end of her multi-colored silk blouse. "I don't have a love for sports, and I can't say that I'm a fan of any particular team. I just got into the habit of watching the games with Emmett, and occasionally, I still watch with Chase."

Although she looked directly ahead and not at him, Neil could see the sadness gradually return to Shaylynn's eyes. "Emmett?" He had little doubt that he didn't already know the answer, but Neil fished for assurance.

Shaylynn took a moment to slip the sunglasses on her face, and then she relaxed her head against the back of the seat. "My husband."

Shaylynn's voice that had once been strong was barely audible when she spoke the two words, but they were loud and clear to Neil's ears. Not her former husband, not her deceased husband, not her late husband . . . but her husband. Neil bitterly took note of that. Shaylynn's body language clearly stated that she didn't want the conversation to continue, but as Neil caught a new sparkle from her wedding set, he knew he had to keep talking. Not necessarily about Emmett. As a matter of fact, he didn't even want to talk about Emmett. But he needed to talk about *something.* He needed to establish a level of trust between them so that he could get to know her better. Neil's fascination was too strong to let go now.

"So is there anything about Atlanta that you like?" He thought he'd take it back to their original conversation, and when Shaylynn turned in his direction and delivered to him a faint smile, Neil figured he'd made a good decision.

"Have I led you to believe that I hate the city?"

"You don't?"

Shaylynn sat up straight. "Of course not. I wouldn't live here if I hated it. I do have options, you know."

"I don't doubt that one bit. I'd guess that you have more choices than most." Neil tried to mask his allusive tone, but from the look Shaylynn tossed him, he knew he'd failed. Quickly moving on, he asked, "So what do you like about Atlanta?"

After a thoughtful pause, she replied, "Well, for starters, I like Kingdom Builders Academy."

Neil couldn't have withheld his pleasure if he'd tried. "That's good to know. I take that as a personal compliment. Whenever the school gets a high mark from a parent, it makes me feel like I'm doing something right."

Shaylynn looked toward Chase, and then back at Neil. "When my son is happy, I'm happy."

Agreeably, Neil nodded. "Anything else about Atlanta that you find . . . attractive?" Now he was just plain flirting, but from Shaylynn's reply, Neil doubted that she'd picked up on it.

"I like the potential for success that a new business like mine has."

Neil leaned forward. "What business is that?"

"I'm an interior decorator."

"Oh?" He never would have guessed, but as meticulously dressed as Shaylynn always appeared to be, a job that involved beautifying and coordinating was a perfect fit for her. "Is it a sole proprietorship?"

"Yes. Now that we've been here a few months, and Chase has adjusted to our new surroundings, I'm laying the groundwork for my company."

"Will it be home based?"

"For starters, yes. Cuts down on the overhead."

"Definitely," Neil agreed.

"I may branch out into a separate workspace later."

"That's economically smart. Have you chosen a name yet?" The more Neil talked to Shaylynn, the more he wanted to talk to her.

"I had the business about a year ago when we lived in Louisiana. It was called Ford's Home Interior and Designs then, so I plan to stick with that name as I restart it."

"Ford's Home Interior and Designs." Neil mulled over the name like a cud-chewing cow. It was too wordy and just seemed too ordinary for the extraordinary woman who would be running the business. Neil's thoughts must have shown on his face.

"What? You don't like that name?"

Neil turned to look at Shaylynn. She had removed her sunglasses and was turned in his direction, leaning forward and looking directly into his eyes as though his opinion mattered. For a brief span, her pecan-shaped eyes grabbed his tongue and held on, not allowing him to form the words for a prompt response.

"What's the matter with Ford's Home Interior and Designs?" she pressed, breaking his momentary trance.

Neil's mouth suddenly begged for moisture. "Nothing's wrong with it," he managed to say, licking his lips for relief, and then continuing. "I think I was just expecting you to say something different. Something with a little more . . ."

"More what?" Shaylynn urged when his voice trailed.

"I don't know. Just something a little catchier, a little jazzier, I guess."

A lasting period was placed on Neil's response when the school bus slowed and came to a brief stop as the driver maneuvered the large vehicle into the parking lot

of the aquarium that had made special al-
lowances for field trip visitors. Generally,
tours such as the one Kingdom Builders
Academy had planned, began at noon, but
the Georgia Aquarium had acquired two
new whale sharks, the only ones known to
be in any aquarium outside of Asia, and
elementary schools from all over the city
were taking advantage of the exclusive
Tuesday morning four-hour tour invitation.

Their tardy arrival forced the driver to
park farther away than most other school
buses had, and the children's excitement
level rose as the engine was turned off and
the driver opened the door in preparation
for their exit. Neil stood and Shaylynn followed his lead. Her petite stature made him
feel taller than he really was. He liked that.

"Children, children, children," Miss Berkshire said in an attempt to gain the attention of those who had marveled by the mere
sight of the outside of the facility. "Have a
seat for a moment and quiet down. We cannot get off of the bus until you quiet down."
When the children complied, she continued
in a tone that seemed mastered by grade
school teachers. It was a slow, rhythmic
speech that paralleled one used when speaking to a foreigner who wasn't fluent in
English. "Remember the rules that we went

over in class. We will do what?"

"Stay together," the children chanted.

"And we will what?"

"Use our inside voices."

"And we will what?"

"Keep our hands by our sides."

"Unless we are what?"

"Given permission to touch something."

Neil laughed to himself and hoped the rookie school teacher realized that for the children, repeating the rules was much easier than following them. He predicted that he, Shaylynn, and Miss Berkshire would have their hands full for the next few hours.

Satisfied that they were clear on the memorized rules, Miss Berkshire stood at the front of the bus and instructed the students to form a line. As the children made their dismount and the line ahead shortened, Neil extended his arm in a silent invitation for Shaylynn to step into the aisle ahead of him. As she did, his eyes automatically scanned her shapely form. Nice. *Real* nice. Now that he knew Shaylynn wasn't the married woman he'd thought her to be before she set the record straight at their first meeting, checking her out in such an exploratory manner didn't feel so out of order.

Resuming their conversation would be difficult now that their duties as chaperones had officially begun, but Neil knew that he had to find a way.

Six

"Three hours and counting. You must be on a roll in here." Theresa approached CJ from behind, massaged her fingers through his short, coarse hair, and then sealed it all with a kiss on his shoulder.

Swiveling around in his dark chocolate leather executive chair where he'd been sitting and jotting down scripture notations, CJ faced his wife of four years with an appreciative grin. He not only liked what she said, but also what he saw. To him, few women could hold a candle to First Lady Theresa Loather. She was top light and bottom heavy, and most days she wore her thick shoulder length hair pulled up into a bun that was held together by some chopstick-looking hair accessory. Brown designer frames sat on her nose, but the frames didn't come close to hiding the prettiness of her face. To most men, Theresa's school teacher–like guise probably wouldn't be the most appealing one, but CJ loved it.

His home office, sparsely decorated with only a fully stocked bookshelf (mostly biblical reference guides and law officer handbooks) and a few family photos and ministerial certificates on the walls, was the one room of the house that Theresa rarely entered. Especially on Wednesdays. That day, more than any other weekday, was when CJ was hard at work outlining what would ultimately become his sermon for the upcoming Sunday. But on those infrequent occasions when his wife crossed the threshold of his study space, CJ always welcomed the intrusion.

"Hey, baby." He reached for the steaming cup of coffee that she dangled in front of him like a fishing lure. "Ahhh. A jolt of java. Just what I need to get me through the second half of my studies. Thank you, Resa." It was the nickname she had been given by her parents as a child, and the name CJ most often used when speaking with her. He took a second to blow into the cloudy brown liquid and to inhale a whiff of his favorite vanilla hazelnut fragrance before placing the mug on his desk to cool.

"I'd like to see what sort of message you're going to come up with that will top last week's. Whew!" Theresa used both her hands to fan herself like the thought of it all ignited a flame in her soul. "It was some kinda hot up in that church Sunday."

Shaking his head, CJ replied, "I wish I could take the credit for that, but it was no doing of mine, that's for sure. If you'll recall, the Spirit took over, and I never got the opportunity to bring the message."

Theresa disagreed. "Oh, you brought the Word, Pastor Loather; make no mistake about it. 'When God Is In The Building' was the Word whether it came straight from a scripture text or not. It was what God gave you and what the people needed to hear. The message might have been short, but believe you me, it was brought. Your daddy was probably up in heaven with the other saints, pointing down at you and going, 'That's *my* boy right there, y'all. That's my boy!' "

CJ's fair skin blushed for two reasons. One, he relished when Theresa called him Pastor Loather. He had never been able to determine why the words sounded different coming out of her mouth than when they were said by one of his congregants. When they said it, it sounded like a term of respect. When *she* said it, it sounded like an aphrodisiac. The second reason the weight of the compliment nearly overwhelmed CJ was because he often wondered whether his father was able to look down from heaven and see his only son standing in the pulpit, leading the worshippers that the elder Loather had faithfully served as their shepherd for so many years. And if his father could see him, CJ wondered if he approved of what he saw and was indeed proud. Charles Loather Sr. had left some mighty big shoes to fill. CJ could only hope that Theresa was right, and his dad was satisfied.

There was no questioning the fact that last Sunday's worship service had been extraordinary, but CJ had never been one to pat himself on the back. He felt far more comfortable praising others. "I don't know who would have made Daddy prouder: me or Neil. Did that Negro sing Sunday or what?"

Theresa reached upward and waved her hands in the air like she was back on the front row of Kingdom Builders Christian Center. "Oh my goodness! Baby, I know the Holy Spirit led you to give Neil that mic. There's just no other way to explain it. I just wanted to pick up something and throw it at that boy." She coughed out a short laugh, then dropped her hands by her side and began pacing back and forth. "I hadn't heard Neil sing in so long that I had just about forgotten that he could. And I think he sings better now than when I last heard him. It's a sin, a straight-up sin that Neil keeps that talent to himself. When God entrusts us with gifts, it is so He can be glorified through them. What kind of glory is God getting from Neil's voice if he muzzles it like it's something to be ashamed of instead of displayed?"

CJ tried to hide his grin behind the cup as he took his first sip of coffee. Theresa often walked the floor when she got worked up about a particular topic, and CJ enjoyed the way her ample butt cheeks bounced when she paced with a purpose. Their preset five-year plan would end in less than a year. Prior to getting married, they had agreed that five years into their union, they'd begin a family. If everything went according to plan, he'd be forty-six and she'd be thirty-eight when they had their first child. The second addition would come very soon thereafter. It was late by most couples' calendars, but they'd gotten married later in life than most couples they knew, and it was important to both of them that they were able to give their children the stable environment that they deserved. The Loathers' spiritual, financial, and romantic lives had never been stronger than they were right now. It was definitely time, and CJ was ready.

"Don't you think it's a shame?" she stopped and asked when her husband remained silent.

CJ stretched his eyes, and the tickertape of his mind did a quick recall to try to find the place where it had zoned out of the conversation. "Absolutely, baby. I totally agree." He furrowed his eyebrows and nodded his head vigorously, hoping the added theatrical effects would hide the reality that he wasn't even certain as to what he was agreeing. "It's more than a shame. A doggone shame is what it is." Lucky for him, his quick response worked.

"I know that's right." Theresa folded her arms in front of her and gave her head a solemn shake. "I'm surprised Neil still has that voice at all. It's a wonder God doesn't snatch it right out of his throat. There are countless people — *willing* people — who would love to have his talent, and he has the nerve to withhold it."

Glad to now be caught up to speed, CJ placed his cup back on the desk and said, "Well, the Word tells us that gifts and callings come without repentance. God's not going to take it just because Neil doesn't use it like he should."

"I don't know about that, baby." Theresa sat in the only other chair in CJ's office. It was an aged but sturdy wingback chair that had once belonged to his father. Theresa crossed her legs at the knees. "Somewhere in the Bible, is there not a story of the servant who hid the one talent he'd been given instead of multiplying it? And if I recall correctly, when his master saw that the servant had done nothing with that one talent, he stripped it from him and gave it to another servant who had not only made good use of the talents he'd been given, but had multiplied them."

CJ appreciated the fact that his wife was just about as well-versed in scripture as he was. She kept him on his toes, often helping him with the outlines for his sermons. "I'm very well aware of that biblical parable, baby. It's Matthew 24:14." He threw in that last part just so she'd know that he still had the upper hand. "But because that servant had his talent taken away doesn't automatically mean that God will hand that same judgment down to Neil. It's not like he has no basis for why he doesn't enjoy singing as much." He scooted closer to the edge of his chair. "When Daddy was alive, he and I used to take the male youth of the church on a fishing trip every year. Remember that?"

"Come on, CJ." Theresa sucked her teeth, folded her arms, and pressed her back into the cushion of the comfortable chair. "I know about those trips, and I know you haven't taken the boys on one of those summer outings since your father died. But if you think that taking kids on some overnight camping trip is to be compared with singing for the Lord —"

"Those were more than *some overnight camping trips,* Resa." CJ stood from his chair and walked the length of his modest-size home office, coming to a stop beside a hanging framed photo of his parents. He pointed to his father's image, and then back at himself. "We did a whole lot more than fish with those boys. We fished *for* those boys. For their souls. We talked to them about more than just growing up to become men of honor; we schooled them on how to become men of God. We read scriptures with them and prayed with them. It was way more than a simple fishing retreat."

The look on Theresa's face said she had no idea. "I'm sorry. I never knew it was so intense. I mean, the boys were always so eager to go, and there were always more of them than there were available seats on the bus. With them being so excited, I never thought much more than fun and games went on." She uncrossed her arms and her legs and clasped her hands together in her lap. Her eyes took on a disconcerted gaze. "But if the outings were so spiritually enhancing for the kids, why did you stop having them?"

Tossing a brief glance toward his parents' photo, and then looking back at his wife, CJ said, "Because my father was no longer around to do it with me." He sighed and his feet were heavy as he made his way back to his chair and plopped on the seat of the leather padding. "That's why I have a heart for what Neil is feeling. As much as I know that those fishing trips blessed those young men, without Daddy by my side, I lost my heart for that particular ministry." He looked at Theresa and hoped she'd get what he was trying to say. "But just because I no longer want to minister in that particular fashion doesn't mean that I'm gonna wake up one day and find out that God has taken away my ability to minister."

"I know that, honey, but there's still a difference between your situation and Neil's," Theresa said. "You still mentor and witness to the young people at the church. You may not take them fishing, but you do other fun things to keep them active in the church while showing them God's will for their lives. Neil, on the other hand, has completely stopped ministering."

"I disagree," CJ insisted. "Neil has stopped *singing,* yes. At least, he doesn't do it without a major protest. But he hasn't stopped ministering. How many parents of the children who have been enrolled in our school have ultimately come to worship with us at the church? When they fill out their visitors' cards, more than seventy-five percent of them say Dr. Neil Taylor was the one to extend the invitation. That's ministry, Resa."

When CJ saw Theresa sit forward in her chair and nod her head, he knew he'd won her over. But he still wanted to finish making his point. "I'm not saying that Neil shouldn't be using his gift of song. I mean, look how God used him Sunday." Rehashed thoughts made the corners of CJ's mouth curl upward. "Man! Just imagine how many souls would be blessed if he sang all the time like he used to back in the day. I wish he would just as much as you do, baby." He looked at Theresa. "But at the same time, I understand why he doesn't."

"I suppose you're right." Theresa stood and smoothed out her khaki Capri pants.

"Well, I'm gonna go and let you finish your studies."

CJ stood too. "You don't have to leave on my account. As a matter of fact, I might want to bounce some scripture expositions off of you and get your input."

Theresa smiled. He knew she'd like that, and he willingly accepted the kiss his wife delivered to his lips. "I'm not leaving the house, just the office. If you need me, you know where to find me," she said. "I've got to get started on dinner because I know you've got to be getting hungry after all this studying."

CJ would have denied it if it weren't true, but it was. He slipped his arm around Theresa's waist, and then allowed his hand to trail the full length of her backside as he pulled her closer. "Okay, I guess I'll let you go." He brushed his lips against the base of her neck and added, "Not that I want to."

"Get your mind back on the Word," Theresa teased as she pushed him away.

Laughing, CJ returned to his chair and handed his cup of lukewarm coffee back to his wife. "Yes, ma'am."

Theresa stopped at the office door, and then turned back to face him. "But don't get too spiritual," she said with a wink. "I saw you checking me out earlier, *Pastor*

Loather, and just so you know . . . I'm only feeding you because you're gonna need the strength later tonight. So finish up so you can fit me in your schedule."

CJ twitched like he'd suddenly been touched by the Spirit. "Hallelujah," he said, then added a sheepish grin as he spun his chair back around so that he faced his desk again.

SEVEN

Shay Décor.

It was Thursday afternoon, and the name had played and repeated itself in Shaylynn's head continuously since Neil suggested it two days ago. During the lunch break given to the children prior to boarding the bus and heading back to school, Neil stood near her chatting on the phone to someone, when all of a sudden, he pulled the phone from his ear and brushed her arm with his fingers.

"Shay Décor." He blurted the words as though a genuine light bulb had all of a sudden been turned on in his head.

Shaylynn didn't have a clue what he was talking about. "What?"

"Shay Décor," Neil repeated. "That's it. That's the name of your business. Shay Décor."

From the satisfied smile that seemed to

cover the entire surface of his face, Shaylynn could tell that he was proud of his own epiphany. Neil actually looked as if he wanted to present himself with some sort of outstanding achievement award for the idea he'd produced in the middle of his telephone meeting. Shaylynn had looked at him, but said nothing more, and he'd gone right back to his cell phone conversation, barely skipping a beat. It took Shaylynn a moment to compute what he had said, but when she did, she liked it.

"It has a sophisticated flair to it," Neil pointed out, still marketing the idea to her on the bus ride back to the campus. "It's so chic and refined and so . . . well, you."

Shaylynn liked that too. She didn't know why, but hearing Dr. Neil Taylor refer to her in such a praising manner made her feel good. With a background as disgraceful as hers, she'd been called a lot of things, but never refined or sophisticated. Emmett's family would certainly scoff at that one.

"If he knew my history, he wouldn't have said it either," she spoke aloud while admiring the second ad that she had placed in the newspaper concerning her new business. The *Atlanta Journal Constitution* was the most popular daily newspaper in Atlanta, and she'd placed an ad in it last week. This time, she took the advice of a television commercial and placed one in the *Atlanta Weekly Chronicles.* It was just as popular as the *AJC,* if not more; however, it was produced on a weekly basis only. The ad from last Sunday's edition stared Shaylynn in the face. It was larger and more prominently placed than her previous ad, and in the past two days, she'd received quite a number of calls. No promised jobs yet, but the calls proved that her investment had stirred some interest in the community.

Shaylynn guessed that the calls were coming as a result of the ad plus her additional personal endeavors to spread the word of her business. Tuesday, after finishing her assignment as chaperone for her son's field trip, she found an express package sitting on her front porch. It contained flyers that she'd ordered online through a company called Papered Wonders that she'd found one day while web browsing. Shaylynn was tired from her aquarium adventure, but she loaded the box of postcard-sized flyers in her car and went to work. She placed them on the windshields of hundreds of cars that were parked in the lots at area malls. She even invaded the lots of Home Depot, Michaels, Rooms To Go, IKEA, Wal-Mart . . . anywhere where people shopped for home improvement supplies and furniture. Shaylynn had spent most of the afternoon passing out business cards and postcards and most of the night massaging her aching feet.

It wasn't until today, when she took the time to read the *Atlanta Weekly Chronicles* newspaper in its entirety that she realized that the owner of the paper was the son-in-law of Reverend B. T. Tides. She'd been introduced to the name of the famed bishop while living in Florida, but had no idea that he had family ties to the weekly paper. And in the same newspaper, she saw a conspicuous advertisement by a company called Papered Wonders. Like her own business, Papered Wonders was a sole proprietorship, and it was owned by a single mother who was also a Christian woman. Now, Shaylynn couldn't brush off the feeling that the positive results she was getting from the news ad and the flyers weren't just because she'd knowingly chosen to do business with people who served the city honorably, but because she'd *unknowingly* chosen to do business with people who served God honorably.

Shay Décor.

There it was again, echoing in her head. It was indeed an engaging name that, admittedly, Shaylynn found more appealing than Ford's Home Interior & Designs; but there was one problem. One *big* problem. The name Ford wasn't in it. For her, it was important that her last name was a part of her company's title. Somehow, having her married name represented kept Emmett's spirit alive and made him a permanent fixture in the business that he had encouraged her to start.

As soon as she thought of her deceased husband, Shaylynn's vision began to blur. Even after all this time, it was hard to believe he was gone forever. It was even harder to believe that his death still distressed her so. Dabbing the corners of her eyes with her fingertips, Shaylynn erased the visible signs of her lingering grief. When Chase was at home, he kept her busy, and she didn't think as much about the permanent vacancy that Emmett's passing had left in her heart. But when the house was quiet, even when she tried to occupy herself with other things, somehow her pain would resurface as though the horrific ordeal had happened just yesterday.

Standing from her living room sofa, Shaylynn walked to the fireplace mantel and admired the last photo that she and Emmett had taken not more than a month before his murder. Admirably, she smoothed her thumb across his image, wishing she could touch him once more; wishing he could touch her in return.

"I miss you, baby," she whispered, forcing back the flood that wanted to rise behind her eyeballs. "I wish you were here to see how beautiful your son is and how much he's grown. He looks just like you, and I pray to God that he grows up to be just like you too." Shaylynn thought about the massive shoes that Chase would have to fill in order to satisfy that wish, and she decided to compromise. "Even if he's half the man you were, I'd be proud."

Her eyes darted to the bundle of violets that she'd preserved by leaving them pressed between the pages of her telephone book for a month following Emmett's funeral. The blue flowers had been her favorite ever since Emmett picked a bundle from an open field and handed them to her as he proposed in a surprising move during a casual Saturday afternoon walk. When Shaylynn closed her eyes, she could still see the look on Emmett's face as he held her trembling hand.

"Baby, I don't care what anybody says," he'd told her. "Not my parents, my friends . . . nobody. It doesn't matter that we come from different worlds. Shoot, if you can stomach my present, which comes with my domineering mama and my superficial daddy, then I can sure deal with your past. What happened to you back then was out of my control, but I can promise you this: you'll never have to worry about trivial things like food, clothing, and shelter ever again. I'm on my way to big things, baby, and you're coming with me."

It was at that moment that Emmett slid a small black box from the right pocket of his slacks and opened it for Shaylynn to see. She remembered momentarily being almost blinded by the sparkle that generated when the overhead sun clashed head-on with the one and a half–carat gemstone that sat atop the white gold ring.

"Emmett." It was all that she could say, and even that was barely a whisper. He didn't even ask her if she would marry him. He must have already known the answer, because without hesitation or a second thought, he removed the ring from the box and slipped it on her finger. It was a perfect fit.

"I'm going to love you forever, Shaylynn McKinley. Nothing's ever gonna change that. You hear me? 'Til the day I take my last breath, I will love you."

And he did.

Opening her eyes, Shaylynn found herself again staring at the violets on the mantel. They appeared distorted through her glossed eyes, and she wiped away the pool of moisture to get a better view. The ringing of the telephone startled her, and Shaylynn took a moment to gather herself. Although she used the same telephone for personal and professional dealings, the numbers were different, and she'd had it arranged so that the business line's ring was unlike the home number's ring. This incoming call was business, and she knew she had to get it together fast before it rolled into voice mail.

"Shay Décor."

Shay Décor? Why did I say that? The words had already come out, and taking it back would make her not only sound unprofessional, but like a babbling idiot who didn't even know the name of her own business.

There was a pause on the other end of the line wherein all that could be heard was heavy breathing. Shaylynn was just about to hang up the phone on someone she figured was some kind of pervert when a woman's voice spoke in her ear.

"Shay Décor?"

Breath.

"I, uh . . . I thought I was calling Ford's Home Interior and Designs."

Breath.

"I think I may have dialed the wrong number."

Breath.

Shaylynn shook away the thought that the poor woman on the other end of the line must be morbidly obese, knowing she had more important concerns. She was about to lose a client if she didn't think fast. For the sake of saving face, Shaylynn had to play it off, even if only this once. "No, ma'am, you have the right number. The business is going through a renovation that will come with a possible name change and currently, I'm using the possible new name."

"Possible new name?"

The breathing sounds weren't quite as labored now, but the woman's tone made Shaylynn feel like a babbling idiot in spite of her efforts. If she tried to explain further, it wouldn't sound any less stupid, so she chose to maneuver the conversation along. "Yes, ma'am. Is there something that I can help you with?"

"Maybe," she said, and then paused. "My name is Eloise Flowers, and I've been trying to do some stuff to my house a little at a time, but I'm giving up now. I've come to the conclusion that I'm just too old for all this work. I need help. Is that what you do,

Ms. . . . ?"

Stupid, stupid, stupid! Shaylynn assaulted herself inwardly. One would think that this was the first time she'd been in business. She knew better than to answer the phone without introducing herself. This was strike two. One more and she'd be out for sure. "I'm sorry. My name is Shaylynn Ford, *Mrs.* Shaylynn Ford, and I am the owner of F . . . Shay Décor." She hoped her near blunder just sounded as if she were holding the "F" sound at the end of the word before it.

"I saw your ad in the paper," the woman revealed. "I was wondering if this was the kind of work you did."

"Yes, ma'am, it is."

"How much is something like this here gon' put me out of?"

Shaylynn almost laughed. Southern people — especially older people — amused her. She hoped to appeal to a more corporate, prosperous crowd, but she had prayed for God to send business her way, and if there was one thing that her grandmother had grilled in her head, it was that beggars couldn't be choosers, and this woman sounded like she was closer to being ready to get to work than most of Shaylynn's prior callers had seemed. So for now, an aging, uneducated woman would have to do. "I'd like the opportunity to meet with you personally so that I can get a better idea of what it is that you desire for me to do," Shaylynn said. "I'm sure that we can find something that fits into your budget."

"Oh, you ain't got to fit it in my budget, honey. You got to fit it in my young-un's budget. That chile been trying to get me to get this house updated for years. Folks say I'm still living in the early nineties, teetering on the edge of falling back into the late eighties."

Eloise laughed, and Shaylynn laughed with her. When she began talking again, Shaylynn noticed that the weighty breathing was all gone.

"Like I said, I saw your ad in the paper, and I thought I'd give you a call. So when can you meet with me, and how long is it gon' take? I ain't got all day, you know."

Shaylynn smiled into the receiver. "I'm very flexible. I don't mind working around your schedule, Ms. Flowers, and the meeting will only take as long as you need."

"How 'bout this evening 'round about seven?"

Shaylynn froze. "This evening?" She hadn't planned to meet outside of her normal office hours. That was her time with Chase.

"You did say you would work on my schedule, didn't you?" Eloise reminded her.

"Uh, yes, ma'am, but I have a son who —"

"Well, bring him on with you, honey. It ain't gon' take long, and I don't bite. If you come hungry, I'll even feed you."

This was the first call Shaylynn had gotten far enough with a potential client to set up an actual appointment. She had no choice but to make the sacrifice . . . this time. "Okay, Ms. Flowers. If you give me your address, I'll meet you at seven."

EIGHT

Once a month on a Thursday night at six-thirty, the men of Kingdom Builders Christian Center gathered for a gender-specific Bible study and chat session. The organized, spiritually strengthening sessions were the brainchild of Jerome Tides, the second son of Reverend B. T. Tides. Jerome had begun the gatherings at New Hope Church just a year ago as a counterpart to Women of Hope, a weekly ministry that his younger sister founded for the ladies of the church. The Hope for Men's impact on the male population of the tabernacle quickly spread throughout the churches under the New Hope Fellowship of Churches. CJ wasted no time building the foundation of KBCC's own Hope for Men assemblies, and so far, they'd been accepted well among the brothers.

Neil had hardly recuperated from his busy day at the school before he had to prepare himself for the meeting. He enjoyed the brief but influential gatherings. Some of the things the men shared in those sessions were mind-blowing, and it was comforting to know that they had a safe place to go where they could talk to their pastor and fellow brethren without feeling threatened. But immediate disappointment settled in when Neil walked through the doors of the church and caught a glimpse of the associate minister who would apparently be facilitating tonight's meeting.

"Dang!" he whispered under his breath. CJ generally led the discussions, and Neil wouldn't have bothered to show up if he had known that Elder Ulysses Mann was going to be in charge. If Deacon Burgess's old Impala hadn't crept into the parking lot at the same time that Neil had shut off his engine, and had the old man not shuffled into the church alongside him, Neil wouldn't have thought twice about backing out the door and making a mad dash for his car.

Elder Mann was quite knowledgeable in the Word of God and had earned his ordination into the ministry, so his ministerial credibility wasn't in question. The problem was that he was one of the most lackluster orators that Neil had ever heard. The sixty-year-old mortician could break down a complicated scripture like a mathematician could break down a problematic fraction. Only an idiot wouldn't be able to understand the verse once Elder Mann got finished explaining it. But the man's humdrum voice was enough to put a chronic insomniac to sleep. He had about as much charisma as the corpses he came in contact with each week, and the only times he ever got the chance to address the congregation were the few occasions that CJ allowed him to lead their regular Wednesday night Bible study sessions.

Hope for Men usually lasted ninety minutes, but because no one felt compelled to participate tonight, the session was cut short. By the time the hour-long assembly was over, Neil had long lost count of how many peppermints he'd eaten in an effort to stay awake.

"Forty-two," Deacon Burgess blurted out at Neil immediately following the benediction.

"Excuse me?" Neil wondered if this was one of the old man's senile days.

"Forty-two," he repeated, flashing four crooked fingers, and then two more as a visual aid. "That's how many times you gapped tonight. Probably more. That's just how many I happened to see."

Neil shook hands with two of the other brothers who passed by him on their way toward the exit, then he turned his attention back to Homer. "Gapped?"

"Yawned," the deacon clarified while his wrinkled hand inched toward his keys that lay on an empty chair. Neil often wondered if Homer Burgess's driver's license was even valid. He found it nearly impossible to believe that the Department of Motor Vehicles continued to renew the man's driving privileges, even allowing him to drive at night. Incredibly thick lenses gave away his failing eyesight, and the Chevrolet that the man drove never moved more than thirty miles per hour on any given day. Deacon Burgess used the keys to scratch his scalp through fat curls of silvery hair that his age hadn't thinned one bit.

He flashed a perfect set of dentures at Neil and added, "Ain't no sense in me beatin' on you 'bout it, though. I was sure I was gonna die sittin' here waiting for that boy to shut his mouth. Jesus, Mary, and Joseph!" the man huffed out. "I ain't saying that I'm ready to check outta here or nothin', but I done lived a good long life, Deacon Taylor, a good long life. I done known love, raised chil'ren, seen grandchil'ren, great grandchil'ren, and great-great grandchil'ren come into the world. I done lived so long that I done buried both my wives, two of my sons, and my only daughter. And just in the past week, I was blessed with my first two great-great grandchildren. Twin boys."

His proud grin vanished quickly and was replaced by a disapproving look that he hurled at Ulysses Mann, who was now kneeling next to his chair like he'd really outdone himself tonight and needed to stop and thank God for how powerfully He'd used him. Shaking his head, Deacon Burgess peered through his glasses at Neil. "While you were nodding off, I was praying for the Lord to call me home to glory. I'm a dime short of being a hundred, and the undertaker was already here, so it would have been easy on everybody. Like I said, I ain't necessarily ready to die, but a quick death would have been a heck of a whole lot less agonizing than sitting through this right here."

Neil's body vibrated as he did his best to withhold an outburst. But inasmuch as the old deacon's words had been comical, Neil didn't fail to take note that he'd learned more about Homer Burgess in those fleeting seconds than he'd ever known about the man in all the time they'd worshipped to-gether.

"You know I'm telling the sanctified truth," Deacon Burgess concluded.

Not wanting to add his own lashes to the verbal beating that the deacon had already given the minister, Neil settled for saying, "Well, I think we'd all rather hear Pastor Loather bring the Word on any given occasion. I don't think we can fairly compare anybody to him. Pastor Loather has a rare gift."

"Compared to that right there" — Deacon Burgess directed a bent finger toward the chair that Elder Mann had made into an altar — "*mildew* has a rare gift."

The classroom was now virtually empty, and acoustics were making Homer's voice bounce off the walls. Neil was certain that Elder Mann could hear the exchange despite the fact that he remained in his bent-knee position. Neil theorized that Ulysses had probably finished his prayer a long time ago. He was probably just too embarrassed by what was being said to get up and face the church's oldest member.

In an effort to end the preacher's torture, Neil began walking toward the exit door. "Come on, Deacon. Let me walk you to your car."

Deacon Burgess needed the assistance of a cane, and even then, the speed of his stride could best be described as creeping. A distance that Neil could have covered in thirty seconds had he been by himself took him five minutes walking with Deacon Burgess. They had barely made it outside the classroom door when the elderly man spoke again.

"Speaking of rare gifts, you got a pair of pipes in that there throat of yours, ain't you?"

Neil knew what Deacon Burgess was talking about, but they still had a ways to go before they would exit the church, so for the sake of conversation, he pretended to be clueless. "Pipes? What do you mean?"

Homer Burgess waved his hand out over the empty edifice and said, "You near 'bout tore up this place three, four Sundays ago."

It was actually just this past Sunday, but Neil didn't bother to waste his time challenging him on it. "Thanks." Neil didn't know what else to say.

"I remember when you used to sing all the time."

Surprised by the declaration, Neil stopped and looked at Homer. He didn't think the old man's long-term memory was strong enough to make that kind of recall. "Yes, I did. I don't do it much anymore, but I'm glad you enjoyed it." He ended the sentence in a lasting period, a tone that said the conversation was over.

They began walking again; only a few steps came before Homer's next words.

"I remember 'cause my grandson got saved on a Sunday that you and your brother sung. That had to be 'bout twenty years ago."

Neil stopped again. Apparently Deacon Burgess's memory was better than his own. Neil couldn't remember this occurrence himself. "He did?"

"Yeah. You done forgot?" At last they stepped outside the church doors, and Homer leaned his full weight on his cane and looked at Neil, who stood on the top step. "Anthony was 'bout sixteen or seventeen at the time, and all his life that boy had done 'bout killed his parents with worry. He got in trouble at school all the time. The older he got, the worse he got. 'Fore long, he was running off from home, smoking pot, getting in trouble with the law. He had just got kicked out of school for fighting a teacher when my son and his wife brought him to church that Sunday."

Deacon Burgess got a faraway look in his eyes. "Yes, sir. Y'all sho' 'nuff sung that

Sunday. 'Near the Cross.' That's what y'all sung. And somewhere in the middle of it, Anthony come a-running down the church aisle, eyes full of water. He fell at the altar, and he was never the same no more. Went on to finish high school, went to college, and he's a doctor right now in the nation's capitol."

Warm tears stung the backs of Neil's eyeballs. He had totally forgotten that day. Forgotten the song that had been sung; forgotten the move of the Spirit; forgotten the face of the boy wearing the ripped jeans who raced to the front of the church and crumpled to his knees; forgotten how Dr. Loather had to revamp the whole service to meet the needs of one lost soul. So much about the days when he and Dwayne shared the mic were buried somewhere in the back of Neil's brain.

It was almost eight o'clock, and there was little to no chance that Deacon Burgess could see his tears, but Neil turned his back to the old man anyway. He pretended to gaze out over the well-lit parking lot where a security guard waited for the final cars to leave so that he could lock the entrance gate.

"Yeah." Neil wiped his eyes with a handkerchief he pulled from his pocket. It was warm tonight, and he could only hope that the deacon thought he was wiping away perspiration. Neil kept his voice steady. "Yeah, I remember that now. That was some kind of Sunday. I'm glad Anthony turned out well."

"He did more than turn out well." Deacon Burgess began the task of walking down the steps. There were only four of them, but for a man of his years, it was a chore. "He's preaching now too, you know."

"No, I didn't know that," Neil admitted.

"Son, a whole lotta folks in the world can sing, but everybody ain't anointed." Homer placed his aged palm flat against Neil's chest as he spoke. "Your voice don't just sound good. God done gave you a voice that can heal. A voice that can deliver. A voice that can *save.* Do you realize how powerful that is?"

Maybe it was all in his mind, but Neil was certain that he could feel heat transmitting from Deacon Burgess's hand. The whole center of his body began to feel like it had just been rubbed with Icy Hot. Neil had used the cream on occasions after he drove his ATV. Depending on his speed and the ruggedness of the surface that he chose to take the 4-wheeler on, he would need the sports cream to ease the resulting soreness that crept in his muscles. It was that same heating sensation he felt now that prompted Neil to step away and distance himself from the deacon's touch.

"You miss your brother, don't you?" Deacon Burgess asked.

Neil looked out toward the parking lot again. He and Deacon Burgess had never had such a long conversation before. Most of the time when Neil spoke to him, it was in passing, and the man seemed to only half-comprehend what was being said. But tonight the ninety-year-old appeared to be sharper than ever. Neil answered the inquiry with a quiet nod.

"I know the feeling. Believe it or not, I've outlived all my brothers," Homer said. "My sisters too. I'm the last of the Burgess baker's dozen. That's what our neighbors used to call me and my twelve siblings when we was kids. The last one to die was my sister, Karen. She passed away . . . uh . . . I guess it was 'bout six or seven years ago. I was the baby in the family, so she was older than me, but younger than Millie, so if Karen was alive today, she would be 'bout ninety-two, I reckon."

Deacon Burgess started making baby steps toward the parking lot, and Neil inched along beside him. "Naw, it ain't no fun to bury your kinfolks, and I done buried a whole heap of 'em. It's hard enough to bury your siblings and your parents, but I think the hardest thing in the world is to bury your spouse or your chil'ren."

Neil was sure that the deacon was right, but it was hard to imagine a pain worse than the one he felt when he had to say good-bye to Dwayne. Bidding his father farewell was hard enough, but Dwayne . . .

"That's why you have to make life worth living." Homer's words interrupted Neil's thoughtful comparison. "You got to love your kinfolks so much that when any one of them dies, you find comfort in knowing that not only did they know what real love was, but so did you. 'Cause the truth of the matter is that as sure as we born, we gon' die one day."

"What about love?" Neil heard himself ask.

"Love? What about it?"

"You said you were married twice."

"Yep. Esther was wife number one, and Odette was number two. After that, I gave up. Marrying gets kind of expensive after a while." He chuckled.

"And both of them died before you?"

"Uh-huh. Burying is expensive too."

Neil knew that his question was a bit off-topic from their original subject, but he took the plunge. "Do you think that you would have ever married Odette if things hadn't worked out with you and Esther? I mean, if she hadn't kept her marriage vows, would you ever have opened your heart to trust another woman?"

They were finally standing at the door of Deacon Burgess's car. Before he answered Neil's question, the old man took the time to unlock his car door and chuck his cane inside. He used the open door as a leaning post when he looked back at Neil.

"Me and Esther were divorced for three years before I married Odette."

Neil's eyebrows shot up.

"Yep. Sho' was," Homer said with a firm nod of his head. "We was married for near 'bout twenty years, but probably wasn't in love but for two."

"Why did you stay together for so long then?"

" 'Cause we took vows, that's why. Back in them days, when folks said they was gonna stay together for better or for worse, they did just that . . . come hell or high water. Most of the time anyway."

"But you didn't, right? You eventually broke up." Neil was fascinated by the story.

"Yes, we broke up. Most people say they stayed together for the chil'ren. You know . . . stayed married till the chil'ren got grown. Well, that wasn't our testimony. We stayed together for our mamas and daddies. I think if we hada broke up early on, our chil'ren woulda been just fine. Me and Esther, we stayed together till all of our parents were dead and buried. If we woulda broke up while they were alive, it probably would've killed 'em. So after Esther buried her mama, we called it quits."

"Twenty years." Neil followed the words with a low whistle. "That's a long time to stay married to somebody you *do* love, let alone somebody you don't."

"Tell me about it," the deacon replied.

After a silent pause, Neil said, "So when you said earlier that you buried both your wives, you didn't mean that literally. You just meant you outlived them both."

"No, I meant I buried 'em both. It was an odd thing that both of 'em died of cancer. Odette died of breast cancer, and Esther had it in her . . ." He looked around as if there could possibly be someone standing close by listening to their conversation, even though there was no one in the parking lot except the security guard. He was at least a thousand feet away, pacing impatiently near the gate, but Homer still whispered when he finally said, "female parts."

"I'm sorry to hear that," Neil responded.

"Yeah. Suffering ain't no fun to nobody."

"So if you weren't married to Esther, why'd you bury her?"

"Just 'cause our marriage didn't work out don't mean I hated her. She died, and she needed burying. What was I supposed to do?"

Neil shrugged. As far as he was concerned, if they were divorced, what Homer was supposed to do was nothing at all. No marriage meant he had no responsibility to her. Surely she had other family members who could have taken care of her funeral arrangements and the costs attached. "She never remarried?"

"Yep, but so what? I didn't have a whole lot of money myself, but for every dollar I had, I had ninety-nine cents more than her husband did. Me and Esther had six babies together, and if a woman thought enough of me to bear my chil'ren, then no matter if our marriage fell apart or not, she deserved to have an honest-to-God burial. And that's what I gave her."

On second thought, Neil reasoned that what Deacon Burgess said made sense. He supposed that if he'd had children with his ex-wife, he would probably feel a sense of allegiance to help with her burial if she died before him. But since they'd had none . . .

"And even if we didn't have chil'ren," Homer added, "she still gave me twenty years of her life. We might have grown out of love, but she stayed until we mutually agreed that it was over. And I'd be lying if I said that just 'cause I wasn't in love with her that she didn't bring me no joy during that time. I'd be lying if I said she never cooked me a good meal, or never cleaned up behind me, or never nursed me when I was sick, or never gave me some good loving when I wanted it. Everything wasn't roses, 'cause if it was, we would have stayed together till the end, but there were some good times in there, and I felt like the good times were enough to earn her a decent homegoing."

Neil didn't want to admit it, but that made sense too. Old man Burgess was right again, but Neil didn't want to talk about that anymore. He wanted to go back to where his conversation was headed before they started talking about burials, funerals, and such. "So your divorce from Esther never made you hesitant about trying again?"

Through an extended laugh, Homer said, "It did till I met Odette." He rubbed his right hand across his mass of soft, curly hair. "I wasn't always old and on a cane, you know. I was probably 'bout the age you are now when I got divorced, and just like you, Deacon Taylor, I was a ladies' man, a heart-breaker."

For a minute, Neil thought that the wide smile that dimpled his cheeks had literally brightened the darkness around them, until he noted the two cars that were passing by the church with their headlights on.

Deacon Burgess continued. "Women used to try to catch my eye when I was still married, so when word spread that I was divorced, the sisters came from every which-a-way. I went out with a few of 'em, but I never saw 'em as much more than pretty faces and pretty legs." Deacon Burgess laughed again. "I was a face and legs man."

Neil laughed again too, mainly because he was starting to see a lot of himself in the old, off-key-singing deacon. The face and legs were two of the first things he noticed in a woman too. Shoving his hands in his pockets and wanting to hear more, Neil said, "So I'm guessing that Odette came in the picture somewhere along the way and changed some things."

Homer confirmed, "She changed the rules, the game, the playing field . . . *everything*. She was the real deal. She had the face and legs, too, but what made her stand out was that she wasn't like all them other girls who were all up in my grill."

Another outburst of laughter was released from Neil at the use of the old man's terminology, but his amusement didn't keep Homer from telling the rest of his story.

"She made *me* chase *her.* That was new for me. And when I finally caught her, I was wore out and breathless, but it was worth it. Two chil'ren and forty-one years of marriage. That's what she gave me. Plus a whole lotta good lovin'. *Real* good lovin'. Yes, sir." Homer patted Neil on the arm like he knew the interrogation had been for Neil's own personal gain. "You wait and see, Deacon. It's gonna all be well worth it."

NINE

"Whoa, whoa, whoa . . . hold up, bruh." CJ held up a hand to stop Neil mid sentence.

Neil watched as his friend removed his eyeglasses, misted the lenses with the heat of his breath, wiped away the moisture with a handkerchief he retrieved from his pocket, and then placed the frames back on his face. It was a calculated sequence that Neil had witnessed on several occasions over the years. Almost every time CJ did it, it was the prelude to a lecture — and this time was no exception.

CJ looked up at the clock on the wall of Neil's entertainment room and used the same handkerchief he'd just wiped his lenses with to wipe away small beads of perspiration from his forehead. "I've been here all of what, forty-five minutes?"

"So?" Neil questioned.

"In that time, you've mentioned this Shay Ford lady's name at least seven times.

What's up with that?"

The conversation between the two men had been flowing constantly since CJ answered Neil's challenge to come to his house for a friendly game of ping pong. Despite it being nearly ten o'clock at night, Neil told CJ that he owed it to him. He needed to work out his frustration of having to sit through an hour-long lecture with Elder Mann.

At times, their competitive natures clashed, and the game didn't seem so amicable. But at the end of any ping pong match, no matter which of them walked away with bragging rights, there were never any hard feelings.

"What's up with what?" Neil hadn't realized that he'd been talking so much about Shaylynn. He hadn't even noticed that he'd begun shortening her name, taking the liberty to call her Shay. Having it all brought to his attention at once embarrassed him. Neil picked up a towel and wiped his face, hoping also to disguise his discomfort.

"With you and Ms. Ford, that's what."

"First of all, it's *Mrs.* Ford, so whatever you're thinking, you can just rethink it." *There. That will put an end to that.*

"Oh." To Neil's delight, CJ's face fell, and he clearly looked disappointed. "So she's married?"

Darn! Neil's victory had been short-lived. He was tempted to lie just to bring an end to the conversation, but he opted otherwise. "Yes and no."

"Yes and no? What kind of answer is that? What's she doing? Shacking? Playing house? Living in sin?"

Neil laughed, as he could almost see the preacher's collar forming itself around CJ's neck. "Calm down, Pastor," he joked. "She's doing none of that. She's widowed."

With a nose crinkled in confusion, CJ asked, "Then why did you say, 'Yes and no'? If she's a widow, then she's not married."

Neil laughed again, but this time there was no amusement on his face. "I know that, and you know that, but can you go and see if you can get that through to her?"

CJ placed his paddle on the table, and in one heave, scooted himself on the green surface of it and sat. Neil tossed him a look of disapproval. CJ knew that he didn't like people sitting on any piece of furniture in his house that wasn't a chair. It didn't matter that it was just a game table. A table was still a table.

"Talk to me, Neil," CJ said, ignoring his friend's lingering glare.

"About what? How your tail is all up on

my table?"

CJ still didn't move. "No, about this issue you have with *Mrs.* Ford."

Neil gave up on trying to stare CJ off of the ping pong table and resigned to grabbing his bottled water and taking a few gulps. "I don't have an issue with her."

"Sounds like you do to me."

"Why? Because of what I said? I was just —"

"It wasn't *what* you said," CJ pointed out, shaking his head from left to right. "It's *how* you said it."

"And just how did I say it?" Neil tried to buy time while he thought of a way out of the hole he'd somehow dug for himself.

"Like you're just a bit miffed that this woman is apparently still grieving and not ready to move on. Everyone needs time to grieve, Neil. You don't know what it's like to lose someone that close —" CJ caught his words and the menacing glare that Neil tossed his way. "Sorry," he mumbled.

"Yeah," Neil said halfheartedly just before he sucked the rest of the liquid from his bottle and tossed the empty plastic container in the bin with his other recyclables.

"But let's build on that," CJ came back. "See how ticked off you got just then? Dwayne's death still hurts you when you think about it. Maybe it's the same for her. How long has her husband been deceased?"

"I don't know exactly, but she told Ms. Dasher that it had been some time ago, so it didn't just happen."

CJ repositioned himself on the game table, and then said, "Well, your brother died, what? Fifteen years ago? It's still not easy for you, so why should it be easy for her?"

"I didn't say it should be easy, CJ, but you can't compare Dwayne's death to her husband's. Dwayne died suddenly. We weren't expecting it. It hit all of us hard — even you."

"True." CJ nodded in agreement. "So how did your friend's husband die?"

Scratching his chin thoughtfully, Neil admitted, "I don't know. And she's not my *friend.* I spent a few hours with her on a field trip. I don't think that's enough time to draw lines of friendship."

"Why not? It was enough time to draw lines of attraction."

Neil released an irritated huff. "Man, what are you talking about? Nobody said nothing about being attracted to Shay. Where are you coming up with this stuff? And get your butt off my table."

"Why does it bother you that she still wears Mrs. as her title?" CJ remained seated.

"Who says it bothers me?"

"You did, Neil. Just not in those words. Come on, bruh. The two of us have known each other for almost two decades. How you gonna try to play me now? I know you, Neil. Whether you've spent a few hours or a few days around this lady, she's gotten under your skin so deep that you can't even reach the spot to scratch it away. Do I need to go put on my clergy garb and come back in order for you to open up about this? If so, I will, but whether you talk to me as your pastor or as your friend, this is something you need to talk about."

Neil shook his head and turned away.

"Am I lying?" CJ challenged.

Neil turned back to face his friend. "Okay, let's get this straight before we even get into this conversation. Shay isn't under my skin, okay? Do I find her interesting? Yes. Do I find her intriguing? Yes. Do I find her attractive? Yes. But is she under my skin? No."

CJ raised both hands in surrender. "Fine."

Neil sat in a nearby chair and took a much-needed moment to be sure that he chose his words carefully. He didn't need CJ jumping to any more unfounded conclusions. "She doesn't just insist on wearing the title, CJ; she still wears the ring too."

"Wedding ring, you mean?"

"Yep. The whole set."

"On the left hand?"

"Uh-huh. She must have had it bad for this guy is all I can say."

"Did you meet her at Kingdom Builders?"

Neil nodded. "She has a son in the first grade. She stopped by the school one day a couple of weeks ago, and I helped her unlock her car door. After that, I didn't see her again until the field trip."

"Have you seen her since?"

"That was just Tuesday, CJ. It's only Thursday. Not hardly. Her son has been at Kingdom Builders Academy since the beginning of the school year, and until a couple of weeks ago, I'd never seen her. I'm sure we won't just arbitrarily run into one another at the school any time soon."

"But you're interested in her, so you're not going to just let it go at that, are you?"

"Man, why do you keep putting words in my mouth? I never said I was interested in her."

"Yes, you did. Just a few minutes ago."

Neil shook his head. "No. What I said was that I found her interesting. That's different."

The clarification didn't discourage CJ one bit. "My question remains the same," he said. "You're not gonna just let it go, are you?"

"One thing I didn't tell you," Neil said, not answering the repeated question. "She's very young."

CJ's eyes enlarged themselves. "Oh? When you say *very young,* what —"

"Twenty-six, twenty-seven, maybe. I don't know."

CJ let out a long whistle. "That *is* young." Silence rested for a brief moment before he added, "But when you think about it, that's not unusual these days. Older women are marrying much younger men. Older men are marrying much younger women. It's like we're taking it back to the old days when age really didn't factor in too heavily. A twenty-year difference wasn't out of the ordinary for our grandparents and great-grandparents, and a twelve or thirteen year difference ain't all that uncommon in the twenty-first century."

"Why are you talking about marriage, CJ? See, that's why I didn't want to get into this with you. I made more progress talking to Deacon Burgess."

"Deacon Burgess?" CJ tilted his head to the side. "You talked to Deacon Homer Burgess about this? When?"

"Well, you weren't at the funeral . . . I

mean the men's meeting tonight, so I had to talk to somebody."

CJ laughed at Neil's faux mix of words. Then he announced, "I said I'm sorry, didn't I? I needed time with Resa tonight."

"Yeah, well, you and *Resa* are like two rabbits. Y'all need to let it rest."

"Don't hate, bruh, don't hate."

"Whatever," Neil mumbled. He was happy that his friend was happy, but he couldn't pretend that he didn't sometimes envy what CJ and Theresa had going.

"So what did you and Deacon Burgess talk about tonight? He must have been having a good day if what he said made sense."

"Oh, he was plenty lucid tonight. I hadn't seen him that coherent for that long in ages. He must be on new meds or something. He talked to me about love and marriage. It was pretty cool, actually."

"So you told him you wanted to marry Shay?"

"No! Dang, CJ. I mention finding a woman interesting and you already have me marching down the aisle."

"The bride marches, Neil, not the groom."

Neil rolled his eyes to the ceiling, and then shook his head.

"Is she saved?"

"Man, I don't know," Neil said with a

laugh. He knew that question would get thrown in before long. "We talked a little about church on the ride back to the school. I invited her to KBCC, and she thanked me for the invitation. She's been visiting at another church, but said she hadn't been led to join."

"Did she use those words?" CJ asked.

"What words?"

"Led to join. Did she actually say she hadn't been led to join?"

"Yeah."

"Sounds to me that she knows something about being in communication with God." CJ seemed pleased as he spoke the words, and he didn't try too hard to hide it.

"Anyway," Neil said, trying to mask his own satisfaction at the notion that Shaylynn had a personal relationship with the Lord. "Even if I were drawn to her in some way, she's made it pretty clear that her name is still *Mrs.* Shaylynn Ford, so I think that's a message that has been delivered loud and clear."

"I hope Resa feels that strongly about me after God calls me home. I mean, if I died young, I'd want her to move on with her life, but I'd also want her to feel so strongly that nobody else can treat her as well as I did, that she'd be very selective. You know what I'm saying?"

Neil didn't particularly want to agree under the circumstances, but he responded with a slow nod anyway. "I guess it *is* a compliment to a man, huh?"

"The highest," CJ said. "So whoever Mr. Ford was, he must have been a great guy."

"Emmett," Neil said.

"Huh?"

"Emmett. That was his first name. As young as she is now — unless he was a lot older than she — Emmett Ford had to be rather young when he died."

"Emmett Ford?" The words dripped from CJ's lips like crystallized honey.

"Yeah." Neil looked at his friend through curious eyes. "You act like you knew him or something."

"I know several guys named Emmett, and the last name Ford is probably way too common for it to be the same one I'm thinking about right now. It's just kind of ironic that the one person that I know of who had both the first and the last name is dead."

"What are you saying? You know an Emmett Ford that also happens to be deceased?"

"I didn't know him personally, but I knew

of him, and so did you. Mayor Emmett Ford."

An oblivious look overcame Neil's face. He shrugged his shoulders and twisted his mouth. "Mayor?"

"Yeah. The one up north who got murdered five or six years ago . . . remember?"

Neil's recollection slowly caught up with CJ's words. He remembered the breaking news story that had taken place too far away to remain a major story for any length of time in Atlanta. *It couldn't be.*

"Probably not, though." CJ voiced Neil's sentiment, and then slid down from the table and into a standing position. "I mean, what are the chances? Ready for another round, old man?" he added while tapping the head of his paddle on the surface of the table. "You should have your wind back by now."

Neil laughed, took his place on the opposite end of the table, and then said, "Let's not forget three very important things here, preacher man. One: we're only eight months apart. Two: you're trailing me two sets to one. And three: you were the one who called time out, pretending to be so interested in my personal life. So now that *you* have *your* breath back, let's do this thing."

147

TEN

"Come on in, honey."

Shaylynn was surprised by the woman who greeted her at the door upon her arrival at the split level home in Powder Springs, Georgia, a suburb of Atlanta. She wasn't at all what Shaylynn had expected: not three hundred pounds, not eighty years old, and not wearing a duster and colorful hair rollers. Instead, Eloise Flowers was an average-sized, somewhat attractive woman with beautiful salt-and-pepper hair, who appeared to be in her late sixties. She used a cane for assistance, but other than her walking crutch, she seemed to be in relatively good health.

With an extended hand, Shaylynn said, "Hi, Ms. Flowers. I'm Shaylynn Ford of Shay Décor. It's nice to meet you." Since the wrong business name had slipped out of her mouth during their phone call, Shaylynn figured that she'd stick with it for now, at least in her dealings with Eloise Flowers.

"I know who you are, honey. Come on in." At her second invitation, Eloise stepped aside to provide more space. "And 'round here we don't shake hands unless it's with the insurance man." She pulled her guest in for an unexpected embrace.

Hugging strangers, or anyone other than her son, wasn't a normal practice of Shaylynn's, but she found Eloise's warm reception surprisingly comfortable. During the brief embrace, Shaylynn's eyes did a complete scan of the living room space. The walls were ivory, very clean, but very bland. The furniture, while sturdy, had been outdated for years, and the plastic fruit, which Eloise had no doubt put in the bowl on the coffee table to bring color to the room, only added age to the space. There were no decorative vases, no live flowers, no framed art, no fragrant candles . . . nothing contemporary to match the spirit of the woman who dwelled there.

"And who do we have here?" Eloise said as her eyes darted downward.

"This is my son, Chase." Shaylynn stroked the child's head, trying to make him feel at ease. His arms were so strong around her hips that Shaylynn was left temporarily immobile.

Eloise backed into the house and sat on the couch nearest her front door. "Come over here, sweetheart, with your handsome self. Ms. Eloise got something special just for you."

Shaylynn closed the front door that the owner of the house had left open, and then looked down at Chase. He hadn't budged. She'd taught him not to gravitate toward strangers, and although she was standing right beside him, and Eloise Flowers looked harmless enough, Shaylynn was glad Chase hadn't immediately loosened his grasp and run to the unfamiliar woman's open arms. Instead, he hesitated for a long while, and then looked up at his mother, mutely asking her permission.

Shaylynn placed a tender hand on his shoulder and gave him a gentle nudge. "It's okay, Chase. Go ahead and greet Ms. Flowers."

Still unsure, Chase put one unhurried foot in front of other until he made his way to the couch. Shaylynn watched his every move — and Eloise's — making sure all of the lady's intentions were pure. Chase came to a stop, still a safe distance away, but the woman brought him close to her and released a delightful moan as she cuddled him. Chase's arms dangled by his side, not pushing the woman away, but also not making an effort to return the warmth.

Shaylynn suddenly had the urge to moan too. Not from the feel of anyone's arms around her, but from the delectable aromas that massaged her nostrils. She closed her eyes and inhaled again. Shaylynn wasn't certain what the meal consisted of, but fried chicken was definitely on the menu. *Southern* fried chicken.

"I told you I would cook," Eloise said. Shaylynn was discomfited that her reaction to the aroma was so obvious. "Smells good, don't it?" Eloise openly bragged with pride, adding an accompanying wide grin. "Are you hungry, Chase?"

Chase looked back at Shaylynn like whether he was hungry depended on whether she said he was. She had taught him not to accept food from anyone other than her and the workers who served in the school cafeteria.

With the help of her cane, Eloise stood, not even waiting for an answer. "Y'all come on in the kitchen, and let's eat while we talk."

"You didn't have to go through all of this trouble, Ms. Flowers." As she said the words, Shaylynn felt like she was floating behind the scents while they lured her into the small dining area.

"Oh, this wasn't no trouble at all, baby. I don't get many visitors besides when that young-un of mine stops in, so I'm glad when I have another warm body to cook for. My daughter will be here Saturday, and she'll be staying with me for a few days, so that'll give me more reasons to pull out the pots and pans. I love to cook, so it ain't never no problem to do it."

"Can you tell us where to go to wash our hands?" Shaylynn asked.

"Uh-huh." Eloise tapped the kitchen faucet with her fingertips. "You can wash them right here, and dry them off on one of those paper towels." She pointed at the towel roll that was positioned on the countertop beside a George Foreman Grill that remained sealed in the box.

Shaylynn couldn't remember the last time she'd used a kitchen sink as a basin for washing her hands. Not since marrying Emmett, that's for certain. He and his family were far too prim and proper for that. Shaylynn allowed Chase to go first, and then washed her own hands.

"Would you like me to do something to help?" Shaylynn offered.

Eloise placed her cane in the corner by the refrigerator, then smiled and nodded toward the table. "I would like you to help yourself to a seat at the table over there with your boy and make yourselves comfy. What kind of host would I be if I put you to work?"

Without protest, Shaylynn sat, choosing the chair right beside Chase. She watched as Eloise maneuvered her way around the kitchen. Without the cane, her limp was a bit more pronounced, but she got around without it a lot better than Shaylynn had expected. One at a time, Eloise brought their plates to the table. Shaylynn could almost feel her mouth sweating on the inside in anticipation of tasting the delicious-smelling food. Aside from the crisp fried chicken, there were collard greens, macaroni and cheese (homemade, not out of the box like Shaylynn often cooked), and cornbread muffins. Shaylynn almost burst out laughing when Eloise brought Chase's plate to the table. There was enough food on it to feed a grown man. Chase was a finicky eater. He never ate in large portions.

"There," Eloise said once she joined them.

"This looks delicious, Ms. Flowers. Thank you."

"Thank you," Chase echoed.

"Oh, so there's a voice in there after all,"

Eloise joked. The corners of Chase's mouth curled upward. "And your lips can smile, too? Oh my! You are a talented little boy, aren't you?" Chase's smile turned into a laugh. "Well, now," Eloise continued, "in my mama's house, the man at the table always led the grace. Chase, can you pray over the food for us, please?"

It was the first request Eloise made wherein Chase didn't look to Shaylynn for permission. Shaylynn didn't expect him to. Saying the grace was a regular assignment for Chase when they ate together at home too.

"Thank you, Lord, for this food we are about to eat. Make it good for our bodies. Bless all the people all over the world who are hungry and don't have the food that we have. Provide for them so that they don't starve, and make us always thankful for your provision. Bless Ms. . . ."

"Eloise," Eloise whispered.

"Bless Ms. Eloise for cooking it, and always keep her cabinets full. In Jesus' name. Amen."

"Well, that's about the biggest blessing that I've ever heard a little boy say!" Eloise exclaimed. "Where did you learn that?"

"My mama."

Eloise turned to Shaylynn. "Well, you

taught him well, honey."

Shaylynn's "thank you" was muffled by a mouth full of chicken. It was delicious, seasoned just right. Shaylynn had taught Chase good table manners, but he was stuffing his mouth too. She imagined that to Eloise, they were acting like two of the less fortunate hungry people that Chase had mentioned in his prayer.

"I'm trying to find you in him, but I don't see much." Eloise looked from Chase to Shaylynn and wiped her mouth with a napkin. "He might have your ears or something, but that face —"

"He looks like my husband." Shaylynn smiled when she said it because she knew that saying so was indeed a compliment to her son.

"I figured as much." Eloise paused, and then looked at Shaylynn. "I been seeing you looking around at my decorations, Mrs. Ford. What do you think?"

Shaylynn took a sip of the tea to wash down the macaroni she'd just put in her mouth prior to the question. The drink was much sweeter than she imagined. Too sweet, really, but she drank it anyway, and the sugar lingered on her taste buds even after she'd swallowed. "You have a very comfortable home, Ms. Flowers." As Shaylynn responded, she slid her hands into her attaché case and pulled out a binder. "We'll walk around in a little bit, and if you just tell me what kinds of upgrades you want to do, I'll get them done for you. I have samples here that you might want to look at. I have some good suggestions in mind, but at the end of the day, everything is left up to you. We can do as much or as little as you like."

"Upgrades." Ms. Flowers chuckled when she repeated the expression Shaylynn had used. "I think that's the same word my young-un used. All y'all new generation folks think alike, I guess. Everything that's old fashioned has got to be modernized."

Shaylynn smiled. "You only have one child?"

"Oh no, baby," Eloise said, vigorously shaking her head. "I gave birth to ten. Seven boys and three girls." Without being asked, she began rattling off names. "Ernest Jr., Alice, Jacob, Eugenia, Wayne, Lester, Evan, Sol, Val, and Clyde." Eloise sealed the list with a smile that said she was proud of each and every one of her offspring. She placed her hand over her heart and added, "Eight of them are still living. They're all scattered 'cross the world, though, so I don't get to see them as often as I'd like; but we all get together once a year for our family reunion. I'm seventy-four years old now, and with every year God gives me, it gets more important for me to see my children."

Eloise looked good to be seventy-four, and Shaylynn told her so.

"Thank you, baby. I don't feel my age either. That's what living for Jesus will do for you."

Shaylynn's mind wandered, and she found herself trying to calculate how old her own mother must be now. She wondered if Lorene McKinley ever longed to see the daughter she abandoned. *Probably not,* Shaylynn deduced.

Eloise looked around her kitchen, and then through the entranceway that gave her a glance of her living room. "Well, I guess a little change won't hurt none. I want to totally change my living room, and this dining room needs some sprucing up too, I guess. But my kitchen, I want to keep the same."

Shaylynn totally disagreed about the kitchen thing, but bobbed her head up and down anyway. The kitchen had a strong country theme that was far too rural for a home in the thriving metropolis of Atlanta. The walls were a nice, soft shade of blue, but everything that accented it, from the pot holders and dish towels to the stove burner covers and the area rug, were decorated with what Shaylynn viewed as an unsightly cow-print. One of the two pictures that rested on the kitchen wall was a faded image of people working in a cotton field as the sun beamed down on them from overhead. The other was an African American depiction of Jesus, wide nose, coarse hair, and all. Shaylynn hadn't seen one of those in years, and she'd never seen one quite like this one.

"My daddy drew that himself," Eloise said when she followed the trail of Shaylynn's eyes.

"Very nice." Shaylynn's compliment was genuine. Eloise's father had to be a gifted artist in order to pay such close attention to detail as he'd done with the "Black Jesus" painting. Once Shaylynn's fixation on the painting ended, she turned her attention back to the cotton field photo she'd spotted earlier. She gestured toward it and hoped that her next question wouldn't be taken as an insult. "Were you raised on a farm?"

Eloise nodded and smiled as if her mind were suddenly overwhelmed by fond memories. "Like me, my parents had ten heads of children, and all of us were raised up on hard work and long prayers. Farm life wasn't an easy life, but it was a good life. This space, my kitchen, reminds me of being at home with my parents." Eloise looked closely at Shaylynn. "You're still young, so you probably can't 'preshate where I'm coming from right now. But when the time comes that you start to see your parents getting frail, or when they finally go on to be with the Lord, you'll want to hold on to things that help you keep them close at heart."

"Not hardly." The words jumped out of Shaylynn's mouth without her permission. She wanted to snatch them back, but it was too late, and now, Eloise was staring at her through eyes narrowed by disbelief and disappointment.

"That ain't a nice thing to say, Mrs. Ford, and certainly not in front of the boy." She shot a look toward Chase, and then locked her eyes on Shaylynn once more. "Those are his grandparents that you're speaking bad about, but even more important is that they are your parents. You may not agree with everything they said or did when they were raising you, but —"

"My parents didn't raise me." It really wasn't Eloise's business as far as Shaylynn was concerned, but if she left the house with the woman thinking she was callously disrespecting her "loving" parents, she'd lose a promising client for sure. No doubt, Eloise would deduce that she was some kind of ungrateful brat who'd found some level of success over the years, but didn't have enough common decency to give her parents credit for all of the sacrifices they'd made to help her get there.

"I don't keep secrets from my son, Ms. Flowers. In my childhood home, every abuse you can name — substance, verbal, and physical — were daily visitors. My grandmother provided for me as best she could, but my parents couldn't have cared less. So while I certainly appreciate your desire to hold on to the good memories that you have of your mother and father, please try to understand why I wouldn't want anything in my home that even remotely reminds me of mine."

"Jesus." Eloise whispered His name as if she were uttering a one-word prayer. "Umph, umph, umph," she grunted, then paused and smiled across the table at Chase. "Well, this little one will have a different testimony. You're gonna want to have stuff in your house to remind you of your parents, won't you?"

Chase smiled and nodded, all while taking a bite of his cornbread. He'd almost cleaned the plate of what Shaylynn thought would be wasted food.

"You'll probably have a scrapbook of your mama's work, showing all the houses she helped to decorate. And your daddy . . . well, you'll probably keep —" Eloise stopped for a brief moment, and Shaylynn held her breath. "What does your daddy do, son?"

"My daddy's in heaven." Chase blurted it in an all-too-chipper voice, like he had been anxiously waiting for her to ask.

Shaylynn swallowed. She'd heard Chase give that answer to one question or another about his father more times than she cared to count. But for some reason, this time, it struck a nerve, and she clenched her jaws and pursed her lips in an effort to hold back an outburst of tears.

Usually when Chase gave his reply, the person he was talking to would be jittery, at least momentarily, and would have to re-group and try to think of something to say that didn't sound as foolish as they felt. But Eloise never missed a beat.

"Oh. Well, then he's in the best place in the world. And you know what?"

"What?" Chase asked.

"Up there with Jesus, your daddy's house is decorated a whole heap better than anything I can pay your mama to do for me down here. So when you start to put your memory book together with stuff that reminds you of your parents, you'll need to find some gold and pearls that represent what your daddy does."

A lone tear found its way down Shaylynn's cheek, and she quickly whisked it away. She was sure that Eloise saw it, but instead of addressing it, the woman kept her eyes focused on Chase, almost seeming to purposefully do whatever it took to keep him engrossed in her words so that he wouldn't have to witness his mother's pain.

Never looking away from Eloise's animated face, Chase stopped eating to ask the question that was pressing in his mind. "Why do I have to find gold and pearls?"

" 'Cause your daddy's daily job is to worship God." Eloise stretched her arms across the table, allowing her eyes to follow the direction in which her hands pointed. Fully held prisoner by the dramatic storytelling, Chase's eyes trailed along as Eloise continued speaking. "And every time he enters the gates of the city, he's pushing on pearls, and when he walks the streets, he ain't walking on grass or pavement like we walk on down there. Do you know what your daddy is walking on?"

With eyes that had widened with captivation, Chase asked, "What?"

"Pure gold, that's what. Your daddy is walking on streets that are paved with pure, solid gold. Now, what you got to say about that?"

Leaning back in his chair, and with a face filled with satisfaction, Chase said, "Whoa . . . cool!"

ELEVEN

Another week was winding down at Kingdom Builders Academy, and Neil sat in his office and stared at his computer screen in disbelief. Rarely did he ever close the door to his workspace, but it was closed and locked as he navigated his mouse with one hand and held his telephone in the other. Today of all days, Margaret had worn her hearing aid, and Neil didn't need anyone to overhear this conversation.

"I'm telling you, man; it's her," he spoke into the phone. "I guess this is why she looked so familiar to me when I first met her. I must have remembered her face from all the reports that were shown on television when the news first broke."

From the other end of the line, CJ released a heavy sigh that was followed by a long whistle. "Wow. God sure works in mysterious ways, doesn't He? When I said that yesterday, I didn't think for a minute that she was really Mayor Ford's widow. I just thought it was poignant that her husband shared the mayor's same name."

Neil didn't quite get the connection between the mystery of God and their current conversation, but he let CJ's comment slide without challenge. "Well, there's no irony in this one. That Emmett Ford and this Emmett Ford are one and the same." Neil clicked to another news article that his Google search had discovered and quickly scanned the wording. "Listen to this," he told CJ. "This is a piece that was written nearly a year after Mayor Ford was killed. It says here that 'the mayor left to mourn his tragic, yet unsolved murder a young wife, Mrs. Shaylynn McKinley Ford, who at the time was carrying their first child. The child, a son she named Chase Elliott Ford, was born five months after the mayor's burial. Mayor Ford's widow and son moved away from the Milwaukee area shortly after the child's birth.' "

"But didn't you say she's only been in Atlanta for a year or so?"

"That's what she told me on the bus. I guess she lived somewhere else between then and now. It's definitely her."

Apparently CJ still wasn't completely convinced. "Is that her son's name? The full name, I mean."

"Yep. I looked up his records earlier when I found the first article, just to be sure that his middle name was Elliott, and it is. CJ, this guy has been dead for seven years, and she's still holding on to her title *and* wearing his ring."

CJ had to agree. "Yeah, that's a long time, but if that's what she chooses to do, there's no sin in it."

"It might not be a sin, but it sure is a shame."

CJ chuckled. "Why, because she's not giving herself a chance to let *someone else* in?"

"I didn't say that."

"You didn't have to."

Neil changed the direction of the subject matter just a bit. "Guess what else I found out when I read Chase's records?"

"Something that, as the school's director, you probably shouldn't be divulging to me?"

"You're the pastor," Neil said. "Your daddy founded the school and the church. When he died, it all went to you, so essentially, you own the school. Nothing in the students' records is hidden from you."

"So if I weren't the pastor and were just your best friend, you wouldn't be telling me this, right?"

"You know what? Church people make me

sick," Neil said. "Do you want to hear this or not?"

"Yeah . . . just like I thought," CJ replied amidst a snicker. "Go ahead and tell me. What else did you uncover?"

"She's thirty. Turned thirty last month."

"Well, that's good. I mean, she's older than you first thought, right?"

"Yeah, but thirty is still young."

"Wasn't your dad ten years older than your mother?"

"Yep," Neil said. "And they were fifteen and twenty-five when they got married."

"Now, *that's* a sin and a shame," CJ said, laughing.

"So if ten years is a sin and a shame, what does that say about an almost fifteen year difference?"

"Oh, you're finally admitting that you're interested?"

Neil released an exaggerated sigh. "No, CJ. I'm still just finding it *interesting,* that's all. Her life, I mean. It's a very interesting story."

CJ laughed. "Whatever, bruh. Listen, fifteen and twenty-five may only be ten years, but that's a whole different kind of ten years. That's a girl and a man being put together . . . literally. And it still worked out just fine for your parents. So although there are more years between you and this love interest of yours, you're both mature adults, and your maturity level alone is way closer than that of your parents when they got married."

"Love interest?" Frown lines creased Neil's face. "Will you stop defining this thing? You're making a mountain out of a molehill."

When CJ smacked his lips, it could be heard clearly through the phone line. "Neil, you'd rather die before admitting that you're taken by this woman, wouldn't you?" he accused. "Listen, bruh, just ask her out."

"Ask her out? Haven't you heard anything that I've been telling you? *Mrs.* Ford ain't trying to be asked out by me or nobody else."

"Maybe. But all she can say is yes or no, and you won't know which will be her answer if you never ask."

Quietly shaking his head in protest, Neil held the line and made no verbal reply. CJ couldn't see his gesture of objection, but when he spoke again, he sure sounded like he could.

"Come on, Neil. What are you afraid of? Are you scared that she'll feel obligated to say yes, or are you afraid that you might be shot down?" Without giving Neil time to respond, CJ offered a solution. "Just ask her when nobody's around. That way, she won't feel any pressure to accept if she really doesn't want to, and you won't walk away with egg on your face if she declines the offer. It's as simple as that, and no one will be the wiser."

For a moment, quiet rested in his office while Neil entertained the notion. CJ's suggestion wasn't the first time Neil had thought about approaching Shaylynn with an invitation to a movie or maybe dinner. He had half a mind to ask her out when they parted ways after Tuesday's field trip, but the diamond on her finger was like a neon sign that flashed the words *don't even think about it* in his face.

"Is the murder still unsolved?" CJ's voice broke into Neil's pondering. He'd probably assumed that his friend's extended silence meant that he was ready to change the subject.

"I don't know." Neil's eyes once again examined the article. "It was at the time of this write-up, but this was six years ago." He navigated to another link and began researching that one for answers. A knock at his office door steered away his attention. "Yes?" he called, placing his hand over the phone so that CJ wouldn't feel that his ear was being yelled into.

"Dr. Taylor? You in here? Why is the door locked?"

Neil lowered his voice. "Church folks make me sick," he whispered into the phone, initiating a laugh from his pastor. "What kind of question is that? She just heard me answer her call, then she gonna turn around and ask if I'm in here . . . and then ask me why my door is locked. Who's the boss in here, her or me?"

Still laughing, CJ said, "From the sound of things, she is."

Neil grunted, then said, "Hold on a sec, CJ." After placing the phone on his desk, he rose from his chair and opened his office door just wide enough to see his secretary and the paperwork that she had in her hand. "Yes, Ms. Dasher?"

"You got a minute? I didn't mean to disturb you if you were busy." Though Margaret was speaking to him, her eyes never looked at Neil. All the while, she was trying to peer around him to see if there was anyone else inside the office.

"I'm just on a call, Ms. Dasher." Neil walked away from the door and back toward his desk.

"Oh, I see." Margaret stepped inside, still scoping the room for a reason that the door

170

would be locked. Finally calling off her search, she looked over the reading glasses that dangled at the end of her nose.

A chuckle rumbled in Neil's stomach as he shook his head at her nosiness. He picked up the phone that lay on his desk. "Hey, Pastor," Neil said to CJ, reverting back to his friend's divinity title, "let me call you later. Duty calls."

Margaret's face brightened at the knowledge of who was on the other end of the line, and all professionalism was temporarily lost. "Hey, Pastor Loather!" she yelled from near the doorway.

CJ laughed upon hearing it. "Tell Sister Dasher that I said hello. Go do your work, bruh. We'll talk later."

Neil ended the call and passed along the pastor's salutations. Margaret grinned in reply. Still curious about the papers in his assistant's hand, Neil looked at them as he asked, "What can I do for you, Ms. Dasher?"

"I didn't mean to make you get off the phone altogether," she replied. "It's almost two o'clock, and I just need you to sign this paperwork so I can make copies to give to the teachers before they dismiss for the weekend. Since it's Friday, I figured it might be a good day to get the reminder letters out so they can be distributed, and so parents can have ample notice about the carnival."

"That's next Saturday, isn't it?" Neil looked down at the calendar that lay flat on his desktop. The date had been colored in with a yellow highlighter. That meant that it was a special date for which he needed to keep his personal calendar free. The same highlighting had been done for tomorrow's date as well. Every time Neil looked at it, the reality that he was about to turn forty-five sank in just a little more. Where had the time gone?

Margaret placed the paper on the corner of Neil's desk. "Yes, the carnival is next Saturday, and we want as much parent and student involvement as possible. We already told them about it and explained that it was a fundraiser fun day, but that was a month ago, and you know how some of our parents are. They're just looking for an excuse not to be hands-on with these kids. Just as sure as my name is Margaret Ann Dasher, if we don't send out a reminder letter, somebody will lie and say they forgot. Or worse, they'll drop their kids off at the carnival and drive off like we're some kind of free Saturday babysitting service. We need to drill it into their heads that we need both them and the kids to be here."

Neil knew that she was right. It had happened before, and it would happen again if they didn't stay on top of the parents. "A reminder letter is definitely needed," Neil agreed as he reached forth and slid the paper closer. He reached in his drawer and pulled out his reading glasses. "Let's have a look."

Margaret stood quietly while he took his time looking over the one-page document. His assistant was the best at creating letters, and seldom were they not perfect by the time she showed them to him, but Neil never signed his name to anything without first reading it. Nodding his approval to this one, he scribbled his illegible signature at the bottom and returned it to her hand. Then he returned his glasses to his drawer.

"What are you doing for the big day tomorrow?" Margaret asked, still looking over her frames. "I can't believe you're not having a get-together so all of your family members and friends can celebrate with you."

"You know me, Ms. Dasher. I'm not one for big parties and such. Ms. Ella Mae already threatened me, giving me the 'I brought you in this world, and I'll take you out' speech if I don't make the drive over to her house. So I'm gonna go and see her early in the morning, and then probably lapse into a coma after she makes me eat a whole cake by myself."

Margaret laughed. "What about tomorrow night?"

"What about it?"

"Your visit to your mother's takes care of your morning. What are you going to do for the rest of the day?"

"I told you: I'll be in a coma." Neil laughed at his own commentary.

"I'm serious, Dr. Taylor."

"So am I. I hadn't planned anything for the evening except to sleep off the sugar I'll ingest in the morning."

"Oh, you have to do something more than eat cake."

"Well, you know I generally visit my favorite restaurant on my birthday, but I was debating whether I'd do that this year. We'll see."

"Come on, Dr. Taylor," Margaret coaxed. "Live a little. A man only turns forty-five once. You deserve a home-cooked meal this year. What do you say?"

Neil looked carefully at Margaret and asked, "Am I hearing an invitation from you?" If his long-time crush was asking him out, Neil didn't know how he was going to react, but he prepared himself so that if she was, he didn't revert back to a school-aged boy.

"I might be," she said. "I think at forty-five, you're old enough to come to my house." Margaret removed her glasses and laughed out loud. "Why not? I'll cook you a supper that you won't be able to stand."

"Oh yeah?" Neil held back a grin. He didn't want to prematurely take it for granted that Margaret's invitation to her place was for an *intimate* evening for two, but that sure sounded like where this little semi-flirtatious exchange was headed. Maybe this was the real reason she'd been so adamant all these years for him to be open to a new relationship. Maybe behind all that family matchmaking mumbo jumbo, she was really hoping for her own chance at his heart.

Margaret placed a hand on her left hip, and then shifted all of her weight to her left leg. "You think I'm lying? Honey, you haven't eaten till you've had my cooking," she bragged. "You're looking at a woman who knows for sure that the way to a man's heart is by way of his belly."

There was no doubt about it now. She was laying it on thick, and Neil nibbled at the corner of his bottom lip in an attempt to downplay his flattered pleasure. "I don't doubt your skills, M— Ms. Dasher." He almost slipped and called her by her first name.

Apparently not convinced that she'd totally won him over, Margaret added, "I cook a pot roast that will make you want to slap your mama."

Laughing at both her facial and verbal expressions, Neil said, "That must be some kinda pot roast."

"Interested?" Margaret asked.

"Keep talking," Neil egged. He was enjoying this far too much.

"Pot roast, smothered rice, corn on the cob, sweet potato pie . . ."

"Okay, okay, you've convinced me," Neil said after swallowing back the water that had gathered in his jaws. He couldn't readily determine whether it was the food or the woman that was making him salivate.

"Good!" Margaret exclaimed. "Then it's a date. Dinner will be ready at seven o'clock sharp. Don't be late, you hear?"

"I won't," Neil said as he watched her sashay out of his office. Even after the door closed behind her, he stared at it, not believing for a moment what had just transpired. *I just got asked out by my assistant.* He felt flushed as he replayed the clearly stated words, *then it's a date,* in his mind. Neil fell back in his chair and looked toward the ceiling. "Lord, have mercy," he whispered into the air. "I just made a date with Margaret Dasher."

By three o'clock, the halls were crowded with students making their way to their transportation. It always amazed Neil how noisy the ordinarily quiet school became at the sound of the final bell. As usual, he stood in his doorway and high-fived jubilant children, spoke to flirting female teachers, shook hands with a few passing male instructors, and carefully watched the end-of-the-day activities unfold.

"Hey, Dr. Taylor!"

Neil turned. " 'Sup, Chase?" They exchanged a high five, and Neil's mind reverted back to his computer screen, where the image of Emmett Ford had been displayed for so long that it had become engrafted in his mind. He instantly noted how much the child resembled his father. "Are you headed home?"

"Yes."

"What do you have planned for the weekend?"

"Mama's got a job."

"Oh yeah?" Neil was pleased to hear that Shaylynn had been contracted. He knew how hard she had been working to get her business off the ground, and when possible, he'd been plugging it to a few people who he thought might need her services. Even without seeing Shaylynn's work, Neil had confidence in her abilities. "So she'll be working on redecorating somebody's house?"

"Yes. We went and saw the house yesterday. Mama said she's gonna have her work cut out for her."

Laughing, Neil said, "That's good. The more work, the more money."

"What are you gonna do this weekend?" Chase asked.

Neil squatted so that the two of them wouldn't have to talk so loud to communicate. "Not too much. My birthday is tomorrow so I thought I'd spend a little time with family."

"Your birthday's tomorrow?"

"Yep."

"Are you having a party?"

"Naaah." Neil shook his head. "I'll have cake, though."

"No presents and music and stuff?"

"I haven't had that kind of a birthday party in years, man."

"Are you too old to have a birthday party, Dr. Taylor?"

Neil laughed. "That could be it."

"How old are you gonna be?"

This was the longest one-on-one conversation that Neil had ever had with the child. For staged effect, Neil looked around to be sure there was no one else in listening range. Then he leaned in close to Chase's ear and lowered his voice to a whisper. "Forty-five."

Demonstrating dramatics of his own, Chase stretched his eyes to the size of quarters. "Whoa! That *is* old."

Neil burst into a hearty laugh and stood to his full height. "Go home, boy. Get out of my school."

Chase giggled. "Bye!"

Neil continued to laugh while he watched Chase's uniform mix in the sea of others as he made a mad dash for the door.

TWELVE

At some point between the time he'd gone to bed last night and the time that he woke up this morning, Neil felt as though he'd been overtaken by a chronic case of midlife crisis. It was that "thing" that people had joked would assail him when he turned forty. However, on that day five years ago, nothing out of sorts had happened. He felt no differently at forty than he felt at thirty-nine. But something odd was transpiring today. Maybe overnight, it had sunk in that once he lived again the time he'd lived already, he would be Deacon Burgess's age. Today, he was halfway to ninety! Or maybe it was the fact that a woman who was fifteen years his senior had suddenly gained the courage to take off the mask and reveal her attraction to him. Why did Margaret wait for him to be on the brink of forty-five before she decided to do that? Was this the magic number that defined him as an old man?

Saturday was the one day of the week that Neil never got out of bed early. Monday through Friday, his job forced him to rise at six, and on Sunday, church obligations stirred him at eight. But on Saturday mornings, even when he had errands to run or chores to complete, Neil's feet didn't feel the cool hardwood of his bedroom floor before ten o'clock. But today was different. His eyelids opened just before five this morning, and Neil had been up ever since.

By five-fifteen, he was standing in front of the mirror counting the grey hairs on his head. By five-sixteen, he'd lost count and given up. By five-thirty, he was fully dressed in a T-shirt and a pair of sweat pants and was heading down LaVista Road toward the comprehensive LA Fitness club located there. By six, Neil was a full-fledged member, and twenty minutes later, he was running on the treadmill, tired and breathless, but refusing to be outdone by the Richie Cunningham lookalike on the apparatus beside him. The gentleman had to be at least twenty years his junior. Thirty-eight minutes in, Neil felt like he was ready to meet his Maker, and prayed that the red-headed devil beside him would tire out soon. Seven more minutes passed before God had mercy, but just to put an exclamation mark on his nonverbal victory, Neil kept running for a full fifteen seconds after the youngster had slowed his treadmill to a brisk walk.

When he was finally able to slow his pace too, Neil struggled not to audibly gasp as he battled for one breath after the next. Pains shot through every molecule of his body, and for a short time, Neil wondered if he were on the verge of a massive heart attack. How ironic it would be for him to drop dead in a place where good health and heightened levels of fitness were the order of the day. It would be highly embarrassing. Well, not really, since he'd be too dead to be ashamed of the news features that would be broadcast all over the local stations. But heart attack or not, there was no way he was going to allow his anguish to show on his face. Taking shallow breaths just to stay alive, Neil aimed to appear carefree as he rocked his head back and forth, trying to appear to be far more engaged than he actually was in the tune of an old Michael Jackson song that streamed on his mp3 player: *Beat it . . . Beat it . . . No one wants to be defeated.*

The words couldn't have been timelier,

and although Neil desperately wanted to turn off the treadmill completely and collapse to the floor, he couldn't help but feel a bit of victory in the fact that he'd challenged himself (and the redhead next to him) and won.

"Ughhhh." Hidden by a shower curtain, Neil saw no need to continue the façade. He groaned as the shower waters in the gym stall pounded on his exhausted body. It had been months — okay, years — since he'd stepped foot in a fitness center, and that was a message that his muscles were communicating to him in high volumes. He was in decent physical shape, but most of it came compliments of the good genetics from his father's side of the family coupled with the fact that Neil ate well on most days. While some guys chose to spend their free summer days in a workout facility, Neil would rather be riding an all terrain vehicle. He used to drive his Yamaha Utility ATV every spring and summer. That was another thing that he and Dwayne used to do together. Another thing that his brother's death had changed. Neil rarely rode it now.

When he stepped from the shower stall, his eyes met those of the younger man who had been on the treadmill beside him. Instantly, Neil's guard shot up, and he straightened his slumped posture and flexed his muscles as he reached for a towel and wrapped it securely around his waist. He walked as confidently as he could to the locker to begin gathering his clean, dry clothes.

As he dried himself and got dressed, Richie Cunningham was tying his shoe-strings nearby. Neil completed the dressing process and was ready to put on his shoes too, but he needed his treadmill challenger to leave so that he could start the painful process of bending down without being under scrutiny.

"Good workout, dude," the boy said, walking toward Neil with an outstretched arm. He towered over Neil by at least five inches, maybe six.

"You too," Neil replied, gritting his teeth through the amplified aches of the firm handshake.

"Not many guys that I run into when I come here can match my pace, at least not for the length of time that you did. Are you a long distance runner?"

Been running for Jesus for a long time. Does that count? Neil almost laughed at his own thought. "Not really," he opted to say.

"Have you ever run the Peachtree Road Race?"

"Never."

"You should think about entering this year," the boy suggested while slipping on a red-and-white windbreaker that matched his pants, then running his hands through his spiked, still-damp hair.

"Man, I'm too old for that." This time Neil did laugh. It was more of a chuckle. The pain around his ribcage wouldn't allow for much more. "I'd be forty-five years old running my first road race."

With a happy-go-lucky shrug, the boy replied, "You'll be forty-five years old regardless, right?"

Neil tilted his head. "True, I suppose."

"I'm serious, dude." The boy slipped his hand into his pocket and pulled out a business card. "I'm Adam Schmitz, and I run it every year. I'm not nearly fast enough to win; don't even come close. But it's fun, and every year I challenge myself to do a little better. I'm in training now, so if you ever want to train with me, give me a call, and we can synchronize our gym visits or meet at one of the local tracks."

Neil looked at the card and saw that Adam was a computer geek. For some reason, it didn't surprise him. "Thanks," he said, knowing full well that he would have no use for the number unless his desktop contracted a virus. "I'm Neil." He didn't see a need to give the boy his last name. They shook hands one final time.

Just as Adam reached the door to exit, he turned around. "Are you forty-five for real, or were you just pulling my leg?"

"Forty-five years old today," Neil said.

"Oh, okay. Happy birthday, dude. You don't look that old, and I know guys who are a lot younger who don't have your wind. You'd be an awesome inspiration for some of the younger dudes I train with."

One more *dude* and Neil was prepared to scream, but the compliment drew a smile out of him instead. "Thanks," he responded. The temporary feel-good sensation that swept over him at the sound of the flattering remark was quickly wiped out by muscle aches when Neil finally began putting on his spare tennis shoes. The process that should have only taken a few seconds took a few minutes, and even while Neil exited the gym, he struggled not to show signs of the lingering pain.

On a weekday, the drive from LA Fitness in Tucker to Neil's mother's house in Powder Springs was about forty minutes. On Saturday, with less traffic, the trip could be made in less. Neil checked his watch upon climbing in his year-old black Toyota

Land Cruiser and strapping on his seatbelt. His mother had asked him to come by early so that he could help her bake his birthday cake. It was a family tradition. Growing up, whenever one of the children had a birthday, they'd be required to help bake the celebratory cake, as though doing so was a privilege and was to be viewed as a part of their gift.

For as long as Neil could remember, his mom rose at six every morning. He would make it there at nine, and although that seemed early to him, he knew she would be in the full swing of things. In a half hour flat, Neil was navigating his SUV in his mother's driveway. She was standing in her open doorway, watching him as he climbed out of the vehicle and walked stiffly toward her porch.

"Boy, what's wrong with you?" she called out, examining him closely as he made his approach. "I know today is your birthday, but you ain't old enough to be walking like a man on social security."

Neil laughed. "I went to the gym this morning and gave my body a workout. Now it's repaying the favor."

"Well, I would hug you, but I'm scared I'll hurt you."

"Oh, come on here," Neil said, giving his mother a big bear-like hug despite his body aches. "How're you doing, Ms. Ella Mae?"

It was what Neil and his siblings had always called their mother. When they were small, Ella, who had no education to speak of, helped support her family by keeping neighborhood children. So that the other children would call her Ms. Ella Mae instead of Mama, she had her children do the same. And even though her babysitting days ended years ago, Ella was still known to many, including her own children, as Ms. Ella Mae.

Ella laughed at her son's question, and then said, "Better than you, apparently. What did you do at the gym that got you so crippled?"

"I ran a few miles on the treadmill." Neil sat on the sofa and pulled a mint from his pocket. "Man, I didn't know I was so out of shape."

"I bet you won't be going back no time soon." His mother made her way to the loveseat and sat. "It ain't like you need to lose no weight."

"I don't know, Ms. Ella Mae. I think I could stand to lose a pound or two. Got to fight this middle-aged spread, you know." Neil patted his stomach as he spoke. "And my body feels like I've been in a car wreck. All of these sore muscles are a big wake-up call. Apparently, I need to be a little bit more active."

Ella flipped her wrist and twisted her lips. "Whatever. You'll be done killed yourself, trying to make yourself healthier."

"I don't know. I'm thinking of entering the Peachtree Road Race this year." Neil had been giving Adam's offer more thought during the drive to his mother's home. "I was invited to train with some other guys. I might just do that if I can fit it in my schedule."

"Leave it to you to wait till you start graying to want to get out in the hot sun and run with fifty thousand other crazy folks."

Neil chuckled as he leaned back against the soft cushions and admired his mother. She wore a flattering, casual blue pants outfit, and he could tell that she'd visited the beautician recently. "What you been up to, sweetie? You're looking good."

Fingering her hair like a bashful schoolgirl, Ella grinned and said, "Nothing much, really. Just serving God and trying to live right. You know we been having noonday prayer at my church on Wednesdays." Eight years ago, Ella had transferred her church membership from Kingdom Builders to Bethel Cathedral. Bethel was a part of the New Hope Fellowship of Churches too, and it was much closer to where Ella lived.

"Yeah, you told me that a few weeks ago. How's it going?"

"Oh, the Lord has really been moving, Neil, but ain't nobody been showing up but the women."

Neil readjusted his position to try to get more comfortable. It didn't work. The movement just brought more pain. "Well, it *is* in the middle of the day, Ms. Ella Mae. Most of the brothers are probably on the clock."

"No, they ain't. They just ain't as faithful as they ought to be. A lot of the women work too, but they be there. Prayer is from twelve to one, and everybody get a lunch break, don't they? Deacon Alford Floyd works at the body shop one block from the church, and he don't even come. He probably be stuffing his face while we be praying. That's why he weighs four hundred pounds now. He needs to fast as well as pray. How 'bout you go down there and invite him to go to the gym with you? Now, that's a man who needs to be running on somebody's treadmill." Ella huffed and sat back in her seat. "Po' treadmill probably couldn't even take that kind of punishment."

Neil burst into a laughter that made his

whole body throb. "Ms. Ella Mae, that's not nice," he scolded when he finally got back his breath.

"It ain't nice to have to look at all that come wobbling into church on Sunday either. You know they call him Fat Al behind his back. If everybody in the church is like me, they be praying to God that all that don't come sit next to them. I be putting anything on the bench next to me so it'll look like somebody's already sitting there."

The ringing of the doorbell cut short Neil's second outburst. He turned and looked toward the front entrance, and then struggled to sit up straight. "You expecting company?"

"You just stay put," Ella said. "Slow as you moving, my old bones can make it to the door faster."

Neil's body was too appreciative to protest.

"Hey, Ms. Ella Mae!"

Neil leaned forward, to be sure that the voice he thought he heard was the voice that he'd actually heard. Momentarily forgetting his soreness, he rose to his feet and broke into a wide, beaming smile. "Val, is that you?"

His baby sister released their mother and ran to Neil, jumping into his arms like a teenaged cheerleader. The pain was excruciating, but Neil was too surprised and delighted not to catch her.

"Happy birthday, old man!"

"Lord have mercy, girl, you're gonna kill a brotha!" Neil yelled.

"Get off him, Val!" Ella ordered while her two grandchildren stood around her legs. "The boy already halfway broke up. You gon' finish the job."

Valerie slid out of Neil's arms, stood back, and examined him closely. "What? Are you hurt? What happened?"

Neil laughed at her unfounded concern. "No, I'm not hurt, at least not like you're thinking. I got the bright idea to go to the gym and work out today, and my whole body is kicking my tail in retaliation, that's all. It's good to see you, girl. What wind blew you into town?"

"The one that said, 'Your brother turns forty-five today.'"

"You came in town just for my birthday?"

Valerie nodded. "And because Ms. Ella Mae threatened to pull out the strap if I didn't." Turning to her children, she added, "Come on over here and speak to your uncle. Why y'all acting like you don't know him?"

"Well, it *has* been a minute," Neil said as

he returned to his seat on the sofa so he wouldn't have to suffer through the pain of bending down to hug Keisha and Tyrese. "You guys have gotten big. How old are you now?"

"I'm five," Keisha said, putting up as many fingers.

"I'm seven." Tyrese announced it like the two-year difference made him eligible to vote or something.

"Man, time flies," Neil said. He'd seen the children at last year's family reunion, but they seemed to have grown by leaps and bounds since then. "Where's Otis?" he asked his sister, referring to her husband.

"He's in New York. He had a load to haul there today, so he couldn't make it. Somebody's got to bring home the bacon, right?"

"He still treating you good?"

"I'm still with him, ain't I?" Valerie said. Living up North hadn't erased any of the Southern country girl from her personality. Not by a long shot. "Boy, you know I don't take no mess. If he weren't treating me right, I'd be out, okay?"

"And what if he wasn't treating her good?" Ella injected. "As tore up as you are right now, you couldn't do nothing about it. All Otis would have to do is pat you on the back, and you'd crumble to pieces."

The truth in her statement was a laughing matter that even the children took part in. It was turning out to be a better birthday than Neil had expected. He was having so much fun that he didn't even mind being the brunt of their jokes. He never got to see Valerie as often as he would like. She was a year younger than Neil, and she and her family lived in New Jersey. Valerie and Otis had recently celebrated their eighth anniversary.

"You think you gon' be able to help make your cake, son?" Ella looked at Neil with motherly concern.

"I'm not that bad off, Ms. Ella Mae," Neil assured, rising from his sandwiched spot between his niece and nephew. "Let's get to it. You know I'm ready to get the baking over with so I can get to the eating."

Neil washed his hands in the kitchen sink, and then spied all of the ingredients that his mother had already laid out on the counter. There were eggs, butter, flour, milk, sugar, cooking oil, and lemon extract: all the elements needed to make a lemon pound cake, his favorite. As customary, Ella did most of the work. All Neil really did was crack the eggs, pour in the milk, and lick batter residue from the spoons after everything had been mixed together.

"Okay, Ms. Ella Mae, you didn't invite a whole bunch of folks over here, did you?" Neil looked at his mother through suspicious eyes when he heard the doorbell ring again.

"I'll get it," Valerie called from the living room.

"No, I didn't," Ella said as she finished dumping the cake mixture in the two layer pans. "I know you don't like big parties, and I want you to enjoy your birthday. I wouldn't plan something that I know you wouldn't want. I knew you'd want to see your sister. That's the only reason I insisted that she come this way."

"Ms. Ella Mae, it's for you," Valerie's voice sang out.

Ella wiped her hands on her apron and pointed at Neil. "Okay, you be careful now. I want you to place both those pans in the oven. And try not to waste none of the batter while you do it."

Neil nodded. "I got this, Ms. Ella Mae. You just go see about your company." Then he dropped his voice to a whisper. "And get rid of them."

Ella laughed before leaving him in the kitchen to follow the orders she'd given. The oven had been preheating, and when Neil opened the door, he had to turn his face away to avoid the hot vapors that came barreling out. There was a sheet of foil wrapping already lying on top of the oven rack. Neil gingerly placed one of the pans on the rack, and then the other. Once he finished doing so without a spill, he felt a sense of pride as he closed the door so the baking process could begin.

The voices from the living room seemed to get louder, and the louder they became, the more familiar they sounded, not just Ella's and Valerie's voices, but also the stranger's. Neil crept closer to the kitchen's entrance and listened. For several moments, all he did was stand glued to the floor and eavesdrop.

"Oh my goodness," he whispered. Wiping his hands on a dishtowel that had been placed on the counter, Neil stepped into the opening for a better view. All of the front room guests were still getting acquainted, and Ella was the first to see him.

"Oh!" she said. "And this is the birthday boy."

It was only at that moment that Neil was one hundred percent sure that their new houseguest was who he thought it was. Ella continued.

"Sol, this is Mrs. Shaylynn Ford from Shay Décor. I hired her to —"

196

"Hey, Dr. Taylor!" Chase exclaimed. "What you doing at Ms. Eloise's house?"

THIRTEEN

So, Ms. Eloise Flowers, my client, is the same person that the rest of the world seems to know as Ms. Ella Mae. And Dr. Neil Taylor, the director of my son's school, is the same person as the child that Ms. Flowers always referred to as 'that young-un of mine,' and also a person that his family calls Sol.

Shaylynn tried to keep straight all the facts in her head as she nibbled on cake, watched Chase interact with his new playmates, and listened to the conversation that flowed between the adults, all at the same time.

"People who have known me from childhood generally call me Eloise Flowers. That's my maiden name," Eloise had explained to Shaylynn shortly after all the introductions had been made. "But folks who call me Ella Mae mostly call me Ella Mae Taylor, which is my married name. My husband gave me the nickname Ella Mae. Legally, my name is Eloise Mae Flowers

Taylor, so both of them are who I am. I don't mind either one."

After Shaylynn had settled in and met all of the houseguests, she and Eloise had gone through her humble abode and talked about the changes Eloise wanted to make. Neil and Valerie followed, giving their input too. The three of them didn't agree on much, but the one thing on which they all concurred was that the bottom floor of Eloise's split level house needed to be upgraded and rearranged so that she had to climb the stairs as little as possible. The stairs were the culprits that made her breathless, and that concerned both her and her children.

Eloise turned to Shaylynn and put an end to her deep thoughts. "Mrs. Ford, I know you didn't come over here for all of this, but thank you for staying for Neil's birthday cake."

"Yes, thank you," Neil echoed.

Shaylynn's eyes met his, but only briefly before she turned them back in the direction of his mother. "You're welcome, Ms. Flowers. The cake is delicious, by the way."

"Ms. Ella Mae makes the best cakes in the world," Valerie bragged.

"I helped," Neil chimed.

"So if you think this cake is good, you should taste one that Ms. Ella Mae bakes by herself," Valerie added.

Neil tossed a pillow across the room that his sister had to duck to avoid. "Shut up." He followed up with a laugh.

Shaylynn laughed a little too. She liked the way Neil's family interacted. They seemed to genuinely like one another. It was something that, growing up, she'd not had in her own family, and although Emmett's family wasn't poor or dysfunctional like hers, they really never seemed all that happy either.

Neil excused himself and walked into the kitchen for his third helping of cake. Stealing a glance that she hoped nobody noticed, Shaylynn did a quick, albeit thorough, evaluation of the man she'd never seen outside of his professional element, or outside of a business suit. The sporty but smart Nike jogging set fell perfectly on Neil, and the red-and-white colors gave him a more relaxed look than the dark clothes he normally wore at school.

"Would you like more cake?"

Shaylynn looked to her right, and her eyes locked onto the fabric of the left leg of Neil's pants. Following the red line that accented the seam, she scanned him all the way up to his face. Shaylynn hadn't even heard Neil exit the kitchen, and now, with him standing so close, she could smell the masculine fragrance of a men's body wash.

"Uh . . . no." She cleared her throat. "No, thank you. I think one is enough."

"Oh, come on," Neil urged. "Eating only one slice of cake is a sin."

"It is not."

"Yes, it is. It's in the Bible."

Shaylynn giggled, knowing that he was teasing her. "What version is your Bible, Dr. Taylor?"

"Okay, so it's not in the Bible, but it is an unspoken rule for anybody black who lives in the South."

Still smiling a toothy grin, Shaylynn shook her head at Neil's silliness. Another slice of cake did sound like a tasty idea, though. She glanced across the room at Eloise and Valerie, who had their own conversation going on, and then at the children, who were sitting Indian style next to one another, absorbed in an episode of *Blues Clues.*

"You can't be watching your weight," Neil pointed out before she could speak. "One more piece won't hurt you. Come on." He reached out his hand, leaving Shaylynn to wonder whether he was reaching for her hand or her empty saucer. Either way, he wasn't going to get it.

"I really shouldn't," she replied.

"Please?"

After more seconds of thoughtful ponder, Shaylynn replied, "Okay, just one." She stood on her own accord and held on to her saucer while walking past him into the kitchen. Neil followed close behind.

"You're a guest. Let me do that." He stepped in front of her and took the cake cutter from her hand.

Determining that his untimely interception had left them standing too close, Shaylynn backed away to put more distance between her and the intoxicating smell of his skin. "Thanks," she muttered.

Neil smiled, but said nothing as he placed the cutter against the double-layered lemon pound cake and began pressing.

"Wait. That's too much, Dr. Taylor. I can't eat —"

"Neil." He stopped cutting and turned to face her. Lowering his voice, he added, "Call me Neil."

Shaylynn felt flushed, and her stomach felt like there were little gymnasts inside vying for a spot on the U.S. Olympic team. "I . . . I'd rather not."

"Why?"

He was whispering now, and something about the sound of his raspy whisper birthed little bumps that raised the hairs on Shaylynn's arms. She took another half step back and refused to look at him.

"You're the director of my son's school, Dr. Taylor. I just think it is more appropriate that I refer to you by your professional title." Shaylynn's mouth was so dry that she could only pray that her lips didn't look like she'd been kissing baby powder.

"But we're not at school."

He made a good point, but Shaylynn insisted. "But still."

"But still what?"

"He will hear me calling you by your first name."

"And?"

"I don't want him to think he can do the same."

Neil leaned his back against the counter and chuckled. "He's been hearing Val call me Neil and Ms. Ella Mae referring to me as Sol all afternoon, but every time he's said anything to me, it's still Dr. Taylor. What makes you think it will be any different if you call me by my first name?"

Shaylynn still had questions about that Sol thing, but for now, it would have to take a backseat. She was becoming too irritated with this war of words she was having with Neil to even be concerned about the root of his nickname. "That's different," Shaylynn insisted. "I'm his mother."

"And?"

Lifting her hands in mock surrender, Shaylynn's whisper turned harsh. "Just forget it." Then she turned away to return to the living room. A firm but gentle grasp held her by the arm.

"Shay, wait."

Shaylynn turned and glared up at Neil. *Shay?* First of all, nobody called her that, and secondly, who'd given him permission to be so casual with her? Thirdly, she liked the sound of it coming from Neil's mouth, and she hated that most of all. "My name is Shaylynn," she stated. "But for you, it's Mrs. Ford." With that, she backed away and stormed back into the living room, leaving the saucer and the cake behind. Without another word, she returned to the seat she'd vacated earlier.

Eloise and Valerie were still busy with their chatter, and the children were now in a competition to see if they could uncover the mysterious clues that Blue and his friend were giving on the television. If her son weren't having so much fun, Shaylynn would have grabbed him, her attaché case, and headed for her car.

"Here you go."

There he was again, standing to her right.

This time Neil handed her a small slice of cake and a fresh glass of milk as though he were handing her a peace offering. She looked up at him, and he gave her a half smile, but in his eyes, she saw injury. Somehow, Neil's feelings had been hurt in their heated exchange. That was not her intent, but he had pressed her, and she had to be firm. However, knowing she'd wounded him made Shaylynn feel unworthy of his kind gesture.

"No, thank you," she whispered, dropping her eyes to the saucer.

"Please, Sh— Mrs. Ford. Take it."

His quick recourse to correct himself before saying her name should have given Shaylynn a sense of victory, but it didn't. Taking the offering, Shaylynn thanked him, and then watched the man return to his place on the couch across the room. She returned his stare as Neil studied her for a moment, but unable to handle the intensity of his searching eyes any longer, Shaylynn picked up her fork and began eating.

"Do you guys want any more of your Uncle Sol's cake?" Eloise suddenly asked the children.

A chorus of cheers filled the room, and the children stood and scattered into the kitchen in preparation for their treats.

Shaylynn never allowed Chase to run in the house, but he followed the others as though Neil was his Uncle Sol too.

"Ms. Ella Mae, don't give Kee-Kee and Ty too much," Valerie said as she stood from her seated position and started toward the kitchen. She stopped in front of Shaylynn and sighed, adding, "My kids will be bouncing off the walls with all that sugar."

Shaylynn's responding smile quickly dissolved when she realized that once again, she and Neil were alone. She turned up her glass of milk and hoped that when she brought it down from her lips, Neil would have found a reason to join the others.

"I'm sorry."

Shaylynn's eyes traced the voice across the room. There was genuine regret in Neil's tone, and he was looking directly at her when he spoke. His eyes seemed to search her face, reaching for her thoughts. Afraid that he might be able to read them, Shaylynn cast her eyes downward.

"I didn't mean to upset you," he continued. "I apologize for doing so."

"It's okay." Even though she didn't look directly at him, Shaylynn could see Neil shifting in his seat. He stretched out his legs and released an uncomfortable moan. It wasn't the first one she'd heard since her arrival. Shaylynn wanted to ask him if he were feeling well, but decided that it really wasn't her concern.

"So you decided upon Shay Décor, huh?" There was a twinge of satisfaction in Neil's question.

"Actually, no," Shaylynn said. She didn't know why she was so determined not to give him any joy. "No decisions have been made."

"But Ms. Ella Mae said —"

"I was pondering over the name when she called me that day, and it just came out when I answered the phone. Legally, the name hasn't changed yet."

"Yet?"

Shaylynn's eyes surveyed Neil for the first time in a while. "No decisions have been made," she repeated, leaving it at that.

Neil's lips parted to reply, but his words were intercepted by the return of Eloise and Valerie. The children had been instructed to sit at the dining room table to finish their desserts. Shaylynn watched the two women walk past her, and then she glanced toward Neil. He was watching her still, and there was a spark of some indefinable emotion in his gaze. It thrilled and troubled her all at the same time. She needed to leave.

"We're going to get ready to go, Ms. Flowers," Shaylynn said as she stood. "Thanks for the cake, and I'll start working on your designs immediately and get back with you when I have some things for you to look at and consider."

"You don't have to hurry off," Eloise said. "Besides, the boy ain't finished with his cake yet."

Shaylynn turned and looked into the dining area. The children were almost done. "Finish up, Chase. We have to go."

"Let me cut you a couple of slices to take with you." Eloise rose and grabbed her cane. "I got some foil that I can wrap a few pieces in."

Shaylynn wanted to tell her not to worry herself. She didn't need any more cake and neither did Chase, but she didn't voice her objection. Shaylynn didn't know if she were following Eloise into the kitchen to keep her company, or to avoid Neil's eyes. Probably the latter. Those brown eyes of his seemed to bore holes into her flesh. Despite Eloise's urging, in a matter of minutes, Shaylynn was heading out the front door to join her son and his new friends, who were already outside, running around the front yard as though the sugar they'd consumed had gone directly into their bloodstreams.

"Chase, be careful," she called from the

open front door when he nearly fell during a high-spirited sprint.

"I'm going to be in town for a while, Shaylynn," Valerie said as the two of them stood together. "My kids are out of school for a few days, so I'll be here until Thursday. Chase is having so much fun. Why don't you let him spend the night?"

Spend the night? Shaylynn thought the woman must have lost her mind.

"I know Kee-Kee and Ty would love to have him stay over. Chase and Ty are about the same size, so I'm sure there is something in my son's suitcase that Chase can wear. We're going to KBCC tomorrow to visit with Neil, and we'll bring him by your house once we're out. What do you say?"

She had to be nuttier than a Snickers bar. Shaylynn tried to make her smile appear genuine, but there was no way she would even consider leaving her son with strangers that she'd only known for a few hours. "I don't think so, but I appreciate the offer."

"Well, okay. But if you want to bring Chase by after school one or two days next week, maybe whatever days that he doesn't have a lot of homework on, you can."

"We don't live on this side of town," was the only thing Shaylynn could think to say that wouldn't be offensive. Hoping to completely change the subject, she turned to Eloise. "Thanks for everything, Ms. Flowers. I'll be in touch very soon."

"All right. I'll be here," Eloise replied.

Shaylynn stepped out onto the porch.

"I'll walk you out," Neil offered.

Shaylynn's words came quickly as she turned to face him. "No, it's not necessary. I can walk myself out."

"You're not from the South, are you?" Eloise asked.

"No, no, I'm not." Shaylynn wondered what that had to do with anything.

"I didn't think so," Eloise surmised, easing onto the couch and offering no further explanation.

Shaylynn walked outside with Neil shadowing close behind. No words were spoken between them, and she wanted to keep it that way. "Chase, honey, come on. We have to go." She hoped he heard her before he disappeared on the side of the house.

"Why are you in such a hurry?"

First taking a moment to slip on her sunglasses, Shaylynn looked up at Neil and replied, "I have work to do."

He grunted a response, almost as though he didn't believe her.

"Some of us don't have the luxury of working a regular five-day, eight-hour schedule and having our weekends free, Dr. Taylor."

"So, Shay Décor isn't closed on weekends?"

Shaylynn peered at him with a critical squint that her eye-wear hid. "Why do you insist on calling it that?"

"Because it is what it is. Shay Décor fits you, and it fits your business. That's why it rolled off your tongue so easily when you spoke to my mother."

"Chase," she called. Her decision had been made now. She hated this man. For a while she couldn't determine whether she liked him. Now she knew that she not only didn't like him, but she hated him. She hated his smart-alecky secretary too.

"Have dinner with me tonight."

She'd disregarded Neil's first remark, but she couldn't ignore this one. Shaylynn froze in a stunned tableau, and then took a quick breath of utter astonishment. She was too startled by his suggestion to offer an immediate reply. When Shaylynn finally looked up, she found Neil looking down at her. Featherlike laugh lines crinkled around his eyes. He seemed to enjoy her struggle to capture her composure. Oh, how she hated him!

She finally found her voice. "What did you say?"

"You heard me."

"Well, how 'bout I just pretend that I didn't." Shaylynn turned away. "Chase!"

"What are you afraid of?"

"*Excuse* me?" Aggravated by what she determined to be an elevated ego, Shaylynn spun around to face him again, daring him to repeat himself. "Just because I don't want to go out with you doesn't mean that I'm afraid of you."

"Then don't see it as you going out with me." Neil shrugged in an almost boyish manner as he spoke. "Look at it like this: today is my birthday, and I'd like to cap off the celebration by treating myself to dinner . . . with you."

Treat himself to dinner with her. The notion replayed itself in Shaylynn's mind. Neil's words made it seem like he considered her keeping him company as a worthy gift. Shaylynn swallowed. In her lifetime, no man had ever put her through such an array of emotions in such a short span of time.

"I can't." Her tone had softened, but not by much. "I have a son, Dr. Taylor. I can't."

"Not a problem. Bring him with you." Neil's tone was matter-of-fact. "He's welcome to be a part of it. It's only dinner, and

212

it's not a school night. You can't tell me that he's not up late like that on weekends anyway. I won't believe you even if you do. Bring him along." His tone had turned pleading.

At that moment, Chase and his friends reappeared from the side of the house, giggling and breathless from their fun.

"Chase, say good-bye to the children," Shaylynn instructed. "We're leaving now."

Obediently, Chase bid his playmates farewell, and then climbed in the backseat of their Chrysler and fastened his seatbelt, waving at Keisha and Tyrese the whole time. Shaylynn reached for her door handle, but Neil's hand arrived at the mark first. He didn't immediately open the door, and Shaylynn stood alongside him in silence.

"I'll be at Sambuca on Piedmont Road in the Buckhead district at ten o'clock tonight," he said in a lowered voice. "I go there for my birthday dinner every year and enjoy the live jazz. If you choose to join me, it'll be my pleasure and my treat."

Remaining unresponsive, Shaylynn allowed him to open her door, and she climbed in. She didn't even bother to thank him for his courtesy before he shut her inside. All that she could think was that she needed to get away from Eloise Flowers a.k.a. Ella Mae Taylor's son and back to the safety of her home as soon as possible. And if Dr. Neil Taylor thought for one minute that she and her son were going to be gallivanting with him in Buckhead tonight, he had another thought coming.

FOURTEEN

"So you're telling me that you have two dates with two different women on the same night? Do I need to be going before the throne of God on your behalf, bruh?"

The weightiness of CJ's tone added to the hilarity of his words. Neil unleashed a liberal laugh, but his lighthearted attitude wasn't shared by CJ.

"I'm serious, Neil. This isn't cool. This isn't cool at all."

"CJ, aren't you the same man who, for at least the last five years, has been telling me that God had a virtuous woman set aside somewhere for me?"

"A virtuous *woman*, Neil. That's singular. Dating two women isn't even tactful, let alone honorable. And if either of them were aware that you were also going out with the other, I'm sure she wouldn't be the least bit amused by it. As a deacon and a scholar of

God's Word, you have to know better than this."

Neil switched his telephone from one ear to the other while he balanced himself to put on his slacks. He'd called CJ just after he'd dried himself after showering and now, pressed for time, he struggled to get dressed and talk to his pastor at the same time.

The bedroom where Neil slept each night was simple but neatly decorated. A small three-tier bookshelf stood in one corner, housing his many books, mostly nonfiction ministerial tools written by prominent preachers like T. D. Jakes, Joyce Evans, Tony Evans, Rod Parsley, and the like. His favorite was Rick Warren's *The Purpose Driven Life*. Reading was a pastime that Neil and CJ shared.

As the centerpiece of his room, Neil's bed was covered with linen in hues of browns and bronzes, his favorite colors. They added masculinity to the walls that were painted a soft green. Only one framed photo decorated his walls. It was a picture of him and Dwayne, one they took shortly after singing together at their mother's fifty-fifth birthday party, just two years before Dwayne died. That was nearly twenty years ago, but it felt like sooner.

"Are you listening to me, Neil?"

The demanding question recaptured Neil's full attention. "You're getting way too deep with this, CJ. You act like I'm playing the role of some kind of pious playboy. It's not that serious, and I never would have told you if I'd known you'd take it out of context. All you know is that I'm possibly meeting both ladies for dinner. You don't know the whole story, so you can't draw fair conclusions."

"Okay, fine. I'm clearing my mind of all preconceived notions. You tell me the whole story."

Neil didn't hesitate to dive in. "Yesterday, as we were wrapping up things in the office, Ms. Dasher invited me to her place for dinner. She said she wanted to treat me to a homemade meal to celebrate my birthday. There was no coaxing on my part. She invited, and I accepted." Neil took a breath for the first time since he began his explanation. "Then I went to my mom's place this morning, and Shay showed up."

"She just showed up unexpectedly?" There was considerable doubt in CJ's reply.

"As far as I was concerned, yes. I mean, the other day, I showed Ms. Ella Mae the ad in the *Atlanta Weekly Chronicles* that advertised Shay's business, and without letting on that I knew the owner of the business, I candidly recommended that she call. As you know, I have been trying to convince my mom to move from that house for years. It's not built to suit her recent health challenges. But since she has so many sentimental attachments and memories there, Ms. Ella Mae refuses to even consider living elsewhere. So, for the past few months, we've been talking about getting some updates done to the house. When I found out what kind of business Shay was in, and then saw her ad in the paper, I suggested that Ms. Ella Mae call. But she never told me that she'd taken my advice, and I certainly didn't know Shay would pop by the house. So yes, it was unexpected."

"Okay. Go on."

"Well, there's not much more to say. She stayed around and had birthday cake with me and my family, and when she got ready to leave, I invited her to dinner."

"Knowing you already had a date with your office assistant."

Neil huffed. "Man, aren't you the one who said I should ask her out?"

"Yeah, but not if you already had a date. Don't try to pin your bad decision on me, Neil. This pickle that you're in has nothing to do with anything that I said."

Until CJ described it as such, Neil had

never viewed his situation as a "pickle." In fact, he'd been pretty keyed up about his birthday plans. Now his excitement was fully deflated. Neil tried to minimize his mounting guilt. "It's just a couple of birthday dinners, CJ."

"It's not just a couple of birthday dinners, Neil. It's a couple of birthday dinners with two women that you actually have some level of affection for. You've had a thing for Sister Dasher for years, and although you're fighting me tooth and nail on the intensity of your attraction to the former Mrs. Emmett Ford, I know the real deal."

"Let's get it straight. I don't have a *thing,* for Ms. Dasher, CJ." Neil sat at the foot of his bed, still having only slipped one leg into his pants. "I just think she's kinda fine for a lady her age, and there ain't no sighted man who could honestly disagree with me on that. But it's not like I want a relationship with her. She looks good for her age, but her age is still her age. Ms. Dasher is too old for me."

"And let me guess," CJ said. "You're going to say that Shay is too young, right?"

Neil was going to say no such thing, but voicing that fact would just open a whole new conversation that he didn't want to venture into. Because of that, he remained quiet and listened as CJ continued.

"Sister Dasher's too old, and Shay's too young. So your excuse for why it's okay for you to be entertaining both these women tonight is that their ages make it right. Is that what you're trying to tell me?"

"CJ —"

"Listen, Neil. The Bible tells us to shun the very appearance of evil. So for the sake of argument, let's just say that your motives are completely pure. Does it really seem like nothing is wrong with you going out with both these women on the same night? If it were Sister Dasher's birthday and you invited her to your house for a nice, intimate dinner that you took the time to prepare, would you be okay if she accepted, but then also made plans to meet another brother at some upscale restaurant a couple of hours later?"

Neil paused and thought about the scenario he'd just been given. After brief consideration, he shrugged. "Actually, yeah. Whether you believe it or not, I can honestly say that I would be cool with that. I mean, Ms. Dasher's a grown woman, and besides, it's not like I'm in —"

"What if Shay did it?"

CJ's new supposition served as a sharp knife, cutting into Neil's comeback and seemingly, into a nerve as well. He felt a blunt soreness in the pit of his stomach, like someone had jabbed him there. Not enough to crumple him to the floor, writhing in pain, but enough for him to squirm and touch the spot where the pain had hit. Neil pacified himself by defining it as just another aftereffect of his morning workout. The tenderness in his calves was still there, so this new ache must have lingered from the fitness challenge too.

Continuing his quest for answers, CJ expanded his query. "Think about it, Neil. For added visual, let's just say today is Shay's birthday, and she's getting dressed right now to go and meet some other dude at his place for dinner. And mind you, this is not just your run-of-the-mill guy, either. This man is attractive, available, and somebody that she's very fond of. But guess what? After she spends some time with him, she's going to head to her favorite eatery to share her leftover time with you. Are you telling me you're cool with that too?"

"You're making it sound like I'm some kind of dog or something, man."

"You didn't answer my question."

"You're making me sorry I even called you," Neil barked. His avoidance of the issue was blatant. "I thought you'd be happy just to know I was getting out of the house and spending quality time with somebody. Now you're making me want to call everything off."

"Bruh, you know that all I want is the best that God has for you. I just think you're going about this the wrong way. I know Sister Dasher, so I know she's a good, decent woman who loves the Lord with her whole heart. She wouldn't exactly be the person I would have lined up for you, but then again, I'm not God. Truth be told, she'd probably be very good to and for you. You've known her for a while, you have good chemistry, you work well together, you're both saved, active members of the same church. . . . What else do you need?"

Neil quietly rolled his eyes to the ceiling. Why did CJ always have to make everything sound so permanent? It was just a dinner, for crying out loud.

"And this Shay Ford . . . well, I don't know her, but by all that I've heard, I'm inclined to believe that she's not only beautiful on the outside, but also on the inside. My instinct tells me that she's both goodly and godly. She clearly has some issues where her late husband is concerned, but it's nothing that God can't mend if she's the woman that He has prepared for you.

Don't get me wrong, Neil. I'm not saying that your attraction to either one of these women is wrong; I'm just saying that I don't agree with the way you're handling your business tonight. I've always prayed that God would change your mulish, not-needing-a-woman mindset, but it's like you've gone from one extreme to another overnight."

In frustration, Neil kicked to free the one leg that he had gotten into the pants. Maybe all this was just a part of his midlife crisis too. Whatever the case, his friend had messed up everything. The second half of his birthday was ruined, and Neil wasn't even looking forward to it anymore. "Goodness, CJ, you're acting as though I'm sleeping with these women. I'm not."

"You don't have to be sleeping with a woman to violate her, Neil."

"Violate?" That was way too strong a word as far as Neil was concerned, and his raised octave reflected that.

"I wouldn't be your friend or your spiritual leader if I didn't tell you the truth, bruh. There's nothing right, neither morally or spiritually, about you spending time with both these women tonight. Especially since they are unaware of your double plans. Shouldn't they at least have a choice in the matter of whether they each want to *share* intimate time with the same man on the same night?"

"Intimate? It's not all that intimate, CJ. I mean, yeah, Ms. Dasher asked me over, but she didn't give any indication that the dinner would be romantic. She could have easily been just being nice to me when she extended the invitation. Did you ever consider that? And Shay . . . well, I'll be surprised if she even shows up. I invited her, but she didn't exactly accept the invitation. As a matter of fact, she all but turned it down."

"This isn't about the ladies' intentions, Neil; it's about yours. Whether Sister Dasher is planning a romantic evening for the two of you or not, if you're honest, you'll admit that that's what you believe it is, and you're going along with it, maybe even with a little bit of hope that your suspicions are on point. Am I right?"

Silence.

"And whether or not Shay shows up is definitely up in the air. But just in case she does, you have every intention of being at that restaurant at the time that you asked her to meet you there, with the hopes of at least cracking the shell of her inhibitions. Stop me when I'm wrong."

Silence reigned once more, and after a short while and the release of a deep, laborious breath, Neil said, "Church folks make me sick. You know I've never liked you, right?"

CJ expressed a soft display of amusement and then replied, "I know. I love you too, man. I wish I could stay on the phone and talk more, but Resa needs to return a call to her mother before it gets too late, and I need to get some studying done in preparation for tomorrow's sermon. I know your mind is made up, but I hope that I've at least given you something to think about. Don't stay out so late tonight that you can't get up to give God His time tomorrow."

Neil hung up the phone, and minutes ticked away on the clock as he sat in silence with his shoulders slumped. This hadn't at all turned out the way he had planned, and to add to his misery, all of a sudden he didn't feel so well. His eyes roamed to the face of the watch on his wrist. It was a few minutes after six o'clock, and he had less than an hour to get dressed and get to Margaret's house. The drive alone would take thirty. Neil could almost smell the appetizing aromas that were floating from her kitchen right now, but instead of tempting him, they made him feel nauseated.

"I knew I shouldn't have had that sixth slice of cake," he grumbled as he eased his back against the mattress and stared at the light fixture above his head. Minutes later, another pain hit, like the one he'd experienced during his conversation with CJ. Neil moaned and turned over to his side, trying to find comfort. But instead of relief, another pain and then another assaulted his abdomen. Just moments afterward, he was clutching his stomach and swallowing back a sudden onset of uncontrolled saliva.

"Ughhhhhh."

Jolting into an upright position, Neil raced to the master bathroom and barely made it over the commode before his body began purging itself. He clutched the sides of the commode and felt the beads of perspiration surface on his forehead and grow bigger until they began rolling down his face. He didn't have the will or the coordination to wipe away the blinding moisture.

"Jesus," he called between fits of vomiting that seemed endless. When the excruciating pains in his stomach finally subsided, Neil felt depleted of all energy. "Is this my punishment or something? Dang. I haven't had a decent date in months, now when I finally get one . . . okay, two . . ." He looked up to the ceiling. "Can't you cut a brotha just a little slack?"

Neil flushed the toilet and dragged his drained body to the sink, where he doused his face with water and dried it with sheets of paper towel that he pulled from the upright metal stand that stood atop the counter. In the mirror on the wall behind the basin, red, watery eyes looked back at him. After rinsing his bitter mouth with Scope, Neil exited the bathroom and mustered just enough energy to make his way back to the bed. The cordless phone was still in the place where he left it when he ended the call with CJ. Picking it up, he stared at it for a second, trying to steady his vision, and then pressed a key and listened to the almost musical sound of the speed dial in action. Neil prayed that he would get the voice mail, but God still wasn't granting him any favors.

"Hello?"

"Hey, Ms. Dasher."

"Dr. Taylor, is that you?"

Neil rubbed his stomach. "Yeah, it's me. Listen, I'm sorry, but I'm not going to be able to make it tonight."

"You're kidding, right?" Her dazed tone just made him feel all the more awful.

"I'm sorry. I was getting dressed and just all of a sudden got very ill. I think it might

227

be something that I ate at my mom's. I ate way more than I should have, and I feel bad — real bad. There's no way I can enjoy dinner feeling like this. I'm sorry," he said for the third time.

"I understand, I suppose. I mean, if you don't feel well, you don't feel well. I just don't know what in God's name I'm going to do with all this food I cooked. And you should see the way I had everything set up. It was going to be a beautiful birthday surprise for you. I've got scented candles, sparkling cider, mood music, and everything."

Neil couldn't believe Margaret was actually admitting how she planned to romance him. He hadn't given much thought to what Margaret had designed for tonight, but Neil never imagined candles, cider, music, and *everything.* For him, the evening was going to more so be the fulfillment of a childlike fantasy. He'd finally get to have a cozy dinner with the woman he'd secretly admired for years, but frankly, Neil knew his shallow attraction to Margaret was nothing on which to build a relationship. *Had she detected something all along? Did I indirectly lead her on?* He felt like the heel that CJ had all but accused him of being, and he searched for words that wouldn't hurt Margaret's feelings or their friendship.

"I . . . I, uh, Ms. Dasher, I —"

"And worst of all, what am I gonna tell my cousin?" Margaret cut in. "She's just gonna be crushed."

Frown lines accumulated on Neil's face and deepened. "Your cousin?"

"Okay, I might as well tell you," Margaret said through a defeated sigh. "My second cousin's stepson's daughter was staying with me this weekend while she attended some kind of big time book festival somewhere in downtown Atlanta. Her name is Danisha, and she's an airline stewardess and one of those avid readers who have met every big time author in the world. Smart as a whip, too. You like books . . . she likes books. Well, I thought the two of you would really hit it off, so I told Nisha that I would —"

"Wait a minute." Neil stretched out his weakened body on the mattress. "So this was a birthday dinner for three?"

"No, it was gonna be for two." The smile on Margaret's face could be heard through her voice. "I was gonna find a reason to sneak out and leave you young folks to yourselves. You're not mad at me, are you, Dr. Taylor? I know that in spite of your stubbornness, some good woman is going to net you one day. 'Cause in the end, we always

229

win, you know. And I just thought it would be nice if somebody in my family got to be the lucky girl, that's all."

Neil was too sick and too relieved to be upset by Margaret's failed ploy. "No, I'm not mad, Ms. Dasher. And even if I had the strength to be, I sure couldn't stay angry after a compliment like that. I'm sorry to disappoint you and your cousin, but I have no plans to go any farther than this bed tonight."

"Well, that's what I get for trying to be sneaky, I guess," she determined. "My mama always used to say that God didn't like ugly," Margaret added with a chuckle. "You go on and get some rest, and I'll say a special prayer for you. I hope you feel well enough to come to church tomorrow."

"Thanks. I hope so too." Neil ended the call and turned over on his side, staring at the numbers on his nightstand clock as though they were dangling from a hypnotist's string. The last thing he remembered seeing before drifting off to sleep was the illuminated digits change to read 6:43.

FIFTEEN

"Ouch!" Shaylynn winced and grimaced from the self-inflicted pain that resulted from her pressing the sharp prongs of her fork into the flesh of the back of her hand.

If anyone had seen her, they would have understandably thought that she was a woman in need of psychotherapy. But Shaylynn was too angry at herself to even care about the opinions of others.

"Would you like more water, ma'am?"

Shaylynn looked up into the face of the tall, thin, pale-skinned waiter who stood next to her, dressed from head to toe in solid black. He had been her server from the moment she was seated and had been nothing but kind. Even so, Shaylynn found herself gritting her teeth and fighting the urge to stand up and slap the smile right off of his face. As far as she was concerned, every man deserved to be whacked today.

"No, thank you," she mumbled, and then

took a gulp from her current supply in a failed attempt to calm herself.

The only reason Shaylynn had even ordered a meal was to save face. Everyone would have guessed that she had been stood up had she sat awhile, and then left, never having placed an order. Now, because of her foolhearted last-minute decision to fight Saturday's late night traffic to get through the party district of upscale Buckhead, Shaylynn had been forced to pay nearly twenty-five dollars for a meal of Atlantic salmon, jasmine rice, and snow peas that she could have cooked at home for a fraction of the price. Using her fork, she picked at the flaky pink fish. The small portion that she'd nibbled was delicious, but just as with the beautiful jazz that was being sung by the man who stood beside the piano onstage, she was too enraged to enjoy it.

As her mind continued to replay all that had happened in the hours before arriving at Sambuca restaurant, Shaylynn cringed. How could she have been so stupid? She'd always prided herself on being a good decision maker, but this colossal farce had certainly proven otherwise. *I'm an idiot. A brainless, dim-witted idiot!* It's what she would have thought of any other woman who had done what she'd done, so Shaylynn determined that the description was perfect. More than two hours ago, driven by some unseen force that she couldn't even identify, Shaylynn had stopped in the middle of planning the improvements on Eloise's house, showered, gotten dressed, and driven a full sixty minutes from her house to the restaurant where Neil said he'd be.

I go there for my birthday dinner every year, she clearly recalled hearing him say. "Liar!" The loud music and Shaylynn's clenched teeth worked together to make her one-word defamation incoherent to those closest around her.

And that wasn't even the worst of it. As up in arms as she was with Neil, she was even more livid with herself. Tears of anger and guilt welled in Shaylynn's eyes, and she blinked hard to force them back. *I left my son with virtual strangers!*

At the time, it seemed like the best idea. After all, Valerie had given her an open invitation to leave him there, and Chase had begged her to allow him to go back. Plus it really was too late to have a six-year-old child out at night, realizing that it would probably be nearing midnight before they would return home. So stupidly, she'd taken Chase to Eloise's house with an overnight bag and placed his wellbeing in the hands of people she barely knew. Shaylynn had never felt unfit as a mother, but right now, she did. At the haunting thought of it, she trembled and closed her hand into such a tight fist that she could feel her French manicure acrylic nails digging into the flesh of her palm. Unable to take the mental lashing any longer, she picked up her purse, pulled three tens from her wallet, tossed them on the table, and stood.

She surveyed the room for a moment, trying to figure out the best way to exit without disturbing the view of those who were engaged in the live entertainment, and without having to navigate around the few couples who had taken advantage of the opportunity to dance the night away in each others' arms. It was going to be one or the other. There was no way to avoid both.

Choosing to take the clearer exit, Shaylynn grabbed her shawl and made a beeline for the door, walking as fast as she could so that whatever blockage she caused was only fleeting. In spite of her quick steps, Shaylynn could hear someone raising their voice to her. The music drowned out the words, but she was certain that they were directed toward her. Even after she'd cleared the front area, Shaylynn could still hear the patron's displeasure.

"Shay!"

It was only then that she realized it was her name that had been repeatedly called in the distance. Only one person called her that, and Shaylynn turned to look up into his face. She was at a loss for words, and for a split second, Neil seemed so too. He found his voice first.

"Hey. Where are you going? When did you get here?"

Shaylynn continued to stare at him without speaking. Where did he come from? How long had he been here? She had her own set of questions, but she voiced none of them. Following the tug of the strong arm that had at some point made its way around her waist, Shaylynn walked to the front corner of the restaurant, near the vacated hostess stand, where it was slightly quieter and there was no one within listening range.

"Where are you headed?" Neil asked her, looking concerned as he searched her face.

"Home." With her one-word reply, Shaylynn twisted her body and stepped away to free herself of his arm.

"Home?"

"Yes, home, Dr. Taylor. I've been here for an hour and a half already."

The bewilderment on Neil's face increased and regret filled his eyes. "I'm sorry.

I didn't know. Where were you sitting? I would have joined you had I known."

"Are you telling me you've been here all that time?"

"Not *all* that time, but I arrived about forty-five minutes ago." Neil glanced at his watch.

"Forty-five minutes ago? You said ten o'clock."

"I know, and I apologize. In a million years, I didn't really expect you to come. You didn't say . . . Had I known . . ." His voice drifted momentarily. Everything he was prepared to say sounded like he was putting the blame for the mix-up on Shaylynn. Neil didn't want to give her that impression, so he started over. "I got sick earlier today. Really sick. It's a long story, but the whole repulsive episode left me so weak that I had to lie down. At some point I fell asleep. When I woke up, it was nearly ten. I was already late and didn't really feel like making the drive, but I was feeling kinda hungry and didn't want to break my birthday tradition, so I got dressed and headed here. I would have called you, but I didn't expect . . . I'm sorry. Please . . . please don't leave."

It bothered Shaylynn that she could never stay mad at this man she hated so much

236

and that he always found a way to soften her heart, regardless of what had happened to harden it. Shaylynn transferred her body weight from one leg to the other. She had already abandoned her table and her hardly-touched meal. She'd feel foolish going back now.

"Did you order?" Neil asked, reaching for her arm again. Shaylynn allowed his touch and didn't immediately move away. "Have you had dinner?"

"I . . ." Shaylynn moved her arm so that her thought process wouldn't be hampered by the feel of his hand. "I did order, but I didn't really eat."

Neil gestured toward the tables in the open floor. "Please stay and eat with me. Whatever you ordered before, I'll pay for it; plus, I have you covered for whatever you get from the menu now."

"I'm not really hungry," Shaylynn lied.

"Then don't eat," Neil responded. "Just keep me company. Please."

His persistent hand was reaching for her again, and Shaylynn saw when it changed directions and found its way back around her waist. Neil gave her a gentle nudge and she complied, following him to a table for two that was situated in the middle of the restaurant. Neil moved the second chair around so that it was right beside the one he'd been sitting in.

"You get a better view of the entertainment from here," he explained.

Shaylynn carefully hovered over the chair that he held out for her, smoothing her red silk dress down in the back before sitting. When Neil took his position in the chair beside her, they were so close that Shaylynn could feel the fabric of his shirt on her arm.

He leaned over even closer. "You look especially beautiful tonight."

The stroke of his warm breath against the side of her face was enough to make Shaylynn want to get up and run for the door. She clutched her purse in her lap and held on as tight as she could in hopes of easing the anxiety. Shaylynn opened her mouth to thank him for his praises, but if anything actually came out, she couldn't hear it over the music.

"Do you want to order something?" Neil offered.

Shaylynn's eyes fell to the New York strip, broccoli, and garlic mashed potatoes on his plate, and her stomach moaned. She'd fed on so much anger earlier that she didn't realize how hungry she still was until now. "Maybe just an appetizer."

Neil flagged a waitress, and when asked,

she knowledgably rattled off the list of offered appetizers, then waited patiently for Shaylynn to choose one.

"The calamari will be fine," she said.

Even with all of the people that sat around them, when the waiter left, Shaylynn felt as though she and Neil were sitting alone in Sambuca. Without looking in his direction, she saw him watching her. The burn of his eyes put her heart in competition with the beat of the music that played from center stage.

"Where's Chase?"

Shaylynn turned and looked directly at Neil for the first time since they'd seated themselves. She would have thought that he'd known, but his expression was too sincere. "He's with your sister."

The transitory look of surprise that covered his face faded into a raised right eyebrow and a half smile. "You left him with Val?"

Feeling the need to erase any misconceptions that Neil might have had, Shaylynn said, "You were right when, at your mom's house, you assumed that I allow him to stay up later on Saturdays than on school nights. But this would have been too late, even for the weekend. His bedtime is at ten on

Saturdays, and I didn't want to keep him up."

Neil broke into a full smile and looked down at his plate. It was as if he were amused by her determination to keep him in line. Stealing an extended glance, Shaylynn noticed the strong structure of his face. Neil had nice teeth and distinctly attractive brown eyes that almost seemed to light up when he smiled. Neil's low-cut hair was sprinkled with hints of gray that he appeared too young to have. Aside from a very thin mustache that barely outlined his upper lip, his face was cleanly shaven.

He turned to her and caught her looking. Embarrassed, Shaylynn turned her eyes back to the stage and immediately began praying that Neil would let the awkward moment slide.

"Why do you keep yourself so guarded?" he asked, ending the silent prayer that Shaylynn didn't even have the chance to finish.

She was given some time to prepare a practical answer when their waiter returned with a fresh glass of water and Shaylynn's calamari. When she bowed her head to say her grace, Shaylynn also beseeched God for the strength she would need to get through her evening with Neil.

"Okay," Neil whispered in her ear. "I'll let the question slide if you go ahead and say amen."

Shaylynn couldn't help but laugh as she opened her eyes and lifted her head. "Was it that obvious?"

Neil didn't laugh with her, but amusement outlined his eyes. "There is a lot of mystery to you, Shay, but your desire not to allow too many people into your personal space isn't one of them."

Shay. He was just determined to call her that, but since it was his birthday, she wouldn't fight him on it tonight. At least not directly.

"Dr. Taylor, I barely know you or anyone else in this city. I would think that my stance would be expected."

"I would like to change that."

"Change what?"

"The fact that you barely know me."

Feeling flushed, Shaylynn looked toward the stage once more. The artist was taking a break from his singing, but the pianist continued to play soft music. She couldn't think of a response to Neil's statement, so, using her fork, Shaylynn picked up pieces of her fried squid and slipped them into her mouth.

"Let's see," he started in a thoughtful,

241

slow tempo. "You've already met my mom and my youngest sister, who is actually the knee-baby of the family."

Knee-baby. Shaylynn tried not to laugh. She knew what the terminology meant. She was aware that it was a brand given to the child right above the baby of the family, but she'd never actually heard people use it on a regular basis until she relocated to this end of the country. It must be a Southern thing. She stifled her smile behind a napkin, wiping her mouth while Neil continued speaking.

"I'm the eighth child and she's the ninth. I have four brothers — three older and one younger, and two other sisters — both older, that live in various states. You know where I worship; you know where I work; you know my age and my birthday, so there's not much more —"

"I don't know your age." The thought in Shaylynn's mind spilled through her lips without the courtesy of giving her warning. Quickly, she added, "But that's not my business anyway." She shifted uncomfortably. "Neither is any of the rest of that information, for that matter."

"Chase didn't tell you?"

"Tell me what?"

"How old I am."

Scrunching her face into a confounded frown, Shaylynn asked, "Why would he tell me something like that? How on earth would he know how old you are?"

"I told him yesterday that today was my forty-fifth birthday."

Shaylynn did a double-take, then put down her fork and altered her seating position so that her entire body nearly faced Neil. Right away, he grinned, and she could tell that he was pleased by her spontaneous reaction. She wasn't trying to be cordial; the revelation had honestly taken her by surprise. Shaylynn knew that her face was a poster of the shock she felt, but it couldn't be helped. She asked the question that she knew he was waiting for. "You're forty-five? For real?"

"Yes, I am." His satisfaction was obvious.

Shaylynn was surprised at how comfortable she felt while carefully studying Neil's face. It was the closest, most thorough examination that she'd ever given him, and she liked what she saw. He had to have a secret for his youthful appearance. The pores on his face were nearly invisible, and crow's feet were held to a minimum. She knew thirty-five-year-olds that didn't look as good.

"What would have been your guess?" he

asked while she boldly continued her visual research of him.

Shaylynn offered a slight shrug before giving her assessment. She didn't want to reveal her true thoughts and swell his ego too much. "Thirty-seven . . . thirty-eight, maybe," she said.

"I know I keep a low haircut, but can't you still see the silver?" Neil's laugh was clearly a flattered one.

"Lots of people gray prematurely. It's never easy to guess someone's age by looking at their hair. Age is generally presumed by skin elasticity and other facial features. You have nice skin and your face . . ." Shaylynn stopped. Somehow she'd allowed herself to get too comfortable with this charming gentleman who, just minutes ago, had her stabbing herself in the hand. It was time to reset some boundaries. She returned to her original sitting position and picked up her fork. Her babbling had left her feeling quite self-conscious.

"My face is what?" Neil urged.

"Nothing." Shaylynn collected more calamari on her utensil. "You just don't look forty-five, that's all." From her side vision, she saw Neil sit back in his seat, and although she couldn't hear him sigh, she felt the breath that he released, and so did the napkin that lay on the table between them. The corners of it rose slightly before returning to its former flattened state.

"What else about me do you not know?" Neil scratched his chin like he was talking to himself. It was apparent that he had no intention of letting her bow out this easily. "Let's see," he pondered. "I like sports, although I've never really played any. I'm left handed. I love seafood and soul food. I grew up in a family of music lovers. I can play the guitar —"

"You play the guitar?" Once again, Shaylynn was taken aback, and she was too intrigued not to ignore her raised guard.

"Yeah. I used to play sometimes when my brother and I sang at church."

Sang in church? This man was getting more interesting by the minute. "You sing too?" She shouldn't have been so surprised by that one. His talking voice sounded like he had the ability to sing.

Neil nodded while he cut into his meat for the first time since he coaxed Shaylynn to his table. "I don't do it much anymore, but I can."

Shaylynn watched him swirl the cut meat into the mashed potatoes before placing the mixture in his mouth. Then she pried for more. "What do you sing?"

Neil waited until he swallowed, and then said, "Gospel, mostly. I have a certain level of appreciation for all music, as long as the lyrics have a good meaning. Most of the secular stuff I've sung, I've borrowed from some other great composer. But a lot of the gospel songs that my brother and I used to sing, we wrote them ourselves."

Shaylynn was studying his face again, this time for hints that he was teasing. "*Write?* You actually write songs?"

After wiping his mouth, Neil noted, "You seem surprised."

"There's a good reason for that."

Laughing, Neil said, "Most of the kids who grew up in the church during the time I was a kid either played instruments, sang, or did both. I'm one of those who did both. I sang and played a lot as a child, and even through my early adulthood. Now it's just every blue moon that my pastor will call on me to sing. Every now and then, a member of the church will put in a request, but not too often. They know I'm not really doing much of that these days."

"Why? You don't like doing it anymore?"

"I actually love to sing. It's just that —" His sentence remained incomplete. "Let's just say that things are different now than when I was younger."

They sat in silence for a little while, and while Shaylynn picked at her food, she watched Neil's healthy appetite at work. The way he ate — mixing broccoli with his meat, mixing meat with mashed potatoes, mixing mashed potatoes with his broccoli, never eating one food item at a time — it was all quite fascinating. Fascinating and engaging, just as he was beginning to be.

"I imagine it must have been nice to be a part of the church at such a young age." Snapshots of Shaylynn's sordid childhood flashed in her head, shattering her earlier trance. "It's important to have Christian values planted inside you during that most impressionable time."

She noticed the way Neil looked at her when he said, "I agree. I can't honestly say that I appreciated it all that much back then, though." He released a reflective laugh. "Today, it's popular to say that you're a Christian. It seems like everybody makes that claim nowadays whether they're living like it or not. But when I was little, church boys like me got picked on quite a bit. We were called soft, punks, and sissies."

"Because you were Christians?"

"Because we didn't cuss, fight, act all tough, grab our crotches, and feel on the breasts and behinds of the girls at school like a lot of the boys did."

Shaylynn scowled. "Those were supposed to be the good things to do?"

Neil quieted his laughter behind a napkin. "I know you're a bit younger than I am, but times haven't gotten better; they've gotten worse. Are you trying to tell me that the guys that did that kind of stuff weren't the most loved when you were in school?"

School was such a painful blur to Shaylynn that she could barely remember going. She treasured her college experience, but memories of elementary, middle, and high school weren't the most pleasant. "I suppose you're right," she settled for saying. "At that age, not many kids try to be examples of holiness."

"Exactly," Neil said. "Being saved wasn't cool, but my mama wasn't trying to raise us to be popular; she was raising us to be peculiar. It was almost like we didn't have a choice, really." He laughed again. "Me and all of my siblings accepted Christ very young. I guess we all figured that we might as well."

Shaylynn nodded in agreement, but could only wish that she shared his testimony. She could never even recall hearing the word *salvation* before she was an adult. "I was very much a grown woman before I ever started going to church on a regular basis. Emmett —" She paused, took a breath, and then continued. "Emmett was sort of an activist, I guess you can say. His passion was to see our young people grow up to make something of themselves. He always strived to be a role model, sort of like the 'if I can do it, so can you' type. I think when I first started going to church, it was because I wanted to establish some kind of connection to God so that I could pray for Emmett's success and well-being.

"He traveled a lot and was rarely home on weekends, so every Sunday, I would go to this little storefront church that was near our neighborhood. Wanda Woods was the pastor's name, and boy, could she preach. I still remember the day I accepted Christ. It was the only day of my life that made me happier than my wedding day. I also remember being nervous about telling Emmett once he got home about the spiritual step I'd taken."

When she quieted, Neil compelled her to continue. "But you did tell him."

"Yeah, I did. He was a bit thrown, but he wasn't angry or anything. As a matter of fact, his only concern seemed to be that my new relationship with Christ might in some way pose a threat to my relationship with him. Emmett's first question to me was, 'So what does this mean for us?' I think that as soon as I assured him that I didn't have to leave him in order to serve God, he was okay."

"I'm assuming that he, at some point, followed in your footsteps, and that's why Chase says his dad lives in heaven."

Shaylynn smiled and looked at Neil. "Yes, he did, but not right away. It would be a couple of years before Emmett made the commitment. He'd only been saved a few weeks before —" She stopped, and then abruptly said, "Let's talk some more about you."

Neil's smile was one of understanding. "Okay. What else do you want to know?"

"You're forty-five and single. Should I assume that you've been married before?" She hoped that her question didn't sound like she had a personal interest in his marital status. Shaylynn watched Neil take in a large dose of water before answering.

"Yes, you may assume that," he said, pausing as if he thought she might need a moment to let the verification settle. "I got married at the young age of twenty-two, and it lasted ten years before life happened and it all fell apart."

He valiantly tried to hide it, but Shaylynn

could hear a dash of pain, and perhaps a smidgen of bitterness in his voice.

"I'm sorry."

"Don't be," Neil responded. Even the slightest grin showed off his alluring eyes.

He offered no further details, and Shaylynn took it as a cue to change the subject, whether he intended it that way or not. "Was your father a preacher?"

"No, he wasn't. But you would have thought so the way he and Ms. Ella Mae kept us in church." He smiled like saying it brought back good memories.

Shaylynn smiled too. "You were born and raised in Georgia?"

"Mississippi."

That was a state she'd never visited before. In fact, all that Shaylynn had ever really known about Mississippi was wrapped up in ghastly stories of prejudice and segregation that her grandmother had told her. In Shaylynn's mind, black people in Mississippi still tap danced and shined shoes for a living, and white people wore pointed hats and burned crosses just for kicks. She resolved to keep those thoughts in her own head, though. They might rub Neil the wrong way.

"What part of Mississippi are you from?" she asked. It was a pointless question, really.

If he said anything other than Jackson or Biloxi, there was a good chance she would have never heard of it.

"Don't even worry about it," Neil said with a fan of his hand and a carefree chuckle. "Even if I told you, it probably wouldn't ring any bells. It's a very small town that most people who are not familiar with Mississippi have never heard of. It was home, though. Still is, I guess. My siblings and I had some good times in that country town. We were poor, but most days, we didn't know it. We were happy. Very happy. When I retire, I plan to move back there. Probably to Jackson."

Shaylynn remembered Eloise saying pretty much the same thing — that they were happy there — so maybe Mississippi wasn't so bad after all. Her mind also compared some of the other information that both Neil and his mother had shared. She'd wanted to ask Eloise one question, but didn't. Now she prepared herself to ask Neil. "You said earlier that you have four brothers and three sisters, including Val."

"Yes."

"But you said the two of you were numbers eight and nine in the sibling line-up, and you referred to Val as the knee-baby," she pointed out.

"That's right."

"Well, four plus three equals seven, and you make eight. The numbers don't add up." Eloise had told Shaylynn that eight of her ten children were still alive, but Shaylynn wanted details.

Neil laid his napkin on his plate. "Pop and Ms. Ella Mae had ten children. One boy, born about four years ahead of me, died when he was only a few days old. Then Dwayne — that's the brother that used to sing with me — died about seventeen years ago."

"Oh." For the first time in her life, Shaylynn had a taste of what other people must have felt like when she revealed the demise of her husband. She now knew firsthand that it really wasn't easy to find something to say in immediate response to someone who admitted to having lost a close loved one. "I'm sorry." It was the same thing she'd said when he spoke of his divorce, and it just didn't seem adequate for his current revelation.

"Dwayne was a great guy who loved God with a passion, and I know he's in heaven now. Probably up there leading the mass choir or something, knowing him." Neil cracked a wistful smile that disappeared as soon as it came into view. "He was five and a half years my senior, and I have two brothers that are closer to my age than he was, but Dwayne was my best friend in the whole world. You asked me why I didn't sing much anymore. The truth of the matter is that Dwayne is the reason I don't sing as much as I used to. It was much more fulfilling when he was there with me."

Shaylynn's mind drifted to Emmett. A lot of things about her life were more fulfilling when he was around. Neil's voice snatched her back to reality.

"I still remember that March day when Dwayne died. It devastated me to the core of my soul. It hit us all hard, but I just don't think anybody was as distraught for as long as I was. Sometimes I still struggle with it. He had been sick off and on, and even though he knew his body was slowly shutting down, he didn't tell us what was really going on. He finally told Ms. Ella Mae, but he kept it from the rest of us and made her promise to do the same. So when he died suddenly of heart failure, we weren't at all prepared. We were just really getting over losing my dad four years earlier, and now Dwayne was gone too. All of us were hurt, but I honestly think that if it weren't for me thinking of what it would do to Ms. Ella Mae, I would have just prayed for God to take me too."

Shaylynn could relate more than he probably realized. She'd felt the same way when Emmett was killed. She'd contemplated jumping off bridges, slamming her car into brick walls, drinking poisonous homemade concoctions — anything to put a stop to the torture of living without Emmett. Her only reason for having even the slightest desire to go on was the son that was growing in her stomach. If she killed herself, she'd kill him too; and she just couldn't do it.

"Death sucks." Shaylynn thought the words were confined in her head, but it was clear from Neil's reaction that they were vocalized. Since she'd started, Shaylynn figured that she might as well continue. "I don't know if being prepared would make it any easier, but I know that not being prepared is an awful, gut-wrenching feeling."

"You weren't prepared for your husband's death?"

Shaylynn shook her head. She'd never spoken openly to anyone about this before, but for some reason, the time just seemed right. "I remember night after night, asking the Lord why. Emmett was a wonderful man who loved God and adored his family, including his parents, who, in my opinion, weren't all that loveable. Emmett just had a good heart. I still find it hard to believe that he was actually their biological child. They were all about money, and because they had it, they didn't feel the need to treat people as equals. They were always rubbing people the wrong way, but Emmett, on the contrary, was a people person."

"What exactly did Emmett do for a living?"

"He was an undercover policeman turned politician."

"Wow. That's a switch."

Shaylynn giggled. "I know."

"What type of politician was he?"

"Mayor." Shaylynn noticed that Neil didn't look too surprised by her response, but she continued. "You wouldn't have heard of him, though. He didn't get the chance to become a household name, although I don't doubt for a moment that he would have. Emmett had just been voted in when he was killed."

"He was involved in an accident of some type?"

Shaylynn drank a sip of her water while at the same time shaking her head slowly from side to side. When she put her glass down, she looked away, scanning the patrons around the popular restaurant, hoping their images would replace the one that was forming in her mind: the image of the day that she had to identify the body.

Shaylynn turned back to Neil and tried to smile, but her lips quivered instead. "It was no accident. One shot was enough to kill him. Emmett was murdered."

"I'm so sorry," Neil whispered, placing his hand on top of hers and holding it there briefly before removing it. "It's up to you, Shay. We can talk about this some more if you want, or we don't have to talk about it at all."

Shaylynn picked up her napkin and dabbed at the water that had pooled around her eyes. She couldn't believe she'd opened up like that. It was a first, and it felt surprisingly good to release some of her anguish. But she needed to fill her head with more pleasant thoughts. Shaking her head no in response, she placed the napkin back on the table. "Why does Ms. Eloise call you Sol?" Now was as good a time as any to ask.

"Solomon," Neil revealed. "That's my middle name, and a few of my family members call me Sol for short. Ms. Ella Mae calls me that all the time, but she's about the only one who does it religiously. It's interchangeable with everybody else. Outside of my family, I'm Neil. I was named Neil in honor of one of my dad's brothers, and most people that called me Sol did it so that there would be no confusion. My best friend's dad — my *pastor's* dad — used to call me Solomon on occasion. He was the only non-relative that did it."

Absentmindedly, Shaylynn said, "I think it fits you better."

Neil looked at her in a manner that only he could. A look that made her like him one minute and dislike him the next. "You can call me that if you want. If that's the name you like —"

"I didn't say I liked it; I said it fits you better."

Conceding quicker than she would have guessed, Neil sat back in his seat and shook his head in slow motion. Shaylynn knew that he didn't know what to think of her, and she didn't blame him. When she was around him, she didn't know what to think of herself. When the couple who sat beside them suddenly began gathering their belongings, Shaylynn looked at her watch. She hadn't realized that it had gotten so late.

"I guess I should be getting ready to go. It's almost one o'clock in the morning, and I told your sister that she could take Chase to church with her tomorrow, but it'll probably be best if I get up early and go get him. I'm sure her hands will be full enough with her two kids."

Neil leaned forward in his chair. He opened his mouth to speak, but then seemed to rethink whether he should speak at all. After another moment, his lips parted again. "Let him stay," he said. "The children's ministry at KBCC is wonderful, and he'll love being a part of it."

Nibbling one side of her bottom lip as she considered it, Shaylynn said, "I'd just hate to have them have to bring him home. And what if you all get out of church before I do? I'd really feel badly if they brought him to my house and I wasn't even there."

"Why don't you come to KBCC tomorrow and worship with us?"

His suggestion pulled Shaylynn's eyes from the table and locked them on him. She couldn't do that. That would mean missing service at her church. Neil must have sensed her quandary.

"It's only one Sunday, Shay. What do you say?"

The services at the church that she had been visiting for the last three consecutive Sundays were more enjoyable than those of the other churches she'd sampled since moving to Atlanta, but no membership commitment had yet been made. Truth be told, Shaylynn was getting her fill of being a chronic visitor and wanted to find a spiritual home for Chase and her. She had all but made up her mind to settle on Community Worship Temple and even thought that tomorrow would be a good time to do it. The female pastor there reminded her of Prophetess Wanda Woods, the woman who led her to Christ, but she didn't want to join without Chase being with her. Shaylynn supposed that waiting one more Sunday wouldn't hurt. She'd visit with Neil tomorrow and wait for the following Sunday to add her name to the roll at Community Worship Temple.

Neil appeared visibly shocked when Shaylynn accepted his invitation. Shocked and relieved. He thanked her twice, and then, without warning, cupped her left hand between both of his and kissed the back of it. Shaylynn was too unprepared to pull her hand away, and when his lips touched her skin, she could feel goose bumps racing to see which ones could appear on her arm the fastest.

"Would you like to dance?" Neil looked directly at her as he asked the unexpected question.

Shaylynn released a nervous laugh. "I haven't danced in years. Not in front of anybody anyway. I don't think —"

"Nor have I." Upon his revelation, Neil stood and reached for her to follow.

With him standing over her, it felt like she didn't have a choice. Looking around, Shaylynn saw a handful of other couples dancing in the spaces closest to their tables. The area where she and Neil sat was dark, and even if she made a wrong step, the likelihood of anyone seeing her was slim to none. Without placing her hand in his outstretched one, she slid her chair backward and stood. When Shaylynn faced Neil, she suddenly became aware of how close they'd have to be in order to dance to the slow ballad the vocalist was singing. The lyrics of the song were beautiful, but when Neil slid his arm around her waist and pulled her in to him, Shaylynn suddenly became oblivious to everything else, including the sounds from the stage.

It felt like an involuntary authorization, but whatever the case, Shaylynn allowed Neil to take the lead, and she glided with him. Her cheek rested on his chest, and his arms tightened around her, forming a gentle but firm hold. Every time Shaylynn inhaled, she took in a manly fragrance that was potent to her nostrils. She could smell him forever and not tire of his scent.

"Thank you for sharing my birthday with me."

It was only when she heard the words Neil whispered in her ear that Shaylynn escaped from oblivion and noticed that new music was playing in the background. She tuned in to the song, but as soon as she did, her eyes overflowed, causing tears to soak into the fabric of Neil's shirt. Her sudden emotional outburst startled Neil, and he stepped away and looked down at her, using his hands to force her chin upward so that she faced him.

"What's the matter?"

Her sobs increased, and Shaylynn could not control them enough to reply. She heard Neil's question, but the words from the soloist on stage rang louder in her ears:

When the eagles forget how to fly, and it's twenty below in July . . . and when violets turn red, and roses turn blue, I'll be still in love with you.

Shaylynn knew that there was no way Neil could understand the profundity of the words that were originally written and recorded by Brian McKnight that the man at the mic now sang, but she was glad that he didn't press the issue. When she didn't answer his concern, Neil simply pulled her

back into his arms and allowed her to weep
freely as they swayed to the music.

Sixteen

Neil sped down I-285, frequently glancing through his side and rearview mirrors, praying that no speed traps would catch him. He had thirteen minutes to make it to Kingdom Builders Christian Center and avoid the guilt of being late for two consecutive Sundays. Being tardy for church was a personal vexation for Neil. In fact, not arriving on time for any appointment served as an annoyance. He didn't like the stigma that many black people attached to themselves, making it seem as though skin color was the deciding factor on whether a person would arrive or an event would start on time. Each time Neil heard the term "C. P. time," meaning colored people's time, he was offended.

Most Sundays, it only took him a few minutes to get dressed, but today he'd gone through five changes of outfits before finally settling on the charcoal suit with the burgundy pinstripes. Neil coordinated the suit with a burgundy button-front shirt and a paisley print tie that matched the ensemble with perfection.

Perfection.

That was the word that described the level that Neil felt his bar had to be raised to today. Dressing up was a way of life for him. He did it at work on a daily basis because it made him feel professional and respected. And Ernest and Eloise Taylor had taught him from childhood that dressing up on Sunday mornings was a way of giving God the best. Neil still clearly recalled the day that he and his siblings finally mustered up the nerve to ask if they could dress like the other kids and wear their comfortable, casual clothing to church. Their dad was shaking his head before they could even finish getting their words out.

"Absolutely not," Ernest had said in no uncertain terms. "It's true that clothes don't make a Christian, but I just believe that you ought to give God the best you got. Y'all get to dress like little savages all week long. The least you can do is dress like you're somebody when you go to the Lord's house. When you go to the hospital, you don't want no doctor operating on you dressed in jeans and sneakers. When you walk in the police station to file a report, you don't expect to see the cop wearing no cotton shorts and sandals. Wherever you go, you expect the people there to look like they belong there, and the same goes for church. When we go to the Lord's house, we ought to look like we're going to the Lord's house. It would be different if y'all didn't have no better clothes, but you do; so get up them stairs and put 'em on before I take off my belt."

Neil unconsciously smiled at the memory as he turned into the parking lot of KBCC and navigated into the nearest available space. He wasn't the only one rushing to beat the call to worship. There were several others who were rushing up the walkway to make it through the doors too. Looking at his watch, Neil saw that he still had four minutes to spare. He popped a mint in his mouth and grabbed his Bible from the seat beside him, and then exited his vehicle to join the throng that was pressing toward the entrance.

As he made the walk to the deacons' corner, Neil saw that he had made it in time to claim an open seat clear on the other end of the pew from where Deacon Burgess sat, but he chose to occupy the space directly by the man. He could tell from the blank stare Homer Burgess gave him that the old man wasn't himself today. It still baffled Neil that someone who went in and out of sensibility as often and as quickly as Deacon Burgess did could qualify for a driver's license. Neil delivered a friendly pat to the man's knee, and the deacon responded with a slight smile and a nod of his head.

From his prime seat location, Neil had a very clear view of the audience, and when the praise and worship team took the pulpit and the crowd stood in applause to welcome them, Neil gave the faces a quick inspection. He wondered if Shaylynn was among them, hoping that the emotional ending to their time together last night hadn't changed her mind. Although Neil remained somewhat confused about her tears, his gut feeling told him that it had something to do with Emmett.

It had been nearing four o'clock this morning when Neil finally drifted to sleep after leaving Sambuca. He'd tossed and turned for hours after getting into bed, battling with the question of what had caused Shaylynn's eyes to overflow. Their conversation had been flowing so well up until that moment. He'd gotten her to reveal to him all that he really already knew from his online web search; but knowing that she had grown comfortable enough with him to talk about Emmett's death had been reassuring. The evening was on a huge uphill swing after the shaky start they had when Neil discovered that Shaylynn had been at Sambuca sitting at a separate table.

It felt amazing to hold her so close in his arms and to dance the night away with her clinging to him, but when reality hit, Neil had to face the truth. Shaylynn wasn't crying because she was blissful from being in his presence, and she wasn't holding to him with such fervor because she desired to be close to him. The common denominator to all of her actions was Emmett, a man who had been buried beneath the earth for seven years, yet still gripped the heart of the one woman Neil knew he was falling for.

Shaylynn had nothing but good memories of Emmett, and at times as they spoke, to Neil, the dead man seemed larger than life. Neil's time with Shaylynn last night made his forty-fifth birthday his favorite of them all, and Neil was certain that there were moments when he could feel that his attraction to her wasn't one-sided. But to know that his one rival was a man who wasn't even alive to make a major blunder that might create an opening in Shaylynn's heart for another to enter, was beyond frustrating.

She still wore Emmett's ring, she still carried his name, and she still loved him. And Neil felt powerless to do anything about it.

Praise and worship was good, but not as spirited as it had been the Sunday before. Or maybe it was. Perhaps Neil had just been too preoccupied with other thoughts during the devotional service to appreciate it in its full worth. He took his seat along with everyone else when the microphone was turned over to CJ to deliver the day's message.

"Let every heart say amen," the pastor instructed, drawing echoes of responses.

Neil responded too, but he did so while giving the crowd one last once-over. In his limited viewing, he saw no signs of Shaylynn. *Maybe it's for the best,* he pacified himself.

"Deacon Taylor, I know you don't want to do this, but I have to ask," CJ said, bringing up Neil's eyes and locking them onto his.

"Let him sing. Let him sing to the glory of God!"

Neil's eyes shot back out toward the crowd. He'd know Ella Mae's voice anywhere, and he immediately knew that she was the one who'd made this morning's request. Whether his mother had requested it or not, Neil had sung last Sunday and had no intentions of making this a habit. His mother knew better than anyone else that he didn't want to do this, and he was both shocked and disappointed that she would put him on the spot. Narrowing his eyes at CJ, Neil hoped the pastor got his silent message: *I told you last Sunday night not to do this again!*

Just as if he'd heard the words, CJ shrugged his shoulders and gave a verbal reply that reverberated through the speaker system. "It's not me, brother. Your voice has been requested."

"Go'n up there and sing, boy!"

Neil felt a knee nudge him, and he looked at Deacon Burgess and saw awareness in his eyes. Just like that, he was back among the living. The deacon wagged a shaky but stern finger at him.

"What did I tell you 'bout your singing? God wants to use you to heal, to deliver, and to save. I'm gonna say it just like Dr. Loather would say, God rest his soul. Sang, Solomon . . . sang!"

Amidst the deafening calls and applause, Neil rose from his chair like spreading molasses. He wasn't prepared for this, and had no inkling of what to sing, but there was no way he could deny a request that had been publicized before the entire congregation. And he definitely couldn't defy Deacon Burgess. Not when he shook his ninety-year-old finger at him like that and topped it off by quoting Dr. Loather. It almost came across as menacing.

The rowdy crowd quieted when Neil accepted the mic, but that was sooner than Neil wanted them to. He needed more time to think, but none was extended. Lowering his eyes, Neil looked into the awaiting microphone, and then bowed his head, praying for a song that he could sing quickly and retire to his seat. But the one that kept coming to mind was one he hadn't sung since before Dwayne passed away. Every time he would attempt to shoo the song from his thoughts, it would force its way back in, like it was begging him, ordering him to sing it.

Neil's heart felt heavy. He didn't want to sing this one. It was his brother's favorite, and he'd never sung it without Dwayne. But God was demanding it, so he freed a lung full of air from lips that were only slighted parted. Opening his eyes, Neil looked into the waiting congregation and said, "Okay, you all are gonna have to help me with this one. It's an old one, and I haven't sung it in quite a while, but I think pretty much everybody knows it. I'm gonna take this one back home to Mississippi, where Frank Williams and the hometown mass choir recorded it and made it famous."

"Sing it, sing it!" someone from the rear cried out.

Starting a cappella and in a low voice, Neil sang, "Your grace and mercy brought me through. . . . I'm living this moment because of you. . . ."

Immediately, the audience rose to its feet and joined in. As if the song needed no accompaniment, the musicians sat still, not pressing a key, plucking a string, or playing a beat until the chorus came around for the second time.

Neil wasn't quite certain why everybody else seemed to get happy only seconds after he began singing, but his own joy mounted because as impossible as he knew it was, coming from somewhere in the sky, Neil could hear Dwayne's voice harmonizing with his.

In a row where she sat near the middle of the church, tears flowed from Shaylynn's eyes, and Chase leaned his head against her arm and stroked her back as if he understood. An usher who was walking the aisles tending to worshippers handed Shaylynn a handful of Kleenex and moved on to assist

272

others. Shaylynn buried her face in the tissues and wept. She tried to never cry in front of her son, but something about this song made her emotions too strong to control. Maybe it was the lyrics that so accurately put into words her sentiments to God. Shaylynn knew that it was only by the mercy of God that she had been able to survive the worst of times that followed her husband's death. She knew that it was only by His grace that she'd been introduced to Jesus Christ and was able to rise from the neglect, poverty, and abandonment that had plagued her for most of her life. Neil had prefaced it as an old song, but it was one that Shaylynn had never heard before. And she couldn't imagine that the choir who made it famous had sung it with any more authority or conviction than did the handsome, raspy-voiced gentleman who insisted on calling her Shay.

Seventeen

"Are you expecting anybody?" CJ looked down at his wife as the doorbell rang for the second time.

"No," Theresa said, sitting up in the bed, where her head had been resting on CJ's chest while they both watched television.

CJ looked at the clock. No one ever dropped by their house unannounced, and rarely did he go to his door after nine. But the persistent ringing continued, and when he didn't answer soon enough, knocking ensued. This had to be an emergency of some kind, and CJ pulled himself into a seated position. He slung his legs over the edge of the bed and began the task of covering his nude body.

"Honey, you need to be careful," Theresa said as she watched CJ button his silk pajama shirt, pull on his matching shorts, and slide his feet into his slippers.

"I will." Although his wife didn't look reassured, CJ gave her a smile, and then quietly walked from the master bedroom to the living room. He stood still for a moment, thinking that he was hearing a voice on the other side of the door.

"CJ . . . open up, man." It was Neil.

Rushing his pace, CJ opened the door and used all of his strength to snatch Neil inside, and then closed and locked the door behind him. "What's up, bruh? Something wrong? Somebody after you or something? You need me to call the police?"

Neil looked at him with inquisitive eyes. "Call the police for what? Man, why you talking crazy?"

Taking into account that all must be well, CJ relaxed and placed his hands on his hips. "Well, when people bang on my front door at ungodly hours of the night, what am I supposed to think?"

"Ungodly hours?" Neil laughed and sat on the sofa, making himself comfortable like it was still noon. "Man, it's still early." He looked at CJ's pajamas as though it were his first time noticing the attire. "Were you in bed already? It ain't even ten o'clock yet, and you're already 'sleep?"

CJ hoped he didn't sound crass, but then again, he really didn't care if he did. "I wasn't asleep yet, but I was in the bed. I'm a married man, Neil. Sometimes we have business to tend to before we go to sleep. You know what I mean? *Business* to attend to. *Business,* CJ." He stretched his eyes and cocked his head to the side for added effect.

Finally getting it, Neil's mouth dropped. "Ohhhh," he said, dragging out the word in realization. "Y'all at it again? I'm sorry, man." Standing to his feet, Neil headed for the front door. "I'll talk to you tomorrow after I get off from work. I didn't know you were in the middle of . . . *business.*"

"Neil, sit down," CJ said, pointing to the spot that his friend had just vacated. "You think if I were in the *middle* of it, I would have stopped to open the door for you?" CJ dropped the full weight of his body on the sofa and beckoned again for Neil to join him. "You're here now; you might as well say what you have to say. And don't come up in here with attitude about me calling you up to sing today. I know you didn't want to do it, but God's hand was too strong on you for me to have any regrets. The way people were blessed today from your singing, you shouldn't have any regrets either."

Just then, Theresa walked into the living room, tightening her robe around her waist. "Hey, Neil. Is everything okay?"

Neil nodded his head. "I'm sorry for busting up in y'all's house like this. I guess I didn't really consider what time it was."

"No problem," she replied. "I'm going to get some water. Do you guys want anything?"

"Yeah, baby," CJ said. "If you could bring us a couple of bottles, we'd appreciate it."

She brought the sixteen-ounce bottles of water and set one on a coaster in front of each man. Pausing to transfer a lingering kiss to her husband's lips, Theresa said, "I'm going to bed. I'll see you in the morning." Then turning to their guest, she added, "Good night, Neil, and happy belated birthday."

"Thanks, First Lady. I promise not to keep him up too late. That way, y'all can get back to doing . . . you know . . . whatever it was you were doing."

Theresa turned and looked at him. "Boy, please. You think that if we weren't already finished *doing whatever we were doing,* we would have stopped to let you in? We love you, but we don't love you that much."

Both Neil and CJ laughed as they watched her disappear down the hall. Once they heard the door to the bedroom close, CJ looked at Neil and waited for him to begin speaking.

"Promise me that you won't jump to conclusions or start with the 'I told you so' speech," Neil requested right off the bat.

CJ leaned forward in his lounger, unscrewed the cap on his water, and took in a few swallows. "I make no promises after nine-thirty. Now, what's up?"

"I just spent nearly five hours with Shay, Chase, and my family. Ms. Ella Mae invited them over for dinner after service, and —"

"Oh . . . so you brought her home to meet the family, huh?"

Neil dropped his head. "See? I knew you were gonna do this."

Hitting Neil on the back of the head with one of the decorative pillows on the sofa, CJ laughed. "I'm just playing with you, bruh. I just said that to get a reaction out of you . . . and it worked." He laughed some more, and then concluded with, "Go ahead and tell the story. I'm listening now."

Neil rolled his eyes, took in a deep breath, and then released it. Settling back against the sofa, he locked his eyes on the ceiling and sat in total quiet, leaving a long, lingering silence in the room before finally speaking. "As I was saying, they came to our house after service and —"

"I enjoyed meeting Shay and her son today," CJ interrupted. "She's the one who requested that you sing today. Did she tell you that?"

Neil turned his face toward CJ, and it was evident that this was knowledge that he hadn't been privy to until now. "Shay did? She's the one who asked you to call me up today?"

"You sound surprised."

"I am. I'm shocked, actually. I would have never expected that from her. I just assumed that Ms. Ella Mae had done it."

"No, it was Shay." CJ noted when his friend's expression changed from stunned to pleased. "Val gave me the note, but she said it was Shaylynn Ford who had made the request. I'll bet any issues you had with me calling on you are gone now, aren't they?"

"Anyway," Neil said, "as I was saying . . ."

"You should have seen the look on your face when I called you out." CJ cut in again, this time with an amused laugh. "Man, you looked like you wanted to strangle me right in the house of God when —"

"I'm gonna strangle you in your *own* house if you don't shut up and listen to me," Neil huffed.

Although CJ knew that his friend was only being facetious, he also noted the exasperation in his voice and saw the struggle on

Neil's face as he stood from the sofa and took steps toward the bay window that faced the front yard. Probably being reminded that it was nighttime and wouldn't be wise to open the curtain for a look outside, Neil changed directions and rerouted to the fireplace, staring up at the oil painting that hung over it.

The abstract print had caught Theresa's eye at an amateur art show that CJ had taken her to during their three-day honeymoon weekend nearly four years ago. The image on the canvas didn't appear to be anything other than a creative mixture of reds, purples, greens, and golds, but Theresa said that the splashes of bold colors represented life, and the curvaceous brush strokes, happiness. While CJ couldn't honestly say that he got the same revelation, he did have to agree that the painting was a great conversation piece, and it complemented the color scheme of their living room with perfection.

CJ watched Neil closely as his generally talkative friend studied the art as though he'd not seen it a thousand times before. He saw Neil shove his right hand in his pocket and retrieve a red-and-white hard candy. CJ observed calculated movements as the wrapper was removed and the peppermint was deposited in Neil's mouth. It wasn't like Neil to struggle with words, but there was little doubt in CJ's mind that Kingdom Builders Academy's head honcho was doing so tonight.

Just as CJ was preparing to say something that might help end the stalling, Neil made an about-face from the fireplace artwork and met his pastor eye to eye. "I need your help with something."

CJ leaned back in his chair and waited for the still unknown request to unveil itself.

Maneuvering the mint so that it became nestled between his teeth and his right jaw, Neil said, "You still have contacts on the force, right?"

The question was an odd one, but CJ managed to hold his face expressionless, trying not to jump to conclusions. "The police force, you mean?"

"Yeah."

"Yes. I have a few. Why?"

Scurrying back to his seat on the sofa, Neil brushed his hands over his face like his thoughts were jumbled, and that somehow wiping his face would arrange them so that they made sense. He took in and released a deep breath for the second time tonight, then said, "I need you to help me find something on Emmett Ford."

"What?" CJ sat up straight. Deep creases in his face said what additional words didn't. Surely Neil couldn't be asking him to do what it sounded like he was asking him to do.

"Just hear me out." Neil held up his hands to interrupt whatever CJ's next words might be, and his voice sounded pleading. "The whole time that Shay was at my mom's house, all she did was harp on this dude. It was *Emmett this* or *my husband that*." His scowl magnified his displeasure. "I've never disliked a living man the way I'm beginning to dislike this dead one. If I had heard his name one more time . . ." CJ could see atypical frustration on Neil's face as he allowed his sentence to drift while he readjusted his seating position. When he continued, he said, "Don't get me wrong; we had a great time of fellowship at Ms. Ella Mae's, but every single time that I feel like I'm getting somewhere with this woman, Emmett somehow rises out of the grave and messes it up. Like last night at Sambuca —"

"Last night at Sambuca?" CJ's echo was filled with discontent. "So you did still meet with both of them to celebrate your birthday? Neil, I can't believe you did that after the long talk we had. I prayed that you wouldn't go through with it."

"Well, you can calm down. Your prayers were answered." Neil's words relaxed CJ, but he remained silent while Neil explained further. "I canceled the dinner with Ms. Dasher, which, by the way, wasn't going to be a dinner with Ms. Dasher after all. And I didn't really think Shay was gonna show up at Sambuca, so I didn't bother to call her at all."

"But she did?" CJ fished.

A satisfied memory must have crossed Neil's mind because although he didn't answer immediately, the pensive smile that invaded his entire face spoke volumes. "Yeah, she did. And we were having a great time — talking, laughing, dancing — then somehow, from the grave, Emmett stepped in and changed everything."

"How so?" CJ gurgled the question while downing more water.

Neil heaved a laden sigh. It had been awhile since CJ had seen his friend so on edge. A part of him wanted to rush Neil through their little mini-session so that he could get back in the bedroom where he knew his wife awaited him, but as Neil slowly unburdened himself of the whole story, CJ was drawn in, and he anxiously awaited the revealing of the plot. He watched Neil's every facial expression, counted every strenuous exhale, and heard every word his body language spoke. When it was all over, CJ had drawn one very big conclusion — one he knew in advance that Neil would contest.

"You're in love with this girl."

Neil dropped his back against the cushions of the sofa. "There you go again, jumping to some crazy assumption! That's why I started not to even come over here in the first place. I knew you'd do this. You *always* do this!"

CJ saw Neil's flailing arms and the rolling of his eyes, but he also noted that none of the theatrics were accompanied by a straightforward denial. "Okay then, what is it?" CJ challenged. "A few minutes ago, you said you wanted me to use one of my contacts to investigate Emmett. Why would you want me to do something like that?"

"I just want to be able to find something on him that proves that he wasn't Jesus incarnate, that's all. I believe that's what she thinks. Shay thinks that man could heal the sick, open blind eyes, walk on water, turn water into wine, take two fish and five loaves of bread and feed five thousand . . . you name it. If our Savior did it, Emmett could too, and could probably do it better,

284

as far as she's concerned." Neil scoffed an irritated laugh. "Heck, if Emmett Ford weren't a stiff himself, she'd probably think he could raise the dead."

"That's not funny, Neil." CJ's voice was stern and reprimanding. "If you really cared anything about Shay, you wouldn't be making fun of something like that. The woman is still hurting from his death."

"But why?" Neil slammed his hand against the soft padding of one of the throw pillows beside him. "It's been seven years, CJ. *Seven!*" For emphasis, he held up five fingers on one hand and two on the other. "That's way too much time to be still hurting over a man's death."

"Who are you to say how long is long enough, Neil? You don't get to draw timelines on how long a person can hurt or grieve. When you stop grieving for Dwayne, when you stop letting his death hamper your ministry of song, then maybe you can start passing judgment on other folks."

Neil sat back hard against the sofa pillows. He crossed his arms and stared straight ahead. CJ knew that Neil didn't like what he'd just said, but it needed to be said, and CJ had no plans to take it back. In fact, he had more to say.

"This doesn't have diddly squat to do with

Shay's grief over Emmett. This has everything to do with your grief over the fact that
you can't love her the way you want to love
her." When Neil turned to him, CJ leaned
forward and looked his best friend directly
in the eyes, holding them there for a short
while, daring Neil to continue his quest to
avoid the truth. When CJ felt he'd intimidated him enough, he asked, "If you don't
love her, why does it matter that she's still
hurting?"

In an instant, Neil was on his feet again.
This time, he paced the floor, back and
forth in short distances, prompting CJ's
eyes to follow him as if he were watching a
ping pong match. For CJ, it was painful to
see his friend struggle with such difficulty
regarding an issue that should have been
relatively simple. In all the years he'd known
Neil, ever since they met on the campus of
Morehouse College, CJ had never seen him
this uncertain of himself. Back then, Neil's
gift for song was no secret, and even though
he wasn't a member of the chorus and
Dwayne wasn't even an enrolled "Morehouse Man," the Taylor brothers were often
called upon to sing at school functions, both
on and off campus. Neil's voice and handsome brown eyes wooed the girls at Spelman
College, the all-female campus that was

located within walking distance of Morehouse. Neil wasn't a ladies' man, per se, but
he wasn't shy about approaching a girl that
he found himself attracted to. It wasn't until
after his broken marriage to his college
sweetheart that Neil took on this new role
as an avowed spinster.

"Do you love her, Neil?" CJ had waited
long enough. He needed to have an answer.
A truthful one.

Without looking at him, Neil said, "No,"
then with a sigh and a shrug, said, "I don't
know." He finished off his confusion with a
solid, "No."

"Is that your final answer?" CJ asked in
his best Regis Philbin voice.

Neil eased back on the sofa. Quiet reigned
again before his voice reclaimed the space.
"Can I just be transparent with you?"

"I really wish you would, bruh."

Neil placed his hands in front of his
mouth in somewhat of a praying position,
like he had to mentally prepare himself for
what he was about to say. "I just want a fair
chance, that's all."

He paused like he was giving his friend a
chance to offer a response, but CJ remained
quiet.

"I haven't been in love in so long that I'm
not even sure what the good part of that

feels like," Neil continued. "I remember the hurt and the anger and the betrayal and the heartbreak of being in love, but the good part is all a blur. Something's going on, but I don't think I'm in love. I mean, I think it's way too soon for that."

"What makes you think that?" CJ threw him a look that he knew Neil would comprehend. And he did.

"Okay, well, it's too soon for most people whose names aren't Charles Loather Jr. and Theresa Rutherford. Most people don't meet and marry inside of eight months, and if they do, they don't stay married. Yours is a special case. Believe that."

"God is good," CJ said.

"All the time." Neil finished with a grin that was sincere but fleeting.

"Tell me more about your desire for a *chance* with Shay."

For the next half hour, CJ sat and listened to Neil pour out his heart in a way that he'd never before witnessed. Neil used phrases like, "I want to get to know her better," and "She has a beautiful spirit," and "When she's around, I don't want the moment to end." CJ's favorite was the ending to Neil's spiel.

"She's like this angel . . . with a broken wing. I know she's wounded, but I kinda just want the chance to help her get back in the air."

You love her, was what CJ wanted to stress, but he didn't want to put Neil back on the defensive. "Why don't you take the chance that you keep saying that you want? Just because she's still — what's the word? — *involved* with Emmett doesn't mean you don't have a chance."

"C'mon, CJ. She's not just still involved with Emmett, she's still *in love* with him. And I think the only way that any other man will have a chance to get any kind of relationship going with *Mrs.* Shaylynn Ford is for her to find out that her beloved husband was not all that she thinks he was."

CJ shook his head in protest. "So you want to make him look bad so you can look good. Is that it?"

"Are you gonna help me out with this or not?" Neil stomped his foot and curled his top lip like a defiant child. "Emmett was in politics, and I ain't never seen a politician that wasn't just a little bit crooked, so I'm sure your detective friends can pull some records and check him out."

"I can't even believe you're asking me to do something like this."

"Is that a yes or a no?"

Everything good within CJ screamed for

289

him to decline the request in no uncertain terms, but his loyalty wouldn't allow him to be obedient. It had been years since Neil had been so consumed with a woman, and CJ reasoned with God that his investigation was only to pacify Neil. Once Shaylynn got to know his friend, she'd open her heart to him regardless. CJ rationalized with his conscience and the Holy Spirit, telling both of them that the unorthodox, immoral, invasive exploration into the dealings of Mayor Emmett Ford would be fruitless, therefore making it harmless.

Don't do it, CJ.

CJ brushed away the voice in his head and listened to the one in his heart. "Okay," he told Neil after a lengthy pause. "I can't make any promises, but I'll see what I can do."

EIGHTEEN

Shaylynn kicked off her shoes, stood back, and exhaled a satisfied sigh. She was more than pleased with the progress that had been made toward setting the plans in motion for Eloise's home improvements. There was no doubt about it. Eloise's would be the makeover that would define Shay Décor . . . Ford's Home Interior & Designs . . . whatever the name would ultimately be. And this one, she was sure, would be the job that would establish her as a force to be reckoned with in Atlanta, Georgia. It had taken nearly three hours of early morning shopping, but the results were worth it.

Yesterday, Shaylynn had gone by Eloise's house and convinced her and her daughter to accompany her to Patterson Furniture Company so that they could view the living room furniture that Shaylynn had found to replace the pieces that Eloise had had for thirty years. The trip to the reputable company, located on Highway 78 in Lilburn, was an entertaining one. Shaylynn found herself laughing more than she had in years as Eloise pumped her ears with stories of yesteryear, raising nine children with nine different personalities.

She described herself as being a blessed mother, praising all of her children in one way or another. "And that Chase," Eloise added, grinning from ear to ear, "he's gonna be a good-un too. I can see it all over him. You watch and see. That's gonna be a blessed little boy."

"A heartbreaker," Valerie interjected. "That's what he's gonna be."

Shaylynn thanked them for their accolades and silently prayed that their words were prophetic, but she wanted to talk more about Eloise's family. She had talked about all of her children except Dwayne, and Shaylynn hoped that she wasn't opening up painful wounds.

"Dr. Taylor told me that he had a brother who passed away. What kind of a child was he?"

"Mean," Valerie said without skipping a beat. That one-word charge evoked laughter from her mother. Valerie joined in and they doubled over together.

Shaylynn smiled, wishing the rough times

in her family life were ones that she could look back on with amusement. The things that went on in her childhood years didn't even deserve a smirk, let alone a laugh.

"That boy wasn't no such of a thing," Eloise defended once she calmed herself, wiping water from her eyes. "You were just always in his stuff; that's why he didn't like to fool with you." She turned and looked at Shaylynn. "Once I was done having babies, Wayne — that's what me and his daddy always called him — was the middle child, and the old folks used to say that there is always something about the middle child that's different from everybody else. Wayne was different; always had his face in the Bible, reading and studying God's Word."

"He sure did," Valerie echoed. "I remember that."

Eloise continued. "If a discussion opened up about anything dealing with the Bible, I don't care what Wayne was doing at the time; he would stop and join in. He should have been a preacher. Probably *would* have been one if he'd lived a little longer."

"And Lord, could he sing," Valerie put in.

"Yes, he could," Eloise agreed. "Him and Neil together could have been big time gospel recording stars if they wanted to. By now, they would have been legendary. No doubt about it." She smiled like a proud mother, but then her eyes quickly drifted into a land of gloominess. "I wish Neil would sing more now. The power of the Lord be all over that young-un when he sings, and I know God wants him to let his voice minister to people. But after Wayne died, well, he just kind of lost some of his desire." Eloise blew out a regretful sigh. "I still can't believe my boy is dead. Gone too soon. Gone too soon."

"Dwayne's in heaven, Ms. Ella Mae. He's happy with Jesus."

Both their voices were starting to tremble, and Shaylynn dropped the subject there. The last thing she wanted to do was feel responsible for rehashing memories that overwhelmed the women with grief.

They arrived at the furniture store only seconds later, giving them fresh, more pleasant matters to talk about. The pattern of the new contemporary yet comfortable three-piece set perfectly blended Eloise's favorite colors of rose and blue. The women were so impressed with the furniture and its sale price that Eloise wasted no time putting it on layaway.

"My young-un will be back to get it soon," she promised the customer service clerk as she signed the paperwork.

Now, as Shaylynn remembered Eloise's smile and pulled brand new curtains, place-mats, area rugs, and decorative vases from her shopping bags, she was reminded of how gratifying she found home decorating to be. Most days, she chose not to, but on those rare occasions when Shaylynn thought back to her childhood, she could easily recall the moment she became fascinated with interior design. As young as five years old, she would close her eyes and imagine that her home wasn't the farce that it was, but instead, a beautiful castle, nestled on one of the hills in the storybooks her teacher had read about.

In Shaylynn's mind, her childhood home had chandeliers and wall-to-wall plush carpet; a vanity mirror in the bathroom with beautiful wallpaper and matching towels; faucets that didn't drip, a kitchen stove with more than one functioning burner; a refrigerator/freezer that stocked more than liquor, cheap beer, frozen pizza, and generic chicken bologna; bedspreads that didn't come standard with cigarette burns; a hand-some prince who would come calling on her, riding a beautiful stallion with a shiny coat, and . . .

Shaylynn flinched at the sound of her ringing doorbell. It wasn't quite eleven o'clock, so it was too early for the postman to be bringing her daily mail, and she wasn't expecting any special deliveries through the United States Postal Service or FedEx.

Too short (without her heels on) to see through the peephole, Shaylynn put her lips close to the frame and asked, "Who is it?"

"It's Neil Taylor," the raspy voice on the other side replied.

Shaylynn gasped. *Neil?* "Just a minute." Using her toes for added assurance, she tried to tread as softly as possible while racing to the decorative oval-shaped mirror on her living room wall and checking her image. She fluffed hair that needed no grooming, smoothed down eyebrows that were not muddled, licked lips that were already moisturized, and then rearranged the pillows on a sofa that needed no tidying. When she was convinced that everything was in order, she raced back to the door, took a quick moment to catch her breath and steady her heartbeat, and then opened it. "Dr. Taylor. Hi. What are you doing here?"

Neil's eyes immediately scanned down to her feet, and it was only then that Shaylynn realized how much taller he seemed today. In all of her rushing, she'd forgotten to put her shoes back on. But a sudden horrific thought made her sock-covered feet trivial.

"What's the matter? Is it Chase? Oh my God. What's happened to him? Is he all right?"

Neil reached out with both hands and touched her arms. "Calm down, Shay. Your son is fine. Nothing is wrong."

"Are you telling me the truth?" She had to be sure. The tone Neil used was the same one that the authorities spoke in when they found her to tell her of her husband's plight. Then, they were deceiving her, only telling her that Emmett had been "in an accident," but knowing full well that he had not only been shot, but was already dead. Shaylynn needed to be sure Neil wasn't doing the same. "Please don't lie to me, Dr. Taylor." Tears were already welling in her eyes.

"Shay," he said, lifting her chin with his index finger, "Chase is fine. I stopped in on his class during my ten o'clock rounds. I'm sorry if my unexpected appearance on your doorstep alarmed you, but I wouldn't lie to you. Chase is fine. I tried to call about half an hour ago to ask if I could drop by, but when you didn't answer, I just took the chance that you may have been on the other line or out taking care of business. So since I had to run out and take care of a few matters of my own, I decided to stop by. I didn't mean to terrorize you." He returned a comforting hand to her arm.

Shaylynn searched his eyes for truth, and when she found it, she released a quiet sigh of relief, and then whispered the words, "I'm sorry."

"There's nothing for you to be sorry about. I guess to some degree, it would be refreshing if all of our parents were as concerned as you." Neil's declaration lessened her embarrassment, but his touch heightened her uneasiness. "May I come in?" His eyes darted back to her feet. "Did I catch you at a bad time?"

Shaylynn felt flushed with awkwardness. "Yes . . . I mean, no . . . I mean, yes." She took a breath and stepped aside. "What I'm trying to say is yes, you may come in, and no, you didn't catch me at a bad time." She hated it when she allowed this man to unnerve her.

Neil's eyes smiled, warming her as he stepped into her home. And while he walked past Shaylynn into her living room, she took that window of opportunity to slip her feet into the ankle boots she'd taken off earlier. For a moment, she watched him take in the view of her décor. When his focal point became the photo on her mantel, it somehow made Shaylynn uncomfortable.

"Please, have a seat," she invited, motioning toward the sofa that he stood near.

"Thank you." When Neil sat, he crossed his right ankle over his left knee, showing off shoes that were either brand new or spit-shined.

"You're not working today?" Shaylynn began gathering the newly purchased items as she talked.

"Yes," Neil revealed. She could feel his eyes following her every move. "I took an extended lunch and thought I'd see if you would join me."

Shaylynn's movement slowed, and her eyes met Neil's for the first time since she welcomed him inside her home. "I . . . I can't. I'm working."

Neil's observation went back to the display on her fireplace mantel, and it lingered there for a moment before he turned back to face her. Shaylynn held her breath, hoping that he didn't turn her mantel's centerpiece into a conversation piece. Not today. She wasn't in the mood to talk about Emmett right now.

After a stale silence, he pointed to the items in Shaylynn's hand. "Are these for Ms. Ella Mae?"

Smiling from relief more than anything else, Shaylynn nodded. "Yes, they are. You like?"

"Yes. Yes, I do. Very much so."

He was looking directly at her when he responded, and Shaylynn had the feeling that Neil wasn't talking about the accessories. She swallowed the rising lump in her throat and avoided eye contact, regretting that she'd wished away a pending conversation about Emmett. Maybe changing the subject was in both their best interests. "Would you like something to drink? I have lemonade, ginger ale, milk, water —"

"I would love some lemonade."

"Okay."

"But . . ."

Shaylynn was preparing to place the items back on her coffee table when the simple conjunction stopped her. She looked at Neil, waiting for him to complete his sentence.

"I'd like to drink the lemonade at Maggiano's. Will you come with me?"

Shaking her head, Shaylynn began, "Dr. Taylor —"

"Please, Shay. I promise I won't bite you. All I'm asking is for you to join me for lunch." It was the same coaxing tone that had her, against her better judgment, driving through thick traffic to Sambuca in Buckhead last weekend.

"I can't, Dr. —"

"We can take this to Ms. Ella Mae while we're out if you wish. It'll save you the trouble of having to drive out on that side of town later."

"But I'm not finished getting —"

"If there are more items that you need to purchase, I can take you wherever you need to go."

Does he have an answer for everything? "But you have to go back to work."

"I'm the head man on campus. I don't *have* to do anything, as long as everything is running well. And it is."

"I have to pick Chase up from school."

"Aw, man!" Neil said in blatant sarcasm. "We'd better hurry up then, 'cause we only have four whole hours."

Even Shaylynn had to laugh at his melodrama. "It's the middle of the day, and —"

"And that's when lunch is generally served."

"I know, but —"

"You owe me."

Shaylynn stared at him. "I owe you? For what?"

"For giving CJ — Pastor Loather — the request to call me up to sing last Sunday."

"Oh." Shaylynn was caught off guard. She had no idea that he knew. "I, uh —"

"Owe me lunch," Neil added, finishing her

sentence with words that didn't even bear a resemblance to the ones she was trying to come up with.

"Dr. Taylor —"

"Neil."

Shaylynn sighed. "I'd rather not call —"

"I know," he intruded again, "but humor me."

An all-out war was going on inside of Shaylynn as she stood, staring at her coffee table and holding the packages that housed two sets of fully lined navy blue curtains. In her peripheral vision, she could see Neil stand from the couch and cautiously erase the space that had kept them at a comfortable distance. Shaylynn could smell that signature manly fragrance that had become synonymous with Dr. Neil Taylor, and the cold chill that resulted nearly made her shiver.

He reached out and took the packages from her hand. "Please."

Still refusing to look at him, but finding the mobility that she desperately needed, Shaylynn backed away, and "Give me a minute," came out of her mouth instead of the "I'm sorry, but you need to leave," that she fished for.

In the secure confines of her bedroom, Shaylynn stood for many minutes with her back against the door, searching for a way out of the situation that she'd agreed to. *Why didn't you tell him no?* She would have scolded herself aloud if she didn't think Neil would hear her. In the past, Shaylynn had never had a problem turning down men and their advances, no matter how persistent, or even handsome, they were. She couldn't even count the number of dinners, movies, musicals, and even church services that she'd been invited to since Emmett's death, and with every one, she'd declined and stuck to her decision. *Why can't I say no to this man?*

Just so the departure to her room wouldn't appear to be the needless excuse for an escape that it was, Shaylynn changed her clothing, taking off the jeans and top that she wore during her shopping spree and putting on a mint green silk sundress. And after moisturizing her legs, she topped it all off with a pair of high-heeled dress sandals, white accented with mint green jewels. Since Neil was wearing a business suit, she reasoned that her new attire wasn't to capture his attention, but to keep him from feeling overdressed.

Yeah, that's it. To keep him from feeling overdressed.

When Shaylynn re-entered the living

303

room, she found Neil standing at her mantel, getting a closer view of the display she'd seen him glancing at earlier. Why was he so fixated with it? To disrupt his focus, she clicked her heels harder than necessary against the floor beneath her feet.

At the sound of Shaylynn's approach, Neil turned and faced her. His lips were quiet and still, but his eyes spoke at deafening volumes as they scrutinized her choice of garment, coming to a rest at her polished legs. Shaylynn had long drawn the conclusion that a woman's legs were two of Neil's favorite parts of the female anatomy, though she was sure that he had other preferences as well. His eyes said that he was pleased with the view, and although she refused to admit it to herself, Shaylynn was pleased that he was pleased.

"Ready?" He swept his arm toward the front door as if to say, "Ladies first."

Nodding, Shaylynn said, "But I have to set my alarm, so you'll have to exit first." Complying, Neil closed the door behind him. "Lord, what am I doing?" Shaylynn whispered while punching in the security code.

NINETEEN

Tuesday afternoon's Italian lunch had
turned into a Wednesday night fine dining
experience. It had taken a little more charm
than normal, but Neil won again, and now,
he could hardly take his eyes off of the
woman who sat across from him wearing
the vast majority of her micro braids neatly
gathered and pinned into an up-do that
made her look even more elegant. Shaylynn's tastefully applied makeup gave her
the appearance of a woman slightly older
than her thirty years. The beading on the
silver cocktail dress she wore caught the
chandelier lighting of the restaurant that
was tucked away along the banks of the
Chattahoochee River in the Atlanta community of Vinings.

A gentle but cool summer breeze that the
nearby waters seemed to purposefully blow
in the direction of the table Neil shared with
Shaylynn had caused her to begin shivering

early in the evening. Neil could tell that she wanted to decline the offer of his suit jacket, but the persistent breezes caused her to graciously accept. As Neil removed his jacket and did the honors, purposefully brushing his hands against Shaylynn's bare arms in the process, and then using his hands to gather her fresh dangling braids and freeing them from the temporary captivity that the draped jacket had placed them in, he made a mental note to thank God later for His unmerited favor.

Back in 2005, Canoe restaurant had been named to the Fine Dining Hall of Fame in *Nation's Restaurant News.* Ever since reading about the eatery's honor, Neil had been searching for a reason to visit. He'd considered taking his mother there on her seventy-fifth birthday, but the setting seemed far too romantic for a mother/son affair. On the other hand, when Shaylynn finally accepted his invitation after four phone calls, three text messages, and two dozen roses (all within a twenty-four hour period), Neil couldn't think of a more effective way of impressing the young woman who had nabbed his affections like a common criminal and placed them in handcuffs. Here lately, with thoughts of her lingering in his head, Neil felt as though his heart had not only been arrested, but the key that could free him from permanent lockdown had been thrown away.

It appeared that Canoe was a good choice. As Neil admired Shaylynn's beauty, she admired the splendor of the open space surrounding their patio seating. While they awaited dessert, she seemed to have just as much trouble taking her eyes away from nature's magnificence as Neil had taking his eyes away from her. Even when Shaylynn finally turned her attention to her date for the evening and caught him gazing, Neil still couldn't force his eyes away.

"You're staring," she said, fidgeting in her seat and tucking dangling braids behind her ear.

"You're stunning," Neil replied.

"Thank you." Her smile was bashful, and just when Neil thought that he couldn't be more attracted to her, he was.

Something about the desires stirring inside of him didn't seem appropriate. Neil took several gulps from his glass of water and hoped the cold liquid would douse the inner smoldering. He needed to strike up a conversation that would ease his mounting passion. "Did you enjoy your dinner?"

She eyed him, and Neil knew why. It was a question that he already knew the answer to, not only because she'd cleaned her plate, but also because —

"I told you that I did," Shaylynn replied. "It was so delicious that my mouth is already watering just imagining what dessert is going to taste like."

Mine too. Neil couldn't believe the level of naughtiness that his mind had reached. It was apparent that talking about dessert wasn't going to help. He'd have to try another avenue. "My mother told me that she loves what you're doing for her house." Perfect. Any man who couldn't snap out of it when talking about his mama needed psychological help.

"Did she?" Shaylynn's smile broadened just as the server appeared with her chocolate mousse torte and Neil's lemon chiffon cheesecake.

"Yes, she did." Neil requested the bill, and once the attendant provided it and left them alone, he continued, glad that he could feel his heightened emotions calming now. "Getting Ms. Ella Mae to incorporate some changes has been quite a job. Me and my siblings have been tussling with her for years. I guess she just needed a professional, someone who would patiently walk her through it instead of badgering her like we were doing." Neil's speech was distracted when Shaylynn reached up with her left hand to tuck away a braid that a new breeze had displaced. Her ever-present wedding set flashed a reminder of her heart's status, just in case he'd forgotten.

God, I need your help. The silent prayer crept into Neil's head while he sank his fork into his cheesecake. He had never wanted to win the love of a woman as much as he did Shaylynn's, and knowing that the memory of a dead Emmett Ford was strong enough to prevent it forever nearly made Neil detest a man he never knew. His heart ached for a love that seemed so close, yet so far away.

"My mother is fond of you as a person too. She says you're easy to work with." The quietness had begun to pound on Neil's eardrums. He had to talk about something.

Shaylynn's expression said she was pleased with his comment. "I like her too. She has a great sense of humor. I imagine she kept you guys laughing when you were children."

Neil smiled. Actually, she hadn't. Eloise Mae Flowers Taylor did a lot more mothering than laughing when Neil and his siblings were growing up. The sense of humor that she had now was a reserved trait that they rarely saw until they got older. Neil didn't tell Shaylynn that, though. He'd let her keep the notion that his mother had always been their footloose and fancy free friend, instead of the strict disciplinarian that he remembered: the one who would pull out a switch in a New York minute if her children even looked like they wanted to get out of line.

"She told me that she hurt her leg in the same accident that killed your father," Shaylynn added.

Talking about the sudden death of his father wasn't nearly as painful as talking about the death of his brother, but Neil didn't like to do either. He hoped to keep this conversation on a path that didn't force him to revisit either of the losses. "Yes, she did. Ms. Ella Mae has been through a lot in life — we all have — but we're still going strong, and much of that is due to my mother. She sees everything as God's plan, and I think that helps her survive every test. Did she tell you that her leg was supposed to be bum?"

"No, she didn't," Shaylynn admitted. Her eyes said she was surprised by this new revelation. "Ms. Flowers did tell me that she was walking by God's grace, but she didn't go into detail. When you say 'bum,' do you mean she was supposed to be lame?"

"In that one leg, yes." Neil took the time to put a piece of cheesecake in his mouth and savor the flavor before continuing. "Ms. Ella Mae had several surgeries on her leg, and the doctors said she'd never walk again; but look at God."

"Amen," Shaylynn said. "What a wonderful testimony. And she's a feisty lady too."

"And very perceptive," Neil added, recalling the knowing glance that his mother gave him when he and Shaylynn stopped by the house, dressed in their evening wear, to drop off Chase. He knew that he didn't have to tell Eloise what was happening. She was fully aware, and even without her saying so, Neil knew she approved. "I think my niece and nephew are gonna miss Chase when they leave tomorrow."

Shaylynn beamed and bobbed her head up and down. "He's definitely going to miss them. Chase talks about them more than he does any of his schoolmates, and I know he's enjoyed the time he's spent with them at your mother's house. He still talks about that overnight stay last Saturday. He had a blast."

"So did they. The kids spend every summer with Ms. Ella Mae, so maybe they can hang out once the school year ends."

"Sure. My son would jump at the opportunity to spend more time with your niece and nephew."

"Would his mother like to spend more time with their uncle?" Neil didn't know where the voice had come from, but apparently it had come from his mouth, because he was the one that Shaylynn was staring at.

"Dr. Tay—"

"Please don't call me that," Neil implored. "It's apparent that you already know Dr. Taylor. I want you to get to know Neil, and I want to get to know more about Shaylynn."

"You do know me."

"Not as much as I'd like to know."

"Well, you know all you *need* to know."

Neil knew he should let it rest. He could see that the atmosphere was changing, and Shaylynn was becoming agitated. But he couldn't let it go. He couldn't just keep letting Emmett run things from the grave. He had to find a breakthrough. "What are you afraid of?" Neil asked the same question he'd asked her on his birthday as they stood at her car door at his mother's house. He didn't get an acceptable answer then, but he hoped to get one tonight. He'd never get anywhere if he didn't know what he was working against.

Both their voice levels were low, but their tones were turning stiff. The eyes of those sitting at the tables nearest them darted in their direction, but neither Neil nor Shaylynn seemed to notice or care.

"I'm not afraid of anything. And certainly I'm not afraid of you, if that's what you're insinuating."

"Then why won't you open up to me?"

"Maybe I don't want to. Did that ever cross your mind?" Shaylynn pushed her dessert away like she'd suddenly lost her appetite for the chocolate she'd been craving.

Neil placed his fork down, but didn't push away his cheesecake. "Yes, you do."

"Well, aren't we the arrogant one?"

"I'm not being arrogant; I'm being honest, which is more than I can say for you."

Shaylynn's eyes widened, and her jaws were clenched when she replied, "I beg your pardon?"

"Shay, a man knows when he's gained a woman's interest." Neil knew he was sounding full of himself, but he didn't care how much she denied it; he knew there was something special between them.

"Does he also know when he's gotten on her last nerve?" Shaylynn's eyes were shooting missiles at him. Maybe the whole notion that she felt something special for him was all in his mind.

"Yes, he does," Neil admitted. "And I'm

very aware that I'm doing that too, and I'm sorry. But I don't know any other way to make you understand."

"Understand what? What do you want from me?"

"I want to love you, okay? Is that too much to ask?"

Shaylynn stared at Neil, and he stared back, just as shocked at the words he'd said as she was at the words she'd heard. Batting her eyes in disbelief, Shaylynn asked, "You want to what?"

Neil had the urge to take back the words he'd blurted, to erupt into laughter, and tell her that it was all a joke. Not because he didn't mean what he'd said, but because he could already feel the humiliation of her total rejection. "I'm sorry," he whispered, staring at the table in front of him.

Why was he apologizing? He'd asked God for an opportunity, and this was it. The door had been opened, and it was up to him to walk in.

It's now or never. Knowing that his thoughts were truth, Neil recanted. "No . . . no, I'm not. I'm not sorry." Finding a spark of courage, Neil leaned across the table, bringing himself closer. "You don't feel this?"

Shaylynn drew back. "Feel what?"

"This," he stressed, pointing from her to himself. "Look me in my eyes and tell me you don't feel anything. Tell me that there's no part of your heart that is begging to belong to me, no part of you that feels like Jesus Christ Himself brought us together to be a source of healing for one another. Tell me that, Shay, and as God as my witness, I'll take you home, and I'll never call on you again." Neil prayed that he wouldn't be forced to cash in on that promise.

Shaylynn's eyes pooled with tears. "I have to leave." She pushed her chair back from the table.

"Wait, sweetheart. Wait." In one quick motion, Neil reached and grabbed her left hand and held it for a long while of silence. Neil didn't move, and neither did Shaylynn, but silent tears were streaming down her cheeks. Neil took the thumb of his right hand and wiped away the moisture while repeatedly mouthing the words, *Please don't leave.* To his surprise, Shaylynn didn't pull away.

Neil tried again. "Listen to me for a minute, okay?" Shaylynn nodded, and he handed her a napkin for her newest tears, then continued. "Whether you know it or not, the two of us are a lot alike." When Shaylynn turned her eyes away, he added, "Hear me out. We've both been through some tragedies that include losing spouses. Mine came by way of divorce and yours by way of death, but both were losses that were not planned and certainly not painless. I'm not trying to lessen the seriousness of Emmett's murder, but your losing him made you draw the same conclusion that my divorce made me draw. That conclusion was that we would never put ourselves in the place to be hurt again. You promised yourself that you'd never allow yourself to love another man, and I vowed to never allow myself to love another woman."

Neil paused and took a long look at Shaylynn's wedding ring. When he touched it, he felt her hand flinch. Looking back at her, he said, "I can't speak for your heart, Shay, but mine is making a liar out of me real fast."

Shaylynn snatched her hand away. "Take me home." She jerked her chair farther from the table, ripped his jacket from around her shoulders, and walked away, leaving his coat partially dangling on the back of her vacated chair.

"Shay . . ." Neil had planned to pay the bill using a credit card, but as he watched Shaylynn take quick footsteps down the walkway, he pulled out a one hundred dollar bill and laid it on the table. The cost of his pork tenderloin and her duck breast meals, combined with the desserts, came to less than seventy dollars, but he didn't have time to get change. The waiter probably deserved the extra tip just for not throwing them out for their minor disturbance.

He grabbed his jacket as he made his exit, and when he called her name again in pursuit, Shaylynn stopped and turned, waiting for him to catch up with her. Neil slipped his arm around her waist and changed her direction, leading her to the walkway where clientele sometimes strolled before or after eating to take in the sights. Neither of them spoke until they were a good distance away from the restaurant, unable to clearly hear any voices from the patrons, but still within earshot of the music that floated through the atmosphere.

"Please." Neil pointed toward an iron bench, and Shaylynn sat without resistance. Her face was expressionless when he sat with her and reclaimed her hand. "Maybe I'm going about this all the wrong way," he started. "Charge it to my head. I'm an old man, and I've been out of the game for a while." He saw a slight smile tug at Shaylynn's lips that caused him to wonder out loud. "Is that it? Is our fifteen-year age difference a factor here?"

Shaylynn sighed, closed her eyes, and shook her head from side to side, giving Neil the impression that she thought he was oblivious. "You're not an old man by any definition. You're attractive, you're a lot of fun to be around, you're smart, strong, talented, and from everything that I can gather, you're sensitive and romantic. You're all those things, and you're also a man who worships God. You could have any woman you want."

"Apparently not," Neil said with a dry laugh.

"I promise . . . it's not you."

"Then what is it?" Neil could hear the desperation in his own voice.

Shaylynn seemed to struggle to find the right words, but he knew in the end she chose to be honest. Neil guessed that she thought he deserved that much. "My heart's not available, Solomon. I know that sounds farfetched to you and to the rest of the world, but it's the truth. My heart is not available to anyone else because I still love Emmett. I would think that you, of all people, would understand." Fresh tears were appearing and making their way down Shaylynn's cheeks. "I mean, you're trying to make it seem like I'm being so unreasonable. I saw the way you were looking at Emmett's photo in my house yesterday when you dropped by. It's like you think I'm crazy for having it there, but Val told me that you have a picture of you and Dwayne hanging in your room, and he's been gone much longer than Emmett. Why is it okay for you, but not for me?"

"Nothing's wrong with you having a picture of Emmett in your house, Shay. I don't think you're crazy for that, and I never intended to give the impression that I did. It wasn't the photo that I found odd; it was the flowers. I was just trying to put the pieces together: the flowers were violets . . . the song that had you crying the other night mentioned violets. I was just trying to make sense of it all. I just couldn't —"

"It means forever," Shaylynn broke in.

Not understanding, Neil asked, "What means forever?"

"The song. That was our song," she explained. "When violets turn red and when roses turn blue, I'll be still in love with you. Those words meant that no matter what, even if the impossible or the unthinkable happened, our love would never change."

When she went on to share the story of how Emmett had proposed to her in a field of violets and how the flowers on her mantel were the same flowers she'd held at his

319

funeral seven years earlier, misery crept upon Neil. He felt as though he was fighting a losing battle and running short on the strength to continue.

They quieted as another couple strolled by hand in hand, taking in the beauty of Canoe restaurant's landscape. Even the darkness of the nighttime couldn't hide its majesty. During his and Shaylynn's conversation, Neil had tuned out the music in the background, but now he heard it clearly and was familiar with the song that played. It was Bill Withers's 1985 hit single, "You Just Can't Smile It Away." Neil leaned his back against the bench and joined in the lyrics, not knowing whether he was singing the song to comfort himself or to send one last pitch to Shaylynn. Either way, it seemed to have worked.

"Let's sit and talk it over and work it out. I love you so. Can't we just talk it over and see what we can do . . ."

As he continued singing, Neil found reassurance in the feel of Shaylynn's head as she rested it on his shoulder, and in the sudden recall that just a few minutes ago, for the first time, she'd called him Solomon.

TWENTY

Growing up, CJ had often heard his mother say that phone calls that came in the middle of the night or in the wee hours of the morning could be nothing but trouble. Whether that was indeed the case would probably forever lie in each asked person's opinion, but tonight, it rang true in the Loather home. CJ sat straight up in his bed with the phone pressed to his ear.

The sound of the telephone combined with his sharp movement stirred Theresa, and she sat up with him. "What is it, honey?"

"Nothing." He responded with the half truth after placing the caller on hold and while peeling back the covers and slipping his feet in his slippers.

"Are you sure, CJ? Where are you going?"

"I'm just going in the living room so I won't disturb you. Go on back to sleep, baby. Everything's fine. It's a business call."

He knew Theresa would assume that it was one of the church members calling for prayer, or one of the many young men that he mentored, needing a listening ear. Those were the only types of calls that filtered into their household at hours such as this one. CJ watched as Theresa lay back down, although she never took her eyes off of him.

When the pastor stepped into the living room, he looked at the clock on the wall. It was two in the morning, an ungodly time to call anyone if it weren't an emergency. But he had told his former force mate, Victor Cross, to call him immediately if any information was discovered. CJ had had to be very careful about who he selected to entrust with this unauthorized assignment. He could get into a great deal of trouble if it were discovered that he'd used contacts he'd made as a public servant for a personal investigation into the life of the late Mayor Emmett Ford. Not only could CJ be publicly bashed for his part, but everybody he brought in on the assignment was at risk of losing their credibility, their jobs, or both. That was the major reason that he chose not to call any of his old buddies who still worked with the Dekalb County police force. It was just too risky.

CJ had spent a day in prayer prior to making the call. He didn't exactly get God's blessing to do what he did, but CJ did feel that in some way, the Lord was offering some grace and guidance so that he made choices that wouldn't scar him for life. Perhaps God was merciful, knowing that Pastor Loather's heart was in the right place.

CJ decided on the independent firm of Kris-Cross, P.I., which was run by the investigative team of Kristoff Nain and Victor Cross, two Jamaican-born cousins who had migrated to Atlanta when they entered college. Both men had worked with CJ on the force for several years before establishing their own private practice. In fact, as a rookie, Victor had shadowed CJ, learning most of what he knew about the business and about Jesus Christ from the preacher/investigator. Although they both eventually branched out to answer their respective callings, the men never lost touch, and CJ knew that if there were anyone he could trust with a mission such as this, it was Victor.

With the call still on hold, CJ walked into the kitchen and splashed his face with cold water over the sink. He could almost hear Theresa scolding him for using the dish towel to dry his face. Now that he was fully awake and confident that he was coherent enough not to misinterpret what his friend was saying, CJ released the call and said, "Okay, I'm sorry, Vic. I had to get somewhere where I could speak freely."

"No problem, mon," Victor said.

That famed Jamaican saying generally tickled CJ, but his mind was too cluttered for it to even calculate its usual humor. "I think I misheard you the first time, so start over from the beginning with what you were telling me before, and talk slower. You know that accent of yours kicks into overdrive when you talk fast."

"This has nothing to do with my accent, CJ. You heard me right the first time," Victor assured. "It didn't take me and Kris no time to get the information that we gathered. Everything was too easy to confiscate and validate for this case to have gone cold. If you ask me, it looks like officials in Milwaukee might be fully aware of who killed their mayor, but if they reveal it, it will blow Emmett Ford right out of the water."

"But that's the part that doesn't make sense. If the truth would make Ford look bad, why wouldn't they just go ahead and tell it?" CJ thought of how elated Neil would be to get this news. "I mean, wasn't the mayoral race divided down color lines? Black folks voted for him, but most white folks didn't, right? Wasn't the general consensus that the whole campaign had a lot of race issues surrounding it? Seems to me like if this were so, and Ford wasn't on the up and up, authorities in Milwaukee would be all too happy to expose it so that the dark cloud of racism, which no doubt still looms in the minds of some, could be cleared once and for all."

Victor agreed. "If that were the case, it would only make sense, right? But look here: that whole race fire didn't start burning until *after* his death, and I think the match was lit intentionally just to make the general population lose sight of the real issue."

"How so?"

"Think about it," Victor said. "If the election were really divided down racial lines, Emmett Ford never would have won. In Milwaukee, Whites only outnumber Blacks by about five percent, but white *voters* outnumber black *voters* by a much wider margin. If a substantial number of white folks hadn't voted for Ford, he wouldn't have stood a chance."

"What was the voter turnout on that day?" CJ asked. "If the white community was overconfident that their candidate would win, maybe they didn't go to the polls to vote as they should have, thinking their guy was a shoo-in."

"I see you haven't lost that analytical ability to rationalize — that annoying gift that you were so famous for on the force." The chuckle that followed was brief. Then Victor added, "Actually, you make a good point, but it's not one that Kris and I hadn't already considered and checked out. Milwaukee had an almost eighty-five percent voter turnout for that race. Emmett Ford won fair and square, but it wasn't on the African American vote alone. Given the statistics, it couldn't have been."

"And you say this info was easy to gather?" CJ scratched his chin, feeling the investigator inside of him rising.

"Yeah, mon. Think about it. Kris and I got this information in twenty-four hours and without doing a full-scale investigation. There's no way on God's green earth that this case should have been so hard to crack that seven years later, it's still unsolved. Unless the investigators in Milwaukee are a pack of idiots, somebody ought to be behind bars, sitting on death row. There was so much evidence, including an eyewitness who heard the single gunshot and saw a man running from the area where the crime took place. Take my word for it when I tell you that there is no way that a real, honest to goodness effort was put forth to make an arrest in this case."

CJ walked from the living room to his home office and sat in the chair behind his desk, running a hand over his head. This was almost too much to grasp at this hour of the morning. When he contacted Victor, CJ had all but assured the man that he wouldn't find anything. The investigation was really just to prove to Neil that Emmett's slate was clean. And after telling him so with the proof of an investigator's report, CJ planned to convince his friend to go after Shaylynn's heart like a man, and not like some hungry vulture, swooping down to feast on the remains of the woman's broken heart and taking advantage of her vulnerability. But the news CJ was receiving was backfiring, and it made him regret his decision to go against his better judgment, not to mention what he knew was God's direction.

"So are you saying that Ford's death wasn't race-related in any manner?" CJ knew the answer before he asked the question.

"Honestly, I don't think racism had one iota to do with this man's murder. Emmett Ford was the Barack Obama of Milwaukee.

He had his haters, no doubt, but people were ready for a change, and he had way more people for him than against him. This wasn't a black/white thing. White folks loved Ford just as much as black people did, and he had mad support across the board during his bid for office.

"And here's the kicker: if you listen to the description that the eyewitness gave the police when he was questioned seven years ago, it'll make you throw the whole deck of race cards away. Mind you, this is a description that never made the news.

"I can't give you the eyewitness's name because I don't even have it to give. We used connections to put word on the street in the area where Ford was shot that we were looking for any possible witnesses. After weeding out all of the fakers and shakers, too many facts lined up for this John Doe not to be telling the truth. And it was obvious that he was scared as a rabbit when he was talking to me."

"But you're sure he was on the up and up?" CJ asked.

"Yeah, I'm sure. He even remembered the name of one of the detectives that he gave his story to. And guess what? That detective was found dead the same day he took the eyewitness report. His car veered off the road somehow and smashed into a tree, and he was found slumped over his steering wheel with fatal head injuries."

"You don't think the accident killed him?"

"I can't say one way or the other. Apparently the injuries were consistent with the impact, but the timing of it all is a bit too ironic for me. Our John Doe must have thought the same, since he never spat a word of what he saw to another soul."

"Well, how did you get him to tell you what he wouldn't tell the media?"

Victor chuckled. "Because the love of money is the root of all evil. You know as well as I know that if you set the right price, you can buy just about any information that you need."

"You paid him?" CJ couldn't believe the lengths that his old chum had gone to just to help him out.

"Don't get misty-eyed," Victor said. "Save the tears for when you receive the bill and see how many zeros are in the bottom line."

CJ wanted to protest, but he couldn't. He'd asked for the service, and the resulting bill was probably God's way of punishing him for his disobedience.

"Let me read you what this guy told the police," Victor said. "The description is a bit sketchy, but it was enough for me to get a good handle on the likelihood of the killer's ethnicity, and the police should have too. The man admitted that it was nighttime and no clear facial features of the killer could be seen, but the man he spotted fleeing the scene was described as wearing an oversized T-shirt and extremely baggy jeans that he was holding up at the waist with his hands as he escaped. He was dark in complexion, approximately six feet tall, one hundred eighty pounds, wearing a baseball cap, and he made his escape in an early model Oldsmobile Cutlass Supreme with large, expensive wheels. Not stereotyping our brothers, CJ, but I'm inclined to believe that this was a black man."

Nodding in silent agreement, CJ said, "So what are you really trying to say about the reason behind this murder, Vic?"

"I'm saying he lived a double life that led to a single death. There was the Emmett Ford who was the doting husband and do-gooder that spearheaded organizations that offered mentoring for kids and launched efforts to clean up the drugs from inner-city neighborhoods, but then there was the Emmett Ford that left a paper trail of conclusive evidence proving that in his early years of politics, and even during the time that he ran for the office of mayor, he went on frequent excursions masked as business trips, where he paid everything in cash — cash that was never withdrawn from his own accounts."

CJ grimaced. "What did he do on these so-called business trips?"

"Illegal gambling, drug laundering, prostitution . . . you name it. If he campaigned against it, he took part in it. I'm telling you, his marriage notwithstanding, this man bought women like we buy suits. I can't judge him on whether or not he loved his wife as much as you tell me that she loved and still loves him. I'm sure the other women meant nothing more to him than a lay, and he meant nothing more to them than a dollar. But he wasn't even close to being a one-woman man, and if his widow knew that, her tears would dry up like an Arizona desert."

"No doubt," CJ said. It would be all that he'd have to tell Neil in order for his friend to get the chance he wanted with Shaylynn.

"The operation that he was a part of was big, CJ. Huge," Victor went on. "We didn't find out names of who were, or maybe still are in it, but I'm guessing that the names on the membership roll would blow our minds. That's why they didn't divulge the information that would blow Ford out of the water, because it would blow them out too. We believe that Ford was a puppet for politicians long before he ran for any high offices. As a matter of fact, his rise to success in government was likely based on the backs he'd scratched while he climbed up the political ladder."

CJ was getting a headache from the overload. This was far worse than he thought. "So you've drawn an early conclusion that Emmett was a crook, and what? His death was the result of some kind of illegal dealing that went bad?"

"Not exactly, but you're on the right track," Victor said. "My early conclusion is that Ford, at one time, was a crook. *Was,*" Victor stressed. "The slanderous paper trail stops right about the time he won the election. The new trail he leaves behind, the one that begins just weeks before his murder, shows something entirely different: no trips, no drug laundering, no gambling, no call girls. We find that he starts being a lot more hands-on in his clean-up organizations, and get this, CJ: he becomes a regular churchgoer. At the church he attended, it's noted on the books . . . the day he joined, the day he confessed Christ, the dates he paid tithe —"

"Are you . . ." Pausing to sit up straight in

his seat, CJ broke his voice down to a horrified whisper. "Are you telling me that Emmett Ford is dead because he got saved?"

"That's exactly what I'm telling you. I'm inclined to believe that the deal turned murderous because Milwaukee's great mayor made a life change, and at some point between the time he won the mayoral race and his early weeks of serving in his official capacity, started to walk the straight and narrow."

"And he was probably about to pull the covers off what was going on," CJ thought out loud.

"Exactly. Mayor Ford's new conscience was probably urging him to tell what he knew, but he never got the chance. Ford wasn't killed by some prejudiced skinhead who didn't want to see the city run by a black man, and he wasn't killed by some drug lord who wasn't willing to sit by and watch the new mayor sweep the streets clean of his kind of dirt. I believe that his killing was carefully orchestrated by the same people, the same dignitaries and VIPs, who endorsed him and convinced the people of Milwaukee that he was the best man for the job. At the time they were supporting him, Ford was one of them, but one decision on Ford's part changed everything."

"The decision to follow Christ," CJ mumbled.

"Exactly. And just like me and Kris found this out, every official that was assigned to this case has had the ability to solve this crime; but they didn't because every one of them is probably still on payroll with the real killers even as we speak."

CJ rubbed his forehead. "Man!"

"The saddest part of all," Victor added, "is that Emmett Ford never needed to get involved with this mess to begin with. I guess he just got caught up in the idea of living in the fast lane and having a big name, because it sure wasn't about the need for money. He wasn't strapped for cash. He had the fortune of being born with a silver spoon in his mouth, plus on his own merit, he had the means of making all the honest money he needed."

"If his folks were so rich, seems like they would have put up the kind of reward that would make somebody come forward," CJ observed.

"After the brutal way Ford was assassinated? Are you kidding me? I don't think any of them would have been that brave. They probably wouldn't have even lived long enough to collect the reward."

"I guess not." The inhumanity of it all saddened CJ. "If only someone had introduced Emmett to Christ before he ever got caught up in that mess. He'd probably still be alive today."

"Yeah, mon. Ford made the decision to go straight, no doubt about it. But his past wouldn't let him live to tell the story. One man pulled the trigger, but I'm convinced that he was just doing what he'd been hired to do. The real killers wouldn't have dared to be directly connected to the murder. They're too smart for that; but a real investigation probably would have brought them all to light, I'm sure. That's why they had to squash it and let it go cold. Too many hands would have been found with blood on them, maybe even the hands of some of the city's top government officials."

CJ exhaled heavily. He wished he could rewind time and erase everything he'd just heard, but he had promised Neil that he would let him know of any discoveries. *Lord, direct my path. Show me what to do.* It almost seemed too late to be praying that prayer. CJ was fully aware that God had been trying to guide him all the while, and because he refused God's direction, CJ had walked into a danger zone. And it was too late to back out now.

"That's all I have," Victor said. "I hope it

answered all of your questions, because I'm done with this one. Don't make me regret it, CJ."

"I won't. I promise."

"Believe me when I tell you that I believe you. If I didn't . . ." Victor let his incomplete sentence trail.

"Thanks, Vic."

"For what?"

"The information," CJ said.

"What information?"

Immediately catching the hint, CJ replied, "Nothing. See you 'round, my friend."

TWENTY-ONE

As if metal springs had been surgically embedded in his back, Neil's body shot into an upright seated position. He hadn't been running, but his heart pounded like he was embarking upon mile five of a steep uphill climb. One hand fluttered to his chest; then both hands synchronized to trace the surface of his cheeks, traveling to the top of his head. All signs pointed to the fact that it was all a dream, but Neil had to check one more thing before he could be absolutely sure. Flipping his left hand palm down, he looked at his naked ring finger. It had been a dream all right, but instead of relief, a deep-seated sense of regret overshadowed Neil.

He used the fingers of both his hands to rub his eyes. Early in the morning, Neil's sight was at its worst. On a normal day, he only needed his eyeglasses to read fine printed matter, but anytime he failed to get his full eight hours of sleep, his need for corrective lenses tended to magnify. Turning toward his covered windows and staring as though he could see straight through the green-and-tan curtains that covered them, Neil focused on the dim early morning light that escaped into the room.

"What in the world was that all about?" he whispered into the atmosphere.

The red glowing numbers on Neil's bedside digital clock said that he still had nearly an hour before he'd have to get up and prepare for work. But when he lay back against the pillows, there was no will to sleep, only renewed visions of the dream he'd just awakened from. The colors had been so vibrant, the sounds so vivid, the tastes so —

Neil sprang up in the bed once more. This time, the unexpected blaring of his telephone was the cause. When he picked up the cordless phone from his cherry wood nightstand and saw his mother's name on the caller ID, Neil's first thought was to panic. Getting a call from Ms. Ella Mae at 5:15 in the morning wasn't normal. "Hello?" He held his voice as steady as he could, simultaneously praying in silence that all was well.

"Sol? Did I wake you? You sound like you

already woke."

"I am. I woke up just a few minutes ago. What's wrong? Why are you calling?" By his mother's response, Neil knew that his best attempt at sounding blithe wasn't working.

"Calm down. Nothing's wrong," she said. "I just thought you might want to holler at your sister before she leaves. Her flight takes off at eight this morning. Remember? She didn't want me to call you because she said you didn't get up before six, but I told her you wouldn't mind getting up a little early to say good-bye to your baby sister."

Neil was relieved that the call wasn't a crisis. The last time he got a call in the early morning hours from a family member, it was from Ernest Jr., his oldest brother, telling him that Dwayne has passed away. "I'm glad you called, Ms. Ella Mae. I would have been mad if Val had left without speaking to me."

"See, I told you," Neil heard his mother call out triumphantly, apparently speaking to Valerie, who was somewhere in the house with her. Then she turned her attention back to her son. "Here. I'm 'bout to put her on so y'all can talk before you have to be rushing to get ready for work."

In the moments of silence that followed, Neil's thoughts floated back to his dream. A large part of him wished that he could revisit it and linger awhile to see what would happen next. The best part of it had to be just moments away, but he'd never experience it due to the tickling sensation on the sides of his face that awakened him.

"Hey, Sol."

Neil smiled. While his siblings addressed him by the name occasionally, none of them made a habit of it. "Hey, Val. I hear you're headed out."

"Yeah. As soon as the kids finish eating the breakfast that your mother insisted on preparing for them and we get the rental car loaded."

"You know Ms. Ella Mae wasn't about to let her grandchildren leave on an empty stomach," Neil observed. "You should have expected that."

"Yeah, I should have."

"You'll have to kiss Kee-Kee and Ty goodbye for me," Neil said. "And I can't thank you enough for being my birthday surprise. It made my day. Your being there was better than the cake."

Laughing, Valerie said, "I think that's the first time I've been compared to a dessert . . . well, not really. There was this time that Otis said I bought this whip cream in the spray can and —"

"Never mind! Never mind!" Neil exclaimed. Then over the sounds of his sister's laughter, he added, "There are some things that I don't need or want to know."

"Anyway," Valerie said, still giggling, "you're very welcome. I'm glad I came too. But I get the feeling that Shay's appearance was the icing that out-sweetened anything that any of us could have said or done."

Not offering a denial, Neil saw this as a good segue to talk about his dream. He was going to wait and call CJ on his lunch break, but figured that his sister's ears would suffice. Maybe a woman's point of view was what he needed anyway. "You got a minute to talk? Do you need to rush off the phone?"

"No." Valerie drew out the word, and then hesitated. "We're all packed, so I have a little time. What's up?"

"I just had a dream that I want to talk about."

"A nightmare?"

"No," Neil said. "Quite the opposite, actually."

"What about?" She lowered her voice, and Neil assumed that she did so to keep their conversation as private as possible.

He pulled his legs close to his body and crossed them Indian-style. "Not about what . . . about who. I dreamed about

Shay." When Valerie remained quiet, he continued. "We were standing outside on what looked like beachfront property, and we were . . . getting married."

Valerie gasped softly then whispered, "Married? You mean married, as in —"

"As in married, Val. We were getting married," Neil said in a matter-of-fact tone. "Come to think of it, we were already married. I don't really recall the details of the ceremony itself, but it was a done deal. I had the ring on my finger and everything. So I guess what I was dreaming about were the moments after the ceremony ended." Neil closed his eyes and relived it as he spoke. "There was music playing in the background, and everybody was dancing. We were dancing too, me and Shay."

"Sounds nice," was Valerie's response. "What were you dancing to? Luther? Celine? Anthony Hamilton? Mariah Carey? Do you remember?"

Those were some of his sister's favorites, but Neil shook his head in response. "No, none of them. I can't remember whose music it was, but —" He stopped short and gasped at the flashback that was so clear it almost blinded him.

"What?" Valerie beseeched from the other end of the line.

"It was me," Neil revealed.

"What was you?"

"Singing. I was the one singing. I wasn't singing where everybody could hear me, though, so I don't know who the guests were dancing to, but I was singing to Shay . . . in her ear."

"Voluntarily?" Valerie sounded shocked. "You were actually singing without her putting a gun to your head or a knife to your throat? This is huge, Neil."

Neil's eyes fluttered open. His sister's wisecrack had distorted the tender image that he had recalled. "Do you want to hear the story or not?" he snarled.

"Of course I do. What were you singing?"

Sighing, Neil said, "I don't know. It was a song I'd never heard before. It was like I was making it up as I went along. It's still ringing in my head now. A love song of some sort. It's been years since song lyrics came to me in my dreams like that. And even more years since original *love* song lyrics came to me. It's weird."

"Neil, you should write the words down before you forget them," Valerie suggested.

Scratching his ear, Neil replied, "I'm gonna have to. I don't think the words will turn me loose until I do."

"Tell me more," Valerie urged. "What else

happened in the dream?"

Unconsciously closing his eyes again, Neil rediscovered more pleasant memories and shared them. "I was dressed to the nine, Val. I was wearing a sharp black tux from the Drop Dead Collexion."

"The who?"

"It's a line created by Ron Finley, this designer I met a few years ago out in Beverly Hills. Anyway, I was wearing a Drop Dead Collexion original, and Shay was gorgeous in a milky white Vera Wang silk gown that fitted her all the way to her waist, but flared from the hips down. She looked simply breathtaking. Like an angel without a broken wing."

"Like a what?"

"Never mind," Neil said. "The braids at the top of her head were pinned up, but the ones in the back were left to fall around her neck and shoulders. And the veil she wore sat on her hairstyle perfectly. God . . . she was beautiful." The last part was spoken as though he were talking to himself instead of his sister.

"Certainly sounds like it," Valerie remarked. "I hate that Ms. Ella Mae woke you out of this dream, Neil."

"She didn't. I woke up before she called."

"What awakened you? What happened?"

Neil thought long and hard. He tried to recall what had taken place in the moments just before his eyes opened and his body jarred into an upright position. What was the culprit that had so rudely interrupted his visit to heaven? "I remember," he blurted, reaching up and touching the side of his face. "Like I said, I was singing to her, and we were dancing. And in the middle of it all, I pulled her to me and kissed her." Neil's heartbeat quickened at the thought of it. Shaylynn's lips had felt like pure love against his.

"And the kiss is what woke you?" Valerie's question snatched him back from being fully swept away by the total recall.

Neil opened his eyes for the first time in a long while. "No, not the kiss. The wind."

"The wind woke you up?"

"A gust of wind blew, and it caught her veil. It blew the veil over both our heads, and when the netting of it touched the sides of my face, I woke up." A new wave of disappointment swept over him. As appealing as the veil had been, he wished now that she hadn't even worn it. Darn that Vera Wang! Perhaps, had Shaylynn not worn the veil, he would have slept long enough to not only see how the wedding festivities ended, but also how the honeymoon began. He could only imagine . . .

"Are the two of you a serious item, Neil?" Valerie asked, invading his thoughts once more. "I mean, I could feel the magnetism and see the attraction between the two of you, but I didn't want to assume anything. Especially not with you, because you've made it very clear that you'd never go that route again."

"I know." Neil turned his body and allowed his feet to dangle over the side of his mattress. He needed his morning cup of coffee. Glancing at the clock, he knew he'd have to end their conversation soon.

"I hear a *but* in there somewhere," Valerie probed.

"*But* . . . things are changing," Neil stated honestly. "Shay has made me want to try again."

"Really, Neil?" The smile could be heard in Valerie's voice. "I've always hoped that you'd change your mind one day. You're such a great guy, and you deserve to know what it means to have a happy, lasting relationship. And I'm not just saying that because you're my brother. I really think you're a great catch, Neil."

He couldn't help but blush at his sister's compliment. "Thanks."

"I mean it," Valerie added. "And I like

Shay. In the little time that I spent with her, I've really come to like her and Chase."

Neil nodded, though he knew she couldn't see him. "Ms. Ella Mae seems to like them too."

"Like them? No, Ms. Ella Mae loves them," Valerie corrected. Then, lowering her voice even more, she asked, "So what now? Are you gonna go after her? Ms. Ella Mae said that Shay is still emotionally attached to her deceased husband."

"Emotionally attached is a watered down way of putting it, Val. She's still very much in love with that man, plain and simple."

"If you really care about her, you'll fight for her." Valerie spoke like she was the older sibling, passing down years of experienced wisdom.

"Fight what? Fight who?" Neil challenged with new mounting frustration. "Who am I fighting, Val? Emmett Ford? How can I win against a dead man? That's not even a fair fight."

"You have to try." His sister's voice sounded earnest. "You'll never know if you don't try."

"You think I haven't tried? I put my neck on the chopping block last night. I told Shay exactly how I felt . . . exactly what I wanted. She knows that I want to form a romantic

347

relationship with her. You know what she told me?"

Valerie sounded like she was bracing herself for the worst when she said, "What?"

"That her heart wasn't available. Those are *her* words, not mine. She's everything I want, but she's not available. When I say that she's still in love with Emmett, I'm not just making up some unfounded hypothesis. Shay told me flat out that she is still in love with him." Neil released a highly perturbed sigh.

"So she didn't respond to you at all? You laid your feelings on the table, and the only response she had was to tell you that she was still in love with Emmett?" Disappointment saturated Valerie's tone.

"Not exactly," Neil confessed. "It wasn't that cut and dry. There were moments when I felt like she was about to open up. She let me hold her, Val. She let me serenade her. Shay let me get closer to her last night than she'd ever allowed me to get before. Then just like that, it was all over. I know she wanted to let me in. I *know* she did, but . . ." The sentence remained open-ended. Neil pounded his fist on his knee. "First woman I've met in years that I have these kinds of feelings for and can see myself sharing a future with, and she's already taken. And by a corpse, no less. Ain't that a pile of nothing? He can't provide for her; he can't support her dreams; he can't help her raise their son; he can't even return her love, yet he's the man who has a permanent hold on her heart. How am I supposed to compete with that?" It was a question he'd asked many times in the past few days, and the question remained unanswered.

"I don't know, Neil. I don't know," Valerie confessed. "But I do know that you can't just give up. Not after the dream you described a few minutes ago."

"I've never dreamed about marrying a woman." Neil rubbed his free hand over his short strands of hair. "I never even dreamed about getting married when I was actually getting married."

"That's why you have to try again. You said that last night there were moments. If there was even one moment of possibility, then there's a chance. I honestly believe that. I saw the way Shay looks at you when you're not looking at her. This ain't over by a long shot. I don't care what it looks like, Neil. If she hasn't told you to kiss her behind and leave her alone, then there's a chance. And if you really love her — which I know you do because I can hear it all in your voice — you won't give up. What kind of man gives up the fight against a deceased opponent?"

"When the deceased opponent is the great Mayor Emmett Ford —"

"Who he was has nothing to do with this." Valerie was the one sounding exasperated now. "I can't even believe you're gonna go out like that. Great or not, mayor or not, Emmett Ford is still dead. The only dead man in the history of mankind who ever had any real power was Jesus Christ — and His death was only temporary. He rose on the third day with all power in His hands. It's been years since Shay's husband was murdered. If he ain't got up by now, he ain't getting up. Just by reason of his death, you win by default.

"If you're too intimidated to go get your prize, then you don't have anyone to blame but yourself. Don't blame Emmett Ford if you let Shay slip through your fingers, Neil. Blame yourself."

TWENTY-TWO

"Keep your eyes closed, Ms. Eloise. Don't peek," Chase said, giggling as he led the woman by the hand into her newly furnished living room.

"I ain't peeking, but you sure better not let me fall, boy," she warned. Eloise's left hand was securely attached to Chase's right, and her right hand used her cane to tap the floor around her as if she were a blind woman. "First, y'all kept me locked up in that room like a prisoner forever; now you won't even let me open my eyes."

"We'll let you open them in a minute, Ms. Flowers," Shaylynn promised. She bounced with excitement, taking in the total view of Shay Décor's first completed job. "Bring her right here, Chase." She pointed to a location in the middle of the floor that would give Eloise a bird's eye view of her home's new facelift.

The truck carrying Eloise's furniture had

arrived at the same time as Shaylynn and Chase. Friday evening's rush hour traffic had delayed Shaylynn, almost ruining the way she wanted to unveil her first decorating assignment. After speaking with the deliverymen, Shaylynn had entered the home first and convinced her client to retreat to her bedroom while everything was set up.

The whole process, including putting up new window dressings, completely revamping the living room to include modern furniture, accents, and centerpieces, and changing the décor of Eloise's beloved kitchen, had taken just over an hour. Shaylynn had finally talked her client into getting rid of the cow print, with the compromise that she wouldn't disturb the wall art of Black Jesus and the painting of the people working in the fields. The master bedroom and bath would have to wait until next week, and as those rooms were being redecorated, the upstairs washer and dryer would be transferred to the bottom floor and placed in the utility closet down the hall for easier access. Once that was done, the only reason Eloise would have to go upstairs was if she just wanted to look in on any stay-over guests that she had. Even those bedrooms would get an overhaul from Shay Décor.

Satisfied with what she saw, Shaylynn granted permission. "Okay, Ms. Flowers, you can open your eyes now."

"Lord . . . have . . . mercy!" Eloise stretched out the sentence as she gaped at her surroundings.

It was just the kind of reaction that Shaylynn had prayed for, making her long hours of planning and shopping worth their weight in gold. And when Eloise dropped her cane and placed both her hands over her mouth at the sight of the special surprise oil painting that hung on her wall as the first piece of artwork any visitor would see upon entering her front door, Shaylynn almost burst with glee.

"Oh my Lord," Eloise said, moving closer and adjusting her eyeglasses for a better view. She gently smoothed her fingers over the surface of the original artwork and asked, "How on earth did you make something like this? You just thought of everything, didn't you?"

"I wish I could say that it was totally my idea," Shaylynn said. "But the day that we went shopping, while you were admiring all of the furniture, Val pulled a photo out of her purse and handed it to me. She said that you kept one just like it in your Bible and carried it with you everywhere you went. She said it was the only professional picture that you, your husband, and all of your children had taken together. Val wanted me to have it blown up and placed into a large frame for hanging. Well, there was no way that the wallet-size picture could have been enlarged to any decent size without losing its quality. So, I took the photo to Wolf Camera and had an enlarged copy made; then I took the copy to a student artist in Midtown Atlanta, and he brought it to life on canvas."

"You like it, Ms. Eloise?" Chase asked.

Eloise had barely begun to nod her head when a river of tears burst from her eyes. She covered her face with her hands and wept openly. Shaylynn knew that they were joyful tears, but she still felt a twinge of grief, aware that the hurt of Eloise's losses also played a part in her emotional outburst.

Just like he had done to Shaylynn in church as she sat crying while Neil sang, Chase walked up to Eloise and began consoling her with strokes of his hand. The child rubbed Eloise's arm until her lamentation subsided. Shaylynn dabbed the tears from her own eyes, and then handed the woman some fresh tissues that she'd pulled from the box that sat atop her television. After thanking her, Eloise wiped her face, and then looked down at Chase.

"And thank you too," she said, rubbing her hand across his cheek, and then sitting on her new couch beside the place where Chase stood. Still looking at the child, Eloise said, "You remind me so much of my young-un when he was a boy. He was a good kid — sensitive, just like you — always trying to make his mama feel better when I felt bad. Dr. Taylor grew up to be a good man too. And you know what?"

"What?" Chase asked, looking wide-eyed and expectant.

"He really likes you."

"I like him too," Chase said.

Shaylynn swallowed, and then pretended to admire the vase on the coffee table that held live roses. Neil had told her that white roses were his mother's favorite.

"Sol likes you too, Mrs. Ford. He likes you a whole lot."

Shaylynn looked at Eloise, and then at Chase. She couldn't believe the woman would say such a thing in front of her son. Chase looked back at her like she was supposed to reply, but Shaylynn didn't know what to say. After their experience on Wednesday night, Shaylynn had asked Neil not to call her anymore. She just didn't think it was proper. At least, that was what she told him. In reality, she was frightened — frightened that for the first time since Emmett's death, she longed for male companionship. Not just any male. Shaylynn longed for Neil.

She thought of him constantly and prayed for him daily. When her telephone or doorbell rang at odd hours of the day, she hoped that it would be his voice or his face that she would hear or see when she answered. And two nights ago at Canoe restaurant, as much as Shaylynn fought him off both verbally and emotionally, she had to inwardly admit that he made her feel like a teenager being romanced for the first time. When she looked across the table, she saw a man who admired her and wanted to take care of her. When they were sitting in the middle of the scenery with the river just a stone's throw away, she saw a man who longed for a chance to love her and longed for her to love him in return. The incident at Canoe wasn't the first time she'd ever felt loved, but before the night was over, it was the most loved she'd ever felt.

Even now, when she closed her eyes, Shaylynn could see Neil as he stood from the iron bench and pulled her up with him. He'd wrapped his arms around her, and the jacket that he had draped around her shoulders fell to the ground as they danced together. They moved to and fro together just like that night at Sambuca, but on the grounds of Canoe restaurant, Neil held her closer and she held him tighter. Feeling his touch and touching him in return sent ripples of delight through the nerves of her fingers and arms. Shaylynn thought that her entire body would liquefy when he placed his lips near her ear and continued his serenade, accompanied by the music that played in the background. But the kisses were what swept her off her feet the most. Neil's lips against her flesh were almost more than she could stand.

He'd kissed her forehead; then his lips found a vacant space near the outer corner of her eye. Shaylynn began losing herself and longed for the strength to push him away, but she couldn't. Neil's next stop was her right earlobe, and though he spoke no words, his mouth caressed the sensitive spot with the tenderness of a whisper. Shaylynn was shocked at her own eager response to the touch of his mouth. She pulled him closer and could feel the muscles of Neil's forearms harden beneath the sleeves of his shirt. It had been seven long years since she'd allowed herself to be kissed by a man in such a sensual manner.

Neil had moaned in anticipation as his lips moved toward hers. Shaylynn saw them coming, and she knew that she had to shake herself out of the spell. The beautiful yet dreadful spell that the man she loved, yet despised, had placed her under. If she allowed those lips to connect with hers, she would melt, and her liquefied heart — the one that for years had belonged only to Emmett — would become one with Dr. Neil Taylor . . . Solomon Taylor. She couldn't let that happen, and from somewhere within, she found the strength to pull away.

And as soon as the make-out session ended, the guilt began. It was that guilt that drove Shaylynn to tell Neil that they could not see one another again. No phone calls, no visits, no dinner dates, no text messages, no roses, no e-mails, no nothing. The only dealings they could have would be where her son's schooling was concerned. Her boundaries were specific, and to her relief — yet her chagrin — Neil agreed to comply. There was a large part of Shaylynn that hoped he'd be his usual persuasive self and insist on reaching out to her. She wanted him to break the rules, but he didn't. Shaylynn hadn't heard from Neil in two days, and because of it, she ached.

"You know he's just a phone call away."

Shaylynn winced, opened her eyes, and was embarrassed to see both Eloise and Chase watching her. Chase looked perplexed, but Eloise peered at Shaylynn through knowing eyes, as though she had just taken the trip down memory lane along with her.

At a loss for words, all Shaylynn could say was, "I, uh . . . I . . ."

Eloise rescued her. "Chase, honey, why don't you go upstairs so me and your mama can talk for a minute, okay? Ty left some of those video games up there in the room where y'all slept. Why don't you go and play awhile?"

With excitement propelling him, Chase bounced up the steps as fast as his legs could carry him.

Eloise patted the cushion beside her. "Grab that tissue box off the television, and come sit down next to me. You need to get a feel of my new sofa anyhow, so you can see what a good choice you made."

Shaylynn already knew the furniture was comfortable. They'd all tested out the showroom model in the store that day. Still, in childlike obedience, she followed Eloise's instructions, handing her the box of Kleenex as she sat.

Eloise placed the box on the sofa space

between them and immediately began speaking. "When your husband, Mr. Ford, was alive, you not only longed for his presence, you longed for his touch. You thought about him constantly in every way. You didn't just want to be with him, you wanted to be with him intimately. Your body craved him just as much as your spirit did. Am I right?"

Not sure where the line of questioning was going, Shaylynn hesitated before saying, "Yes."

"That's what being in love is. You felt that way because mind, body, and soul, you were in love with your husband. Now, before you answer my next question, I need you to really give it some thought. Okay?"

A nod served as Shaylynn's reply this time.

"Do you still have that kind of yearning for him? Do you still walk around your house every day, wishing he was there to talk to you; sit at your dinner table, wishing he was there to eat with you; lie in your bed at night, wishing he was there to fulfill your every desire? Do you still long for him in the same manner as you always did?"

Shaylynn wanted to blurt out an emphatic, "Yes!" but she couldn't. Not honestly, anyway. There was a time after his killing when Shaylynn did still have the same level of desire, in every way, for Emmett as she did before his death. In fact, it wasn't that long ago that those feelings had remained. But as Shaylynn now mulled over Eloise's words, she realized that somewhere along the way, that type of pining for Emmett had subsided. She couldn't pinpoint the precise time of diminishment, but at some point, it had. Eloise didn't even wait for her to answer.

"The reality of it is, you're not in love with him anymore, baby. You're trying to convince yourself of something that you know ain't still so."

Shaylynn turned away to try to hide the new flood that was rising in the dam of her eyes. The truth made her want to crumble to the floor in theatrical fashion, kicking and screaming like Kimberly Elise did when she played the role of Helen McCarter, the dutiful wife who was being physically thrown from her house in *Diary of a Mad Black Woman.* Shaylynn had never wanted to fall out of love with Emmett, but here she was, seven years later, forced to admit to herself that she had. *Oh my God. What happened?*

"It ain't nothing wrong with it, baby." Eloise spoke like she was a mouthpiece for the Lord. She pulled tissues from the box and pressed them into Shaylynn's hands. "You're not disrespecting your former husband, and you're not doing anything wrong. You're just still living, that's all. And in life, everything changes in its due season, even the heart."

Shaylynn dabbed at new trickles that raced down her cheeks.

"You still love him, Mrs. Ford, and you probably always will. But you're not *in love* with him. If you were, it wouldn't hurt so much that you pushed away my young-un."

Just like Shaylynn figured . . . Neil had told her. Eloise knew everything. Again, Shaylynn's mind reflected on Wednesday night. Neil was visibly shaken when she told him that she couldn't return his affections. He said nothing to her on the ride back to Eloise's house to pick up Chase, and although he did the gentlemanly thing in walking her to her door, carrying her sleeping son in his arms, Neil barely even looked at Shaylynn when he said good night. The feel of Eloise grabbing her hand brought Shaylynn's thoughts back into the living room.

"Change is good when God orchestrates it." The woman tapped Shaylynn's wedding set as she spoke. "When I removed the old furniture out of the house, I wasn't removing the deceased son or the deceased husband that used to sit on that furniture with me. It's in the heart where all the love and the memories hold dear, not in material things."

Shaylynn looked at Eloise and caught the double meaning of her words.

"My son is a good man; and I'm not saying that just because he's my young-un. Everybody who knows Sol knows he's good. Even Audrey knows it."

It was Shaylynn's first time hearing the woman's name, but she immediately knew that it belonged to Neil's ex-wife.

"If that girl could take back the decision she made to walk away, she would. All he would have to do is call, and she'd come a-running. He loved her once, and he might even still love her to a certain degree. But he's not *in love* with her anymore. She had her chance and she blew it. I ain't saying that my son is perfect, and I'm not trying to say that their failed marriage was one hundred percent Audrey's fault, but there was a time when she could have had him back, and she blew it. And because of it, she's all by herself and unhappy." Eloise released a huff and added, "Every year, she shows up at our family reunion like a dunce, trying to keep ties to a family that ain't even hers no more. Just stupid. That's what regrets will do to you. Don't let that happen to you."

Having had her say, Eloise stood from the sofa and limped her way into the kitchen, leaving Shaylynn to her own thoughts. Eloise's home decorating and Neil's persistent wooing had kept her quite busy over the past few days. It had been a while since Shaylynn reminded herself of her grief. Robotically, she inhaled and exhaled. Inhaled and exhaled.

Inhaled.

Exhaled.

The pain that simple deep breathing had brought to her chest for seven years was gone.

TWENTY-THREE

"Dr. Taylor, are you okay?" Margaret knocked and spoke at the same time. "You've been in a funk for two or three days now, and it's sure not like you to be hiding out on the inside while the school's annual carnival is going on outside." She stepped closer, realizing Neil's eyes were focused on his computer screen. "What kind of working are you doing on a Saturday?"

Without looking up from his task, Neil replied, "Just finishing up on some evaluation forms that I got behind on while wasting my time on other matters." Neil didn't even try to mask the sourness in his voice.

"Sounds like there's a story behind that. You want to talk about it?"

"I'd rather not." What Neil really wanted was to be left alone. He knew that Margaret's concerns were genuine, but still . . .

"Are you going to answer that?" she asked, watching his cell phone dance across the credenza behind him as it vibrated, indicating an incoming call.

"I have voice mail," Neil mumbled. Why didn't she just take the hint and leave him alone? Margaret was good at a lot of things, but minding her own business wasn't one of them.

"Dr. Taylor, I don't like seeing you like this. Is there anything I can do to help?"

Neil looked up, but the smile he offered was cheerless. "I'll be fine, Ms. Dasher. It's just one of those days." His eyes returned to the screen in front of him.

"Does this have anything to do with Mrs. Ford?"

"What?" Margaret had his full attention again. Where had that question come from?

"My hearing might not be the best, but ain't a thing wrong with my eyes," Margaret said, like bifocals weren't permanently perched at the end of her nose. "Every time y'all are around each other the air gets thick like taffy. She can't keep her eyes off you. . . . You can't keep your eyes off her. I saw her sneak in the back door at church last Sunday. Whatever happened to the other church she was attending? She got reason to want to attend KBCC now?" Margaret didn't wait for an answer, not that she would have gotten one anyway. "And I saw the way you

366

two were exchanging looks after the benediction. This has something to do with her,
doesn't it?"

Neil rubbed his eyes. He needed to be
wearing his own reading glasses, but hadn't
yet chosen to remove them from his desk
drawer. Truth be told, the nagging throb
that was rhythmically beating behind his
eyes had little to do with eye strain. The
tension of the past few days was beginning
to get to him. "I really don't care to talk
about it right now, Ms. Dasher. Do you
mind?"

"No, I don't mind." She took a few steps
backward. "But you know I'm here when
you're ready."

A half smile tugged at the right corner of
Neil's lips. "Thank you."

Margaret turned away, but stopped at the
mouth of the doorway. "Do you plan to
come out at all? The children have been asking for you."

"Have they?" A flicker of light brightened
Neil's face. He wanted to be with the
children, but he needed solitude. "I'll come
out a little later; maybe."

"Dr. Taylor . . . are you in here?"

The words were sung from a child's
mouth and echoed through the almost
empty building. Margaret turned to find its

source. "See," she said, "you're not out there, so the children are going to start coming in here."

"I'm in my office," Neil called out to whoever it was. "Come on in."

After a short wait, Margaret stepped aside and revealed the face that went with the voice. "Hey, Dr. Taylor."

Neil broke into a wide grin. Outside of brief classroom checks on Thursday and Friday, he hadn't seen Chase since he and Shaylynn had picked the boy up from Ella Mae's house after their dinner date. "Hey, Chase, what it do?" The standard high five was exchanged. "Are you having fun?"

"Not yet. I just got here. When I win some prizes, I'll have some fun."

Neil laughed. Until now, he'd never really noticed the resemblance that Chase bore to his mother. Shaylynn harped on how much he looked like Emmett; and he did, but Neil could see some of Shaylynn too. Or maybe he was just missing her, and his eyes were seeing what they longed to see.

"What are you doing inside the building?" Margaret asked. "All the prizes are outside."

"I had to use the bathroom and Mama said I couldn't use the potties outside."

"Can't blame her for that," Margaret replied.

Neil steadied his voice in an effort not to sound anxious. "Are you here with your mother?"

"Yes." Chase nodded his head, and then spun around on one foot, like he'd suddenly gotten a burst of energy. "She's outside."

"Is she?" Neil clicked on the button to shut down his system and distanced his chair from the desk. He tried to make his motions flow smoothly and seem casual, but he could sense Margaret's eyes locked in his direction.

"You coming now?" Chase asked, giving his body one last spin for good measure before stopping to wait for an answer.

"Yes, Dr. Taylor, are you?" Margaret's question was cynical, and Neil made a conscious effort not to look at her. She continued her mocking. "I thought you had to work, Dr. Taylor. Chase must have said something to change your mind, because clearly, it was set just a moment ago."

Neil still didn't reply, but he shot his assistant a look that warned her of the repercussions to come. While he turned his attention back to the computer, another familiar voice joined them.

"Chase Elliot Ford. There you are. Didn't I tell you to come right back?"

"I came to get Dr. Taylor."

Neil kept his eyes glued to the computer screen for as long as he could, but when the machine powered off and the screen went black, it was no longer a valid avoidance tactic. He stood from his desk and looked toward his crowded open door. "Good afternoon, Mrs. Ford. How are you?"

"I'm okay." She offered a faint smile. "You?"

Not even possessing the strength for propaganda, Neil shrugged. "I've been better." He then turned to Chase and mustered the best smile he could. "Ready to go?"

"Ready!" Chase had more enthusiasm than all the adults in the room combined.

Neil stepped around his desk and paused when he noticed Shaylynn's eyes examining him. She'd never seen him dressed quite this trendy before, and she appeared to be both pleased and fascinated by his attire: a pair of Sean John jeans and a matching denim jacket by the same designer. The button-front pinstriped shirt Neil wore under the jacket was loosened at the neck, giving it a casual but stylish look, and he wore a black New York Yankees baseball cap. There was no allegiance to the team. He'd purchased it yesterday after making the decision to take Adam Schmitz up on his challenge to train for the Peachtree Road

Race. When Neil stepped into Sports Authority to buy new training gear in preparation for next week's gym visit, he saw the hat and thought of his chat with Shaylynn as they sat in the back of the school bus on the ride to the Georgia Aquarium.

When Shaylynn looked up at his headgear, she must have thought of their conversation too, because she smirked just a bit at the sight of it. Neil stood there a moment longer to give her a few extra seconds to take in the view, and then he restarted his trek to the door.

"May I have a word with you before you leave, Dr. Taylor?"

Neil stopped and looked at Shaylynn. There was a tingling in the pit of his stomach, and he didn't know whether it was a good sign. "Now?" he asked.

Shaylynn's eyes darted briefly toward Margaret; then she nodded and added, "Alone . . . please? It'll only take a few minutes."

There was a long and thick silence that Neil's voice eventually ended. "Ms. Dasher, do you mind taking Chase into your office space for a moment? We'll be out shortly."

A perceptive smirk crossed Margaret's lips. She took Chase by the hand and led him out of the office, giving both Neil and

Shaylynn one last clever glimpse before closing the door that separated her space from Neil's.

Neil didn't move from the place where Shaylynn's voice had seized him. He looked at her, and every time her gaze met his, Neil's heart turned over in response. The suspense was unbearable. "You wanted to talk?"

"Yes. I . . . I wanted to show you something." She reached into her purse and pulled out a card. Her hand was trembling a little, and though Neil noticed it, he didn't make mention of it. Instead, he took two steps forward so that he'd be just close enough to reach the card in her outstretched hand. His eyes scanned the bold lettering that was printed on the faded backdrop of a photo of Shaylynn's own meticulously decorated living room.

"Shay Décor. Shaylynn Ford, interior designer." Neil looked up at her, not quite sure why she'd given him the card. He already knew about her line of business.

"The name," she pointed out. "I had it legally changed."

"Oh." It was all clear to him now, and he smiled when he looked at the card again. "Shay Décor."

"Yes."

"Good choice," Neil said. He brought his eyes up from the card again. "Is that what you wanted to tell me?" He was glad she'd chosen to use the name he'd suggested, but it wasn't exactly the reason that he hoped she'd requested to be alone with him.

"Part of it." She took a breath. "I also wanted to thank you."

Neil's eyebrows rose in perplexity. "For?"

"For wanting to love me."

When she said those words, Shaylynn fidgeted, reaching up to touch her neck before allowing her hand to fall back to her side. It was a swift and simple movement, but during it, Neil noticed something that caused his feet to unglue themselves from the space where they'd been planted. He strolled forward and erased the remaining space that separated them. Neil extended his arm, grabbing Shaylynn by the hand and staring at her vacant finger.

Sundry feelings surged through Neil's body, his mind a crazy mixture of hope and fear. "What does this mean?"

Shaylynn looked up at him, and Neil saw the same frightened affection in her eyes that he saw after she pulled away from him on the property of Canoe restaurant. It was a look that said, "I want to stay, but I need to go." Afraid that she'd turn and run as she'd done that night, Neil slipped his arm around her waist and held her in a secure but tender embrace.

"Talk to me," he pled with her. "Tell me what it means."

"I don't know what it means, Solomon." A lonely tear fell from Shaylynn's right eye. "I can't make any promises."

It wasn't exactly the response that Neil wanted to hear, but she had called him Solomon, and that made it good enough. At forty-five, though, Neil was a man who wasn't looking to play games. He didn't want to pressure Shaylynn or scare her away, but there was more that he needed to know.

Before speaking his mind, he pulled her so close that he could see his own reflection in her watery eyes. "I've never asked you to promise me anything, Shay. All I've ever asked for is a chance. Can you give me that? And I mean a *real* chance." Neil inhaled, braced himself for the whatever, and took the plunge. "Am I the kind of man that you think you could love?"

Behind the force of one blink, a tear from her left eye evened the score, and Neil exhaled when Shaylynn nodded her answer. He wanted to grab her in his arms and never let her go, but what she struggled to reveal next momentarily held him hostage.

"I . . . I guess I've felt . . . *something* for a while now. I hoped that it was nothing, but when we were together the other night . . . when you sang to me . . ."

She allowed her voice to drift, and Neil allowed his mind to do the same. Had Dr. Charles Loather Sr. been right all along? Had God gifted his singing to have some type of supernatural power? People had testified in the past that they found healing in his song, and Deacon Burgess said Neil's song was anointed to save souls. But was it also anointed to win hearts? It all sounded unbelievable, but sometimes that was just the way God worked, right? In mysterious ways. Ways that blew people's minds. Maybe this was one of them.

"I tell you what," he whispered, using his thumb to whisk away a portion of the moisture that had gathered on Shaylynn's face. "I'll promise to keep singing if you'll promise to keep feeling . . . *something.*"

She laughed a little and nodded again. "Okay."

Joy bubbled in Neil's belly and shone in his eyes. His phone was vibrating against the credenza again, but if it thought it would get answered now, it had another think coming. This moment was perfect to do something he'd wanted to do since the day he sat across from Shaylynn on the back of the school bus. Completely ignoring the persistent humming of his cell, Neil's face slowly descended to meet Shaylynn's. Under the circumstances, he was fairly confident that she wouldn't leave him hanging as she'd done at Canoe.

Neil longed to know if her lips were as delectable on a Saturday morning as they'd been in his Wednesday night dream . . . if they were as soft in his real-life office as they'd been in the wedding in his dream. Making the long-awaited connection, he wasted no time to use his lips to part hers in a soul-reaching massage. She readily responded, and in a matter of seconds, it was difficult to determine who was in control: perhaps both of them, perhaps neither. Neil hungrily ran his fingers through Shaylynn's braids, and then nearly lost his footing when he felt her slender fingers press into the flesh on the back of his neck, forcing his mouth to crush harder against hers.

Good God from Zion! The dream couldn't even compare. Neil couldn't help but wonder how long Shaylynn had been waiting for this moment.

"Dr. Taylor . . . Mama . . . are y'all

finished talking yet? Can we go outside now?" A knock to the door supplemented Chase's innocent voice.

Shaylynn gasped, jumped backward, and wiped her hands over her lips to remove the telltale wet evidence that the ravenous, thorough searching of Neil's mouth had left behind. Then both her hands shot to her eyes, where they made quick work of erasing residue tears.

Neil's eyes shot toward the door. His head swooned, and he struggled to catch his breath. He knew that it wasn't Chase's idea to knock on the door and interrupt whatever was going on in the office of his school's chief administrator. "I'm gonna get you for this, Ms. Dasher," he whispered.

"Dr. Taylor? Mama?" the boy called again.

Neil took a quick look at Shaylynn to be sure she had gotten herself together, and when he was sure she had, he raised his voice and said, "Come on in, Chase." As the door opened, he distanced himself more from Shaylynn and returned to his desk to gather a few belongings that he pretended to need to take outside with him.

"Y'all okay in here?" There was so much laughter in Margaret's eyes that Neil wanted to pick up something and hurl it at her.

Ignoring her question, he looked across

the room at Chase instead. "Give me one minute and I'll be ready."

While he collected a few folders, Neil reached for his cell phone, then balanced it between his ear and shoulder and listened to the one message that had been left:

"Hey, Neil. It's CJ. I tried your cell earlier, then called your house, but I got voice mails on both, so I'm calling here again. When you get this message, you can call me back if you want. If not, I'll understand."

Neil heard CJ pause and release a sigh, and from the heaviness of it, Neil knew that what he was about to hear was something his friend didn't define as positive news. Neil didn't need anything to ruin his current ecstasy, but he was too curious not to hear him out. "Listen, bruh, I know you're gonna be outdone with me, but I won't do it. I won't feed you any detailed info on Mayor Ford that will help you destroy Shay's image of him. It's not that I can't do it. . . . I just won't do it. Yes, my sources unearthed a boatload of dirt on Emmett. They found it, and I know every sordid detail of it. But I won't share it with you.

"I've disobeyed God's orders enough in gathering this information, but I can't make it worse by passing it along. I know how much it means to you to be able to mar this man's image, but you'll just have to find another avenue to Shaylynn's heart. If this sister is truly meant for you, then you shouldn't have to play these kinds of undermining games. God has equipped you with everything that you need to get the victory in every aspect of your life, including matters of the heart. Use what you got, Neil. Dad once said that you could get anything you wanted if you'd just sing. So sing your way to victory, Neil. Sing your way to victory."

Neil rolled his eyes, smiled, shook his head, and then saved the message before closing his phone. Church people made him sick, and he'd call CJ later to tell him so.

Sliding a mint from his pocket, Neil popped it in his mouth and tossed the wrapper in the trashcan beside his desk. Then he raised his eyes and looked toward the open doorway, where a beautiful lady stood talking softly to her son. Where *his* beautiful lady stood talking to *their* son. This was his future, and for the first time, Neil thought those words in confidence. CJ could keep the dirt he'd discovered on Mayor Ford, and Shaylynn could keep the unflawed memories of her beloved Emmett — however misguided they apparently had been found to be. Neil wasn't going to let any of it intimidate him anymore.

He would no longer be bullied by the man, his picture, or the violets that decorated Shaylynn's mantel in commemoration of her undying love for a husband she'd buried seven years ago. In time, just like the ring she'd worn for so long, those memorials would be removed too. And if they weren't, so what? Emmett Ford had been an important part of Shaylynn's past life, but that's what Emmett was: the past. Neil would have to be confident enough not to let that threaten the present or the future. Period.

"Ready?" Chase held up an eager hand, and Neil answered the call for a high five.

When he looked down into Shaylynn's longing stare, he saw snapshots of the dream he had two nights ago. God, how he hoped the "something" she felt was the same emotion that was causing his chest to swell. What he felt was love. No doubt about it. A long courtship with this lady was out of the question. He had already fallen too deep to wait too long. He needed to share every part of him with every part of her. He was ready to experience that "real good lovin' " that Deacon Burgess told him about.

As Chase charged toward the exit door, Neil slipped his hand in Shaylynn's and gave it a quick squeeze; then he gave the answer to Chase's question, an answer that the boy was too far away to hear.

"I'm ready whenever you are." Neil hoped she got the true meaning that was hidden behind the words he whispered. If not, soon enough, she would.

READING GROUP DISCUSSION QUESTIONS

1) How powerful is grief? Do you think that it can be so great that it overtakes a person's existence and hinders them from moving forward with their lives?

2) Why do you believe it was so difficult for Shaylynn to recover from her personal tragic loss?

3) With the magnitude of her initial grief, do you think Shaylynn would have killed herself had it not been for her son?

4) In your opinion, were there times when she was obsessive with her need to shelter Chase, or was she just being a typical cautious mother?

5) Margaret commented that Neil could possibly be the only positive male role model that the children at Kingdom Build-

ers Academy had in their lives. How important do you think it is for children to have strong male figures as mentors in their upbringing?

6) What do you think of Neil's pursuit of Shaylynn? Did he go overboard?

7) How accepting are you of "May-December" relationships? Should men date/marry considerably younger women or vice versa? Can romances such as this last a lifetime? Would you get involved in such a relationship?

8) Neil had trouble dealing with grief as well, and the time-line of his mourning had far exceeded Shaylynn's. Is that realistic? Do you think that coping with death is easier for men, or more difficult?

9) It is indicated throughout the story that Neil's gift of singing had been anointed by God to heal, deliver, save, and bring victory. Do you believe that God gives people special gifts that contain such abilities?

10) What do you make of CJ's choice when, in the name of friendship, he carried out Neil's wishes to launch an unethical

investigation? What did you think of the decision CJ ultimately made once he gathered all of his findings?

11) Neil alluded to the fact that he didn't believe there was such a thing as a clean (or honest) politician. Do you agree?

12) Even though Neil wasn't told the sordid details that led to Emmett's death, should Shaylynn have been made aware of the findings? Why or why not?

13) The subject of Alzheimer's was implied in this book when speaking of Homer Burgess. Do you believe people struggling with illnesses such as his should be allowed to hold an office (such as deacon) in the church? Why or why not?

14) On one of his "sane" days, Deacon Burgess told Neil about both his wives and how he felt a certain level of responsibility to the first wife even after the marriage failed. Do you agree with the extent of his allegiance?

15) Several of the Christian characters in this story had been married and divorced, including Margaret, Homer, and Neil. What

is your opinion on the divorce rate within the church? Should divorced Christians be treated differently (such as not be allowed to serve in certain leadership roles)? Why or why not?

16) Neil and Shaylynn were both dedicated Christians, but there was never any indication that either of them had access to professional grief counseling as a part of the ministries where they worshipped. How important is it for churches to have these types of specialized in-house services in place to meet the needs of their congregants?

17) Did any part of this story surprise or disappoint you? If so, please share how and why.

18) Who was your favorite character and why?

19) Who was your least favorite character and why?

20) If you could rewrite any part of this tale, would you? If so, what part would it be?

ABOUT THE AUTHOR

Kendra Norman-Bellamy is an award-winning, national bestselling author as well as founder of KNB Publications, LLC. Beginning her literary career in 2002 as a self-published writer, Kendra has risen, by the grace of God, to become one of the most respected names in Christian fiction.

She and her titles have been featured in *Essence, Upscale, Hope for Women,* and *E.K.G. Literary Magazine.* Kendra has been a recurrent contributing writer for *Precious Times* magazine, *Hope for Women* magazine, and *Global Woman* magazine. She is a motivational speaker, and the mastermind behind two distinct writer's organizations: The Writer's Hut (*www.writershut.ning.com*), an online network for published writers of African American literature; and The Writer's Cocoon Focus Group (*www.writers cocoonfocusgroup.ning.com*), a national, multi-cultural support network set in place specifically for aspiring and new writers. Additionally, she is the visionary of the I Shall Not Die motivational ministry (*www.IShallNotDie.org*) and the founder of Cruisin' For Christ (*www.CruisinForChrist.org*), a groundbreaking cruise that celebrates Christian writing, gospel music, and other artistries that glorify God. As a famed publication that celebrates African American achievements, *Who's Who In Black Atlanta* has featured Kendra for five consecutive years.

A native of West Palm Beach, Florida and a graduate of Valdosta Technical College, Kendra is an active member of the Iota Phi Lambda Sorority, Inc. She resides in Stone Mountain, Georgia with her husband, Jonathan, and younger daughter, Crystal. Her firstborn daughter, Brittney Holmes, is also a national bestselling author and a full-time student residing on the campus of the University of Georgia.

Feel free to visit Kendra's official web home at *www.KendraNormanBellamy.com* or connect with her on MySpace at *www.myspace.com/kendranormanbellamy* or on Facebook at *www.facebook.com/KendraNormanBellamy.*